The Wife Swap

The Wife Swap

Jack Heath

First published in Great Britain in 2024 by

Bonnier Books UK Limited
4th Floor, Victoria House, Bloomsbury Square, London, WC1B 4DA
Owned by Bonnier Books
Sveavägen 56, Stockholm, Sweden

First published as an Audible Original under the title
Kill Your Husbands in 2023

And originally published in print by Allen & Unwin under the title
Kill Your Husbands in 2023

A CIP catalogue record for this book is available from the British Library.

ISBN: 9781471417504

This book is typeset using Atomik ePublisher.

Embla Books is an imprint of Bonnier Books UK.
www.bonnierbooks.co.uk

For my wife, Venetia

Dear Isla,

I'm leaving—don't pretend to be surprised. I'll be seeking full custody of Noah. Please don't fight me for him. You know full well that any magistrate would side with me if they found out the truth.

Oscar

Evidence item #438. Description: letter, bloodstained

—FELICITY, stand-up comic, married to Dominic (trophy wife?)
—DOMINIC (Dom), finance bro, gave $10K to Cole (gift or loan?)
—COLE, gym owner, married to Clementine (but attracted to Isla?)
—CLEMENTINE, fitness model, Isla's best friend (find someone who's done IVF, see if story is credible)
—ISLA, full-time mum, married to Oscar (what 'truth' was he referring to?)
—OSCAR, real estate agent (but didn't rent the house?)

From the notebook of Detective Sergeant Kiara Lui

Prologue

She stumbles downhill through the bush in the pouring rain, dressing-gown flapping, puddles splashing under her slippers. The beam of the torch is thin—she can point it at the trail before her feet or the branches in front of her face, but not both. The terrain is dangerous, sharp sticks and slippery rocks hidden just under the mud. She should have snatched up her walking shoes before she fled, but she hadn't wanted to stay in that house a second longer. Another mistake to add to the list.

The cold scorches her lungs. Her cheeks are numb. Her toes ache; she can already picture them turning black and popping off. The mountain is 130 kilometres from Warrigal, and most of the journey is dense bushland. If the weather stays this bad, she'll soon join the dead she's left behind. The voice in her head, which started as a whisper, has become a scream: *what if you're going around in circles?* At any moment, she could break into a clearing and find herself facing the house: those two big windows like glowing eyes, the twin chimneys like horns.

Her thoughts no longer make sense—probably a bad sign. She's been running downhill this whole time, so she can't be back at the top of the mountain. *Unless you're in hell already. Running for eternity, ending where you began.* She's never been very religious, but in her delirium, anything seems possible. The house on the mountaintop had felt safe when she was one of six. Then there had been five, and then four, then three. Now it's just her and God, out here in the dark.

She hears a creak behind her and whirls around. The trees watch her, as silent as jurors.

Has she been followed? She's left behind a trail of muddy footprints and blood-smeared leaves, but that wouldn't be obvious in the dark.

She chews her chapped lips. If she moves, she might be spotted; if she doesn't, she might be caught—

A sound like a gunshot rings out from above. She looks up. A bough has broken off one of the gum trees and is tumbling towards her, crashing through other branches on the way down. She throws herself aside, leaving a slipper behind, as the slab of wood hits the ground with a mighty crash.

That limb probably held on to the trunk for fifty years or more. Was she unlucky to be underneath when it finally snapped, or lucky that it didn't pulverise her? Is she being punished, or conspicuously forgiven?

Suddenly she feels wet tarmac under her feet. She looks around. The trees are gone. She's reached the road, flanked by paddocks. It's not midnight anymore—dawn is spreading from the horizon. Shivering, she tries to remember how she got to the bottom of the mountain, but her mind is quicksand, the memories already submerged.

Her phone chimes in her pocket—a sound she hasn't heard in three days. It keeps chiming as the backlog of messages comes through. She struggles to get her frozen hand into her pocket. When she pulls out the phone, it slips from her fingers, hitting the road with a metallic *splink*. 'No!' She scoops it up, frantically prodding the fractured glass. The lock screen glows, but she can't type in her PIN. When she tries to swipe up, the image—her husband, smiling crookedly, his arms around her—keeps bouncing back.

Headlights wash over her. She whirls around, holding up a palm against the glare. Tyres squeal against the wet asphalt, drowning out her scream.

Kiara

The body lies in the middle of Victoria Street, knees folded backwards, arms splayed. At first it looks like the victim's jaw has fallen off, but as Senior Constable Kiara Lui leaps out of the car and sprints over, she sees the jaw has actually been smashed upward, flattened against the palate.

Kiara reaches for her radio, but she's off-duty, dressed in a denim jacket over a flower-patterned dress: no equipment belt.

The man lying on the road makes eye contact with her.

'Stay in the car,' she shouts over her shoulder, not wanting Elise to see.

Undeterred, Elise unfolds her long legs from the passenger seat and jogs over, carrying the first-aid kit from the glove box. Brushing her fringe out of her eyes, she stares down at the dying man. 'Well,' she says, 'we can't exactly give him mouth-to-mouth.'

It's the sort of joke Elise has been making a lot. Gallows humour is common among paramedics, but after the trauma Elise endured last year, Kiara is worried the nihilism runs deeper.

Kiara looks around. No pedestrians. No sign of the car that ran this man over. Just a flickering streetlight and a row of shuttered shops—a cafe, a real estate agency, a jeweller's. Only the King George pub on the corner is still open. The chalkboard out the front says, GET SCHNIT-FACED! CHICKEN SCHNITZEL AND BEER $10.

'Call an ambulance,' Kiara says.

Elise is crouched over the man, feeling for a pulse. 'You better do it.'

Kiara grabs her phone and dials Rafa.

The dying man is in his fifties, white, beanpole-thin, with a sharp widow's peak and sad grey eyes. Elise starts chest compressions. Blood squirts from the gaping neck onto her silk skirt. She clamps one hand over the wound.

As the phone rings in her ear, Kiara looks down at the ruined fabric. Elise hardly ever gets dressed up. Tonight was supposed to be special—a chance to hit the reset button. Kiara can't afford to take her partner to a decent restaurant, but she thought a picnic dinner next to the Murrumbidgee River would be nice: a secluded spot where no one would be around to stare at them; a small bottle of sparkling, a tube of mozzie repellent, cheese and salad sandwiches with mud cake for dessert. Kiara imagined kissing Elise on the picnic rug, rolling around like teenagers. She'd hoped Elise might finally tell her what's been going on these past few weeks.

As usual, things haven't gone to plan.

Kiara scans the empty street. She can see the whole thing in her mind's eye: someone walks out the back door of the pub, spinning a car key on one finger, telling themselves they have no choice but to drive. It's too far to walk, they can't afford a cab, and anyway, how would they retrieve their car tomorrow? So they get behind the wheel and zoom around the corner, just as this unlucky guy happens to be crossing the road, camouflaged in his grey jumper and black jeans. The driver hits the brakes, but the alcohol has dulled their reaction time. The pedestrian disappears under the vehicle. The driver looks at the body and pronounces him dead, or as good as. Now they ask themselves, what's the point of sticking around? If they go to jail, their kids will starve, their business will go under, whatever—there's always some excuse. So they drive home, wipe the blood off the bull bar, and go to bed. Maybe they feel guilty, like that counts for something.

Kiara will do her job. She'll photograph the tyre tracks. She'll see if the security camera in front of the pub has finally been fixed, and request the footage if so. She'll ask the owner who was in tonight, and check if they saw the accident. She'll tell Bill at the local garage to report any suspicious damage to the front of a vehicle. But in all likelihood, she'll never find out who did this. Even if she does, and can prove it, a sympathetic magistrate will let the driver out in a year or two—and in the meantime, the bodies will keep piling up. Around here, drink-driving is the rule, not the exception.

Once, Kiara spent all weekend in a patrol car on this very corner, breath-testing people. Some of them said she was 'cheating' by doing it so close to the pub.

Rafa finally answers the phone. 'G'day, Detective.'

'Got a hit-and-run on the corner of Victoria and Phillip streets,' Kiara says, without preamble. 'By the time you get here, I think you'll be picking up a body.'

In the background of the call, she can hear several shouted conversations, clinking glasses and the tootling of poker machines. She realises he's in the pub just behind her. It would have been quicker to walk in and grab him.

'Be right out,' Rafa says, and the line goes dead.

Elise is still doing the chest compressions. But the man's skin has gone grey. His eyes are no longer focused; the pupils dilated. Soon the cloudy film will form over them. He's gone.

While Elise works, Kiara goes to the other side of the body to search his pockets. Phone, keys and a receipt from the pub: chicken Caesar salad and a Cascade Premium Light, order number thirty-nine. When she flips open the leather phone case, she finds a pair of twenties and a selection of cards: driver's licence, Medicare, a couple of bank cards. Anton Rabbek, born 3 February 1971, lives at 15/3 Barton Street, banks with Macquarie. Apparently he wears glasses;

Kiara spots them a few metres away, an arm bent and a lens cracked. The photo on the driver's licence is a good match for the corpse, at least from the nose up.

She pushes a button on his car key: no reaction from any of the vehicles nearby. Barton Street is about a kilometre away and perhaps the only area of Warrigal you could describe as 'upmarket'—a lot of fancy townhouses. The guy was probably doing the right thing and walking home from the pub after his light beer. Another good bloke killed by a bad one who Kiara will try and fail to catch, while the rest of the town keeps drinking itself to death.

She has long since resigned herself to care for this place, however little it cares for her. Her family has been here for tens of thousands of years. She endures the violence, the racism and the homophobia. But Elise has been through so much already. Doesn't *she* deserve better?

It's not the time to discuss this. But it never is. On those rare afternoons when neither of them is working and they're sharing the hammock under the pergola, Kiara never wants to spoil the present by mentioning the future.

She squeezes Elise's shoulder. 'Do you want to get out of here?'

Elise is still doing compressions. 'Should wait for Rafa,' she puffs.

'I mean, we could move.' Kiara tries to keep the desperation out of her voice. 'To a different town.'

They can't afford to go anywhere. But the thought of staying is unbearable.

Elise takes a break, sagging back onto her knees. She wipes some sweat off her brow and looks up. Her grim smile chills Kiara to the bone.

'What?' Elise gestures at the pub, the blood-spattered road, the dead man. 'And leave all this behind?'

ONE MONTH LATER

Kiara

The house has a rustic look, with a weathered brick exterior and dark wood trim. There's a low-maintenance garden out the front, typical of short-term rentals: no lawn to mow, no veggie patch to water, just rose bushes herding visitors onto the path with their thorns.

The building is two storeys high, which is unusual way out here, where land is plentiful and it's cheaper to build out than up. Kiara supposes that if you're going to put a house on a mountaintop, you may as well go a couple of metres higher so the upper windows have a view over the tree canopy. Part of the roof has been damaged, perhaps by hail. A brown tarpaulin covers the hole, billowing in the breeze.

If anyone has been in the upstairs bedroom over the past several minutes, they might have seen the Tactical Response Group driving up the hill. If so, they've had some time to prepare for the raid.

Kiara adjusts her stab vest. She's gained some weight since she was fitted for it, creating gaps in front of her armpits. She's also very aware that it doesn't protect her arms or throat.

'I'm going to knock on the front door,' she says.

The commander looks at her like that's the dumbest idea he's ever heard. He's dressed more like a soldier than a police officer, with knee and elbow pads, and various tools dangling from a chest rig. Behind the visor of his riot helmet, his nose is crooked and his grey-flecked beard is patchy.

Kiara first met him at a critical incident eight years ago. A terrified teenage girl had called triple zero because her drugged-up boyfriend was threatening her with a samurai sword, which he'd duct-taped to his own hand so he couldn't be disarmed. When the response group broke into the townhouse, the boy whirled to face them, and the squad commander blasted him with a shotgun. He died, never having to explain his actions or reveal who'd sold him the meth and the sword. The group commander didn't care about any of that, but Kiara did.

She hasn't met the rest of the team: three other men and one woman, huddled around the commander. He says, 'You want to give them *even more* warning?'

'I want to give them the chance to surrender peacefully,' Kiara says.

'According to your witness, they're armed and dangerous.'

Early this morning, a woman stumbled down the mountain in a dressing-gown, and was nearly hit by a car on the highway. The driver took her to hospital, where she babbled about knives and killers but also about God and falling branches. She's still recovering from hypothermia.

'My witness is barely coherent,' Kiara says. 'Let me try to talk them down before you go in, guns blazing.'

'Listen to me. You've been a detective for what, a month?'

It's actually been less than three weeks. This is Kiara's first case since her promotion, and she's only leading because it's a public holiday, and Rohan, her sergeant, is visiting his parents in Queensland. If he'd been the one to interview Ms Dubois, she's sure he would have sent a more senior officer.

'What's your point?' she asks.

'They might kill you.'

Usually this idea wouldn't rattle Kiara. It's a risk every time she puts on the uniform—and even when she doesn't. She once spent four nights hanging around a Wagga Wagga car park in fishnets, trying to catch a rapist who'd targeted sex workers in the area.

But Elise is already fragile. What will happen to her if Kiara doesn't come home?

Kiara swallows the thought. 'I'm more concerned about *you* killing *them*,' she says.

The commander jabs a stubby finger at her chest. 'You're making this operation unnecessarily difficult and dangerous for me and my men.'

Kiara's gaze flicks to the only woman on his team, who doesn't seem offended. She looks like she's in her fifties, with cracks around her mouth and greying curls. Kiara is thirty-three and has learned not to expect support from older women in the job. Having put up with worse sexism in decades past, they expect her to *suck it up, princess*.

'Noted,' Kiara says, and walks towards the front door, hands up.

It's finally stopped sprinkling, but the cobblestones are still slick. The afternoon sun isn't warm enough to dry them. Ahead of her, a wind-chime dangles from a rain gutter, wooden tubes clacking in the breeze.

Kiara edges around the front veranda, with its bench seat on the left, a door on the right, and muddy footprints everywhere. The boards squeak under her feet. The doormat is printed with banksia flowers and a slogan: *bless this mess!*

After knocking on the door, she steps to one side out of habit, even though Ms Dubois told her no one in the house had a gun. 'My name's Kiara,' she calls. 'I'm a police officer. You okay in there?'

No answer.

'I just want to make sure everyone's safe. Do you need first aid? Water? Something to eat, maybe?'

The classic siege strategy is to offer pizza, but the nearest pizza place is in Warrigal, more than an hour away. Kiara is pretty sure she has a banana in her patrol car, though; it wasn't too spotty last time she looked.

'You know what always helps me get some perspective? Fruit.'

Still no sound from inside. She pulls on a pair of latex gloves and tries the handle. It turns—Ms Dubois must not have locked it when she fled.

Kiara looks back at the commander. He glares at her, warning her not to do what she's thinking about doing.

She calls out, 'I'm coming in, okay?' Then she opens the door and steps inside.

Kiara finds herself in a narrow hallway. There's a window on her right, along with some coat hooks and a spot to hang skis, even though Kiara thinks there's not enough snow and too many trees for skiing. A few suitcases and saggy backpacks are lined up against the opposite wall, open as if their owners only got halfway through packing them.

Kiara walks to the end of the hall, where there's a framed poster with a collage of comforting words—*holiday, family, home, love, happy*, et cetera—and turns left.

In the living and dining area, two cream couches sit near a modern-looking fireplace. A glass dining table is surrounded by high-backed chairs. Big windows look out into the bush, and there's a giant TV for those who don't like the view. Only two Blu-rays occupy the shelf: *The Silver Brumby* and *The Man from Snowy River*.

A copperish scent lingers in the air. Blood and urine.

Still turning left, Kiara takes in the kitchen, separated from the dining area by an island bench made of white granite, dirty plates stacked on one corner. Wineglasses are everywhere, puddles of red at the bottom. There's a brushed-steel fridge with a built-in ice machine, an oven big enough to roast a whole pig in, and a body on the floor. Face up, throat slit.

Kiara says into her lapel mic, 'Got a body here.'

The commander comes on the radio immediately. 'Time to go.'

He's right. She's confirmed the house is a crime scene—now it's her job to walk back out the door without touching anything, then summon forensics. But there could still be someone alive in here, meaning the Tactical Response Group will have to clear the building first. They'll trample all over the bloody footprints around the body, and probably shoot any witnesses they find. Then Kiara will never figure out what happened.

'In a minute,' she says.

'For fuck's sake,' the commander mutters.

The lake of blood around the corpse is dark red, almost black. A long smear leads to a nearby hall—it looks like the man was dragged from there to here. The volume suggests his heart kept pumping for a while. There's more on his upturned hands, like he clamped them to his throat, trying to save his own life. The medical examiner will confirm.

Kiara isn't deceived by his peaceful expression. The facial muscles have slackened after death, but his last moments would have been horrifying.

She gets as close as she can without stepping in the blood. The man has a wedding band. A dress shirt, once salmon-coloured, now dirty and torn. Leather shoes with formal uppers and running soles: sales-assistant footwear. He's white, medium build, and about thirty, give or take five years.

Kiara looks around for signs of the murder weapon. Nothing on the floor. A silicone spatula and a wooden spoon are drying next to the sink. When Kiara spots the knife block, she sees not one empty hole but four.

She remembers Ms Dubois in the hospital bed, fingering the crucifix. Her croaking voice: 'Don't go in the house. He nearly killed me. He'll kill you.' It sounded paranoid, insane—less so, now that Kiara is standing over a man with his throat cut.

She swallows. 'Can we talk?' she calls. 'I'm here to help.'

Her voice echoes through the house. No response.

She has a Taser on her belt but doesn't draw it. In her experience, suspects are more likely to attack an armed officer than an unarmed one.

She follows some bloody footprints to a sliding glass door, and opens it without touching the handle. There's an expansive back deck, with a gas barbecue, another dining table and a hot tub shaded by an umbrella. No prints out here, probably washed away by the rain. She approaches the safety rail and peers over. The house is built on a slope, so even though the front door is at ground level, there's a five-metre drop from the back deck to the forest floor, where there's a garden bed, an axe next to a woodpile and a mud-spattered bicycle. The landscape is better suited to mountain biking than to skiing.

Before leaving the deck, Kiara lifts the lid of the hot tub and dips a finger into the water: still warm.

Back in the house, she finds another hallway. Three doors, all on the left-hand side. The first door leads to a bedroom, and another corpse. This man is tucked into the blankets of a queen-size bed, arms out, chest in. He's also about thirty, but he's wearing a suit and tie. There's an ostentatious watch on his wrist, the type men wear to indicate that their time is valuable. The hands have stopped moving, so it's probably an automatic watch, powered by the movement of the wearer. The guy's been dead at least twenty-four hours. His suit is wet, leaving a dark grey stain on the mattress around his body.

There's a halo of blood on the pillowcase. Kiara circles around the bed and sees that the right-hand side of his head has been caved in. Baseball bat, maybe.

This man, too, is wearing a wedding band.

Two dead husbands, Kiara thinks. A long centipede of unease crawls up her spine. If these men were married to each other, this could be a hate crime. She knows all too well how common those are in Warrigal—but way out here?

'Got another body,' she says into the radio. After checking that no one is hiding under the bed or in the closet, she leaves the bedroom.

The second door along the hall leads to a bathroom tiled in grey stone, veined with black. Four toothbrushes are on the sink: three electric, one manual. Four travel bags hang from towel rails; two overflow with lotions and hair products, while the others are smaller, containing only deodorant and razors. There's a double shower, the drain in the middle clogged with hair: not like someone has been shaving—more like they were running a salon. Kiara opens a cupboard to reveal a large washer-dryer and some laundry baskets.

The third door leads to another bedroom, identical to the first except the bed is empty, and there's a sliding door for easy access to the back deck. No curtains. There's more uninspiring art on the walls: a print of a mermaid singing for a ship on the horizon.

There's blood on the thick grey carpet. Maybe more footprints.

'Ground floor clear,' Kiara says, then hears a scuffle upstairs. 'Hello?' she calls.

No response.

She exits the bedroom and walks to the staircase at the end of the hall. 'Let's get out of here, shall we?' she says, as she climbs the stairs. 'We can go somewhere safe—and warm! The forecast is for eighteen degrees back in town.'

She reaches the narrow landing at the top of the stairs and tries the door with a gloved hand. It's locked.

'Can you let me in?' she says. 'I promise I'm just here to help.'

She presses her ear to the door. Silence.

Kiara goes to touch her lucky ring, the one her mother smuggled here from Vietnam. But her finger is bare, because she couldn't find the ring this morning: a bad omen.

'I'm coming in, okay?' she says. 'Stand back.'

She's not quite tall enough for this. Ideally, you want to kick *down* on a door, not up at it. Kiara braces her hands against the walls, plants one foot and channels her inner cheerleader. Her heel slams into the wood next to the handle.

An external door wouldn't have budged, but internal doors aren't built with security in mind. The locking mechanism snaps out of the soft wood, leaving a fist-sized hole, and the door opens—but only a centimetre. Whoever's inside, they haven't just locked the door. They've barricaded it.

Kiara puts her shoulder to the door and pushes. A heavy object grinds along the floor inside. When the gap is wide enough, she squeezes through.

The master bedroom has no carpet, just twin rugs on either side of the king-size bed. A lacquered chest of drawers has been dragged in front of the door. A bedside table has an open bottle of sparkling wine on top. There's a small hole in the ceiling, maybe from the cork. No glasses anywhere, though. Another door looks like it leads to an ensuite.

A man is backed up against one wall, palms flat against it, as if he's on a ledge over a long drop. A woman is standing a couple of metres away, pointing a paring knife at him.

'Hi.' Kiara puts a hand on her chest. 'I'm Kiara.'

The occupants of the bedroom ignore her, staring at each other. The woman's knuckles are white around her weapon.

Despite the cold, the man is in running shorts and a muscle shirt. He looks just like the corpses downstairs—same athletic body type, same short hair. There's blood on his hands. The woman is in leggings and a figure-hugging long-sleeve top, with flecks of vomit around her mouth. Both of them are pallid and trembling.

The man has a wedding band, and Kiara has the sudden superstitious feeling he's doomed unless he takes it off.

Kiara eases deeper into the room. 'I'll be honest,' she says, 'I have no idea what's going on here. Maybe one of you could explain . . . ?'

The woman's gaze flicks over to her. Her expression is serene. Maybe she's in shock.

'Those two blokes downstairs are in a bad way.' Kiara edges closer. She can't use the Taser—the woman is likely to stab herself when she falls. 'And Ms Dubois is in hospital, scared out of her wits. I think it's time to . . .' she stops herself from saying *end this* '. . . take a break.'

She steps between the two of them. Now the blade is pointed at her.

'How about you put that down?' she suggests.

The woman doesn't lower the blade.

Have it your way, Kiara thinks.

She punches the back of the woman's hand and, at the same moment, slams a palm against the inside of the woman's wrist. The woman's fingers pop open and the knife goes flying sideways. It lands with a soft *plop* on the rug. Kiara keeps a firm hold on the woman's wrist with one hand and whips the other back to parry any oncoming blows.

The woman just stares dumbly at her empty hand, like she can see the ghost of the knife.

'Don't hurt her,' the man says softly, from right behind Kiara's ear. 'She's fragile.'

'No one's going to hurt anybody.' Kiara reaches for her lapel radio with her free hand. 'Tactical, you can come in now. I'm upstairs with two unarmed suspects—I repeat, *unarmed* suspects. They need to be escorted from the building ASAP so forensics can come in. Don't touch anything.'

The woman suddenly grips Kiara's collar. Her eyes are wild; her breath foul. 'You can't trust him,' she whispers.

Now that both suspects are talking, Kiara has plenty of questions. But before she can ask any of them, the emergency squad bursts in.

They clear the room and check the ensuite, which Kiara realises she should have done. Then they drag the suspects out the door, handling them more roughly than they need to, perhaps to compensate for being forced to wait outside.

'I have serious blue balls,' mutters a male officer, looking forlornly at his unfired gun.

'You must be used to that, though, right?' the female officer says, with a smirk.

Kiara peeks into the ensuite: a bathtub this time, and two more toothbrushes on the vanity. She unbuckles her stab vest and inhales deeply, like a diver who's just surfaced.

The squad commander is behind her. 'The building's clear,' he says. 'All suspects in custody.'

'Wrong,' Kiara says. 'Two dead, two in custody, one in hospital. That's five people.' She points at the vanity. 'But I've seen six toothbrushes.'

Kiara

'Basically,' Jennings says, 'it's a mess.'

Everything about Jennings is thin: his hair, his stringy body and, most of all, his skin. If Kiara doesn't choose her words carefully he'll storm off, and she'll find herself reading a vague, hastily written report.

'How many people were at the house?' she asks.

'Impossible to know.' Jennings leans on his desk as he talks, leaving little smudges of moisturiser from his pink elbows. 'It's a rental, and it wasn't cleaned well between visitors. The sheets had been washed and the carpet vacuumed, but that was about it. In addition to the prints of the guests we know about, there are partials from hundreds of other people. DNA will take a while, but it's likely to be the same story.'

Kiara sighs. A defence lawyer will love this.

She's already in a bad mood. On Monday she missed dinner with Elise because she was interrogating the two suspects she'd found in the upstairs bedroom. The woman, Mrs Kelly, had accused the man, Mr Kelly, of killing both victims, but said she hadn't actually seen him do it. Mr Kelly, meanwhile, had blamed the missing guest, Ms Madden—the owner of the sixth toothbrush. But he hadn't witnessed the murders either, and provided no evidence to back up his claim.

Then, on Tuesday, the deputy commissioner returned from his long weekend in Tassie to have a go at Kiara for clearing

21

the house herself instead of letting tactical do it. He said this was strike one, and implied that if she took too long to wrap up this case, that would be strike two.

It's now Wednesday. Search and rescue has found no sign of Ms Madden, and it seems less and less likely that Jennings' evidence will include the smoking gun she was hoping for.

'What about the cutlery?' Kiara asks. 'That would be washed regularly, right?'

'The death of Victim A was—'

'Mr Woodleigh,' Kiara interrupts. The two victims have been identified now.

Jennings shrugs, as though the dead man's name doesn't matter. 'According to Gregor he was killed by a single sideways swipe, left to right, from a short, non-serrated blade.'

Jennings is only responsible for collecting evidence from crime scenes—the autopsies, fortunately, are Gregor's job. He may be creepy, but at least he's competent, unlike Jennings.

'Three knives consistent with the wound have been recovered.' Jennings slides three photographs across the table. 'All three have Mr Kelly's prints on them. This one has additional partials from Ms Dubois. And this paring knife here . . .' he taps the photo '. . . features prints from Mrs Kelly and blood matching Mr Woodleigh's blood type. That's the knife you knocked out of Mrs Kelly's hand. Are you following?'

Insulted, Kiara just raises an eyebrow.

'One of your colleagues found the key to the Tarago,' Jennings goes on. 'It was in a bush five metres off the driveway. Two AA batteries were nearby. No footprints, though. Best guess, someone threw it all from the front door.'

'I don't want guesses,' Kiara says, but he's probably right. The killer wanted to strand the victims at the house. Throwing away the batteries for the cordless phone and the key to their only vehicle was a simple way to do it.

'We tested the sheets in the downstairs bedroom—'

'Which one?'

Jennings glares at her. 'Are you implying I didn't notice there are two downstairs bedrooms, Detective Lui?'

Kiara wasn't implying that, but she wouldn't have been surprised. Jennings used to work forensics in Newcastle. At one murder scene, he'd taken some photos, bagged all the evidence, then released the scene back to the victim's family—who found a suspect's knocked-out tooth in the carpet. In court, the suspect claimed to have lost the tooth when he was assaulted by a masked man in an alley. Since forensics had missed the tooth at the scene and the family couldn't prove where they'd got it, the defence argued that the evidence wasn't admissible. The suspect had to pay for some expensive dental work, but he didn't go to jail. And Jennings was transferred to Warrigal. Postings in rural towns are sometimes meted out as punishments.

Her gaze wanders around his office. Jennings seems to have framed and hung up every diploma he's ever received, including his high school certificate: class of '96. On his desk, rather than a photo of a family member or a pet, there's a picture of himself shaking hands with a former prime minister.

Jennings sees her looking and waits for her to ask for the story.

She doesn't. 'Which bedroom?' she says again.

'The west bedroom, closest to the kitchen. Where Victim B was found.' Victim B has a name, too, but this time Kiara doesn't interrupt. 'Quite a lot of blood on the pillowcase, suggesting he was moved to the bed shortly after his death. We found some spatter on the wine bottle upstairs, and the circumference of the base matches the dent in his skull. It's his blood type, too, though again, we'll have to wait longer for DNA.'

'He was killed by a single blow?'

'Indeed.'

In Kiara's experience, most murderers hit the victim several times, in a frenzy. A single blow suggests she's looking for a calm, confident criminal.

Disquieted, she asks, 'Why wasn't the bottle broken? I'd have thought a human skull would be tougher than glass.' She once saw someone smash a pint over a man's head at one of the poker machines in Kingo's.

'Wine bottles typically have a punt—a conical depression at the base. The punt catches sediment for a cleaner pour but also makes the bottle surprisingly strong. And this was a 2004 Margaret River sparkling white. Bottles of sparkling are made with thick glass, to withstand the pressure of the gas.' Jennings may not know much about forensics, but he seems to know a lot about wine. 'I suspect, someone swung the bottle like a baseball bat just as the victim was turning to see who was behind him, and the rim connected. Ordinarily the angle would suggest the killer was shorter than the victim, but you think he was attacked while sitting down in the hot tub, correct?'

'Possibly.'

'Then it's likely the killer was crouching behind him when he or she swung the bottle, so it's hard to speculate about height.'

'Any prints on the bottle?' Kiara asks.

'Partials from . . .' Jennings peers down his nose at a sheet of paper. 'Mr Kelly, Mrs Kelly, Mr Woodleigh and an unknown fourth individual.'

That'd be right, Kiara thinks. 'What about the axe?'

Jennings looks nonplussed. 'None of the wounds suggest an axe.'

'Obviously not, but there was one at the house, and according to witness statements, the killer used it.'

'Ah, yes.' Jennings acts like he knew this all along. 'I'm looking into that.'

'Check it for prints. How about the hair in the bathroom?'

'I noticed that,' Jennings says, bristling.

'I wasn't suggesting you didn't. Whose hair is it?'

'We can't be sure. It's cut hair, so the follicles aren't attached. Follicles can give you DNA, but the hair itself can only give you colour and thickness—very unreliable.'

Kiara knows this. Plenty of convictions have been overturned because they depended on hair matching, which was exposed as a pseudoscience a few years ago.

'Based on the colour, though,' Jennings continues, 'I'd guess it came from Victim B.'

'Footprints?'

'Everywhere. But the footprints with blood in them—the impressions made *after* the stabbing of Victim A—match three pairs of shoes and one pair of slippers.'

Ms Dubois was wearing slippers when she fled. 'What about the shoes Mr and Mrs Kelly were wearing?'

'Blood on the soles. We couldn't find the third pair.'

Ms Madden, Kiara thinks. *The missing woman.* 'What about semen?'

Jennings clears his throat. 'In two of the beds.'

'Which two?'

'Upstairs, and downstairs east.'

'How much?'

'Hardly any.'

This is like pulling teeth. 'So, consistent with condom use?'

'Right.' Jennings is pink now. He's perfectly comfortable discussing murder with a lesbian; sex, apparently, is another matter.

'Does any of it match Mr Kelly?'

'It'll be at least a month before we have DNA—there's a backlog at the lab.'

'Any condoms in the rubbish?'

Jennings looks blank.

Kiara raises her eyebrows. 'You checked the rubbish, right?'

'I think someone emptied the bins,' he says. 'I'll see where the bags ended up.'

'Jesus,' Kiara says. It just slips out.

'I will not be condescended to!' Jennings stands up. 'You can wait for my written report. Good day.' He storms off and slams the door behind him.

'This is *your* office, you prick,' Kiara mutters, wondering if he'll hide somewhere, waiting for her to leave. She misses her old forensics guy. He was good—so good, unfortunately, he was rewarded with a city posting.

She pulls out her phone and calls Elise. Her partner has a way of turning a frustrating situation into a funny one.

Elise picks up. 'Hello.'

As always, Kiara feels a little glow when she hears Elise's velvety Aussie drawl. 'Hi, hot stuff. Are you busy?'

'A bit.' Hospital machines beep and clatter in the background of the call.

'Oh.' Kiara feels a twinge of disappointment. 'We can talk later—everything okay?'

'Fine.' Elise sounds tense. She never talks about it, but Kiara knows she's sometimes harassed by strangers who want to talk about what happened last year. It seems to have gotten worse lately. Elise has been on edge, secretive. This morning Elise's phone rang on the bench—a private number—and when Kiara went to answer it, Elise snatched it out of reach and rejected the call, muttering something about telemarketers. Kiara pretended to believe it, but she was thinking, *Why won't you let me help you?*

Now, Kiara says, 'I'm waiting for some people to get back to me about some things. Not a lot I can do in the meantime. Early dinner tonight?'

'Doubt it. You're about to have a witness to interview.'

Kiara's breath catches. 'Ms Dubois?'

'Got it in one. She's about to be discharged.'

Elise

At the Warrigal hospital, paramedics share the same lounge as nurses, doctors, and other staff. Elise ignores them all, sitting on an L-shaped couch, her legs crossed at the ankles, drinking a cappuccino from a paramedic-themed mug Kiara bought for her. The slogan reads: *drive carefully, or I get to see you naked.*

She watches through the window as two police officers lead Ms Dubois to their patrol car. They help her into the back seat, their hands on her elbows. She looks frail, moving like someone three times her age. Elise has read somewhere that the cold keeps you young, but it must only work up to a point.

In the ambulance on Monday, Elise had simply wrapped the woman in a heated blanket; once they reached the hospital, things got more high tech. The nurses treated her hypothermia with blood rewarming: her blood was pumped out, cooked in a haemodialysis machine and then pumped back in, raising her body temperature.

Elise doesn't need to turn around to know Rafa is behind her. He breathes loudly; it's like he's snoring even when he's awake.

'You want something, boss?' she asks.

'No.' He settles into the couch next to her. He's bearded and squat, with bulging eyes and sleeve tattoos.

'Checking on me?'

'Yeah.'

This isn't uncommon. Last year, Elise endured a horrific trauma. She was abducted and held prisoner for almost a week in an underground septic tank on a disused sheep farm. She barely escaped with her life. She wants to forget the whole thing and move on, but she can't, because people keep checking if she's fucking okay.

She swallows the anger. 'How's Daisy?'

'Don't see much of her at the moment,' Rafa says. 'She's at work all day, I'm at work all night—you know how it is.'

Most people would accept this excuse. But if Rafa wants to spend more time with his wife, Elise wonders why he's playing the pokies at Kingo's almost every evening.

'She's a special lady,' Elise says.

'She is.'

'You're a lucky man.'

'I am.' He changes the subject. 'You okay? You seemed jumpy this morning.'

Elise is still anxious after the near miss. Her phone rang, and Kiara nearly answered it. If Elise hadn't got to it first, she doesn't know what the man on the other end would have said—pretended he'd dialled the wrong number, maybe? But that would have made Kiara suspicious, because wrong numbers don't really happen anymore.

'I'm fine.' Elise points at the police car, which is shrinking as it cruises away down the hill. 'What do you think happened?'

'I think it's none of our business.'

She nods. But she's seen how rapidly things can *become* your business. You don't ignore a bushfire just because it's on the other side of a fence.

A siren screams overhead: another car accident, or a drug overdose, or something else involving clammy flesh and wails of pain. Elise sculls the last of her coffee and stands up, ready to work.

Kiara

'My husband wasn't supposed to die,' Ms Dubois says.

She pauses.

'No one was,' she adds. 'Obviously.'

Kiara reclines in her squeaky swivel chair. Interviewing suspects is like rowing—you lean forward to apply pressure and back to release it, propelling the conversation further along. Forward, back, forward, back: an eight-hour interrogation is a gruelling core workout.

The interview room has no windows and no one-way mirror. Just brick walls, peeling blue paint, and a camera recording from the corner. There's no AC, because the sound can obscure the recording. The air is stale, cold, oppressive.

Ms Dubois is wearing clothes a friend brought from her home: a sleeveless silk shirt with pleats around the neckline, tucked into high-waisted suit pants that look expensive. A ruby sparkles on her finger, flanked by oval diamonds. She looks a lot better than she did in hospital on Monday. There's more colour in her cheeks, no grime in her hair. Her voice is flat but no longer raspy.

She has straight white teeth, perhaps thanks to cosmetic dentistry. Her angled brows are plucked. Her slightly upturned nose looks too perfect, maybe the result of surgery. But beneath all these changes, the overall shape feels familiar.

Kiara tilts her head. 'Have we met before?'

Dubois blinks. 'I don't know. Have we?'

Warrigal is a town of only a few thousand people, so Kiara has met most of them at some point. Nothing turned up on the police database when she ran Dubois' name, though.

Kiara lets it go. 'Hmm. Just a bit of déjà vu, I guess. Let's talk about the house. Renting it for the long weekend—that was your idea, right?'

Dubois looks wary. 'Who told you that?'

No one. Kiara is guessing; she makes a meaningless squiggle in her notebook.

'We were all having dinner at Botticelli's,' Dubois says, 'for my birthday. I'd ordered spaghetti carbonara—'

The hairs rise on the back of Kiara's neck. Irrelevant details are a red flag; they can mean a suspect is stalling.

'—and Dom mentioned the time he tried to cook it for everybody, when they were all down the coast. He overheated the sauce, and it pretty much turned into scrambled eggs. So we were having a laugh about that, and Cole suggested we should take another holiday together. Or maybe it was Oscar . . .? I can't remember.'

Kiara leans forward, applying pressure. '*Try.* Two people are dead.'

'Two?' Dubois repeats. Apparently no one has told her about the second body.

'Your husband,' Kiara says, 'and Mr Woodleigh.'

'Oh.' Dubois stares blankly.

Mr and Mrs Kelly—the couple Kiara found in the upstairs bedroom of the house—are still in hospital, being treated for shock. Mrs Kelly has some bruising around her wrists and throat. Mr Kelly is uninjured. The blood on his hands belonged to Mr Woodleigh, the dead man in the kitchen.

In Warrigal, the homicide rate is low: one or two bodies a year. Last year was an outlier with six, three of whom died on the farm where Elise was held captive. That case was Kiara's worst nightmare, both professionally and personally. But once it was closed, she hoped things would settle down—she hoped *Elise* would settle down. No more jumping at sudden noises, no more gallows humour, no more tossing and turning all night, then looking haunted all day. But Elise doesn't like doctors, and refuses to see a psychiatrist; Kiara isn't sure how hard to push.

Now there are two more bodies and a missing woman, so this year is shaping up much like the last.

Six friends rent a house on a mountaintop. Two are murdered, one vanishes, and three come back with conflicting stories. It's pure clickbait, so the media have descended on the town like locusts. Fortunately, many of the reporters went to Warr*agul* in Victoria rather than Warr*igal* in New South Wales. Kiara hopes to solve the case before they realise their mistake.

She doesn't watch crime shows or read crime novels. Too many seem to glamorise awful people, like drug kingpins or cannibals. Others painfully skew what it's like to work a homicide case, oversimplifying some things and making others needlessly convoluted. In real life, working out what happened is often easy. There'll be a curious neighbour who saw the event, or the killer will have left prints or DNA at the scene. *Proving* it is the hard part—the process takes years, rather than forty-five minutes divided neatly into cliff-hangers and ad breaks.

But in this case, the rental house is so remote that no one lives or works nearby. There are only four suspects, but they were all at the scene, so their prints and DNA are everywhere. Even if Kiara figures out the truth, proving it is going to be a nightmare.

She leans in again. As with rowing, it's best to work backwards. 'Let's start at the beginning,' she says.

LAST FRIDAY

Oscar

'Did you put in a phone charger?' Isla asked.

'Yes,' Oscar replied, dumping another backpack into the boot.

'How about sunscreen?' She was talking to him as though he was her child rather than her husband. As though he couldn't be trusted.

'It's the middle of winter,' Oscar said.

'Have you packed it, or not?'

He hadn't, but he nodded, because a nod wasn't really a lie. He'd duck back into the house and get the sunscreen later, when she wasn't looking.

She must have noticed he was tense. 'I was just asking.' Her throat was hidden by a fluffy scarf. Aviators concealed her thick eyebrows and charcoal eyes. She wore her ponytail pulled through the back of her cap, in a way that Oscar had once found sexy.

He was only wearing a T-shirt under his coat. The cold wind swept up the driveway, slithered into his sleeves and soaked deep down into his bones. The sooner they got out of here, the better.

He dumped the last suitcase into the boot. The three bags were inversely proportional to the weight of their owners. His backpack contained only three changes of clothes and some toiletries. Isla's bag was twice as big, for reasons that were a mystery to him. Noah's suitcase was gigantic, crammed with picture books, stuffed animals, changes of pyjamas and a mattress protector.

'Where are we going?' Noah asked, for perhaps the eleventh time that morning. He was holding a deck of Pokémon cards instead of the water bottle Oscar had filled up for him.

'*We* are going on holiday in the mountains. *You* are off to stay with Uncle Ken and Uncle Raymond.' Oscar tried to ruffle Noah's mop of hair. As usual, the boy shrank away like he expected a beating—even though Oscar had never hit him, not even once, no matter how much the kid deserved it.

'But *why?*' Noah whined.

Isla turned up her collar against the cold. Between that and the sunnies, she looked like a movie star avoiding the paparazzi. She crouched next to Noah. 'Because Mummy and Daddy don't go to school anymore, so we hardly ever get to play with our school friends.'

You mean your *school friends*, Oscar thought.

'That's sad,' said Noah, suddenly a beacon of emotional intelligence.

'Being an adult is sometimes sad,' Isla agreed.

'Being a kid is sometimes sad, too,' Noah said.

Oscar opened his mouth to say how ridiculous that was. Kids didn't have to go to work or pay rent. They had endless leisure time. They recovered from injuries and illnesses with incredible speed. They got buried alive in gifts at birthdays and Christmases, and no one ever expected anything in return. Everyone was friendly to them, even strangers.

But Isla got there first. 'I know, sweetie,' she said, and wrapped Noah up in a hug.

Oscar just stood next to the car, shivering. He checked his watch; they were going to be late, again.

In their youth, he and Isla had been punctual. When they first met, they'd both been waiting for other people at Chili's, just off the University of Wollongong campus. Isla had been sipping a Coke, wearing black leggings and a huge purple jumper that revealed nothing of her figure but nevertheless made her hard to ignore. Oscar surprised himself by sitting next to her and ordering a drink; it wasn't like him. But his eyes kept getting drawn to the side of her face, and he had this feeling that if he didn't start a conversation, he'd regret it for the rest of his life.

After he introduced himself, it turned out Isla was a politics student, like him. A better one—she spoke confidently about Locke and Rousseau in a way that made him feel ignorant, even though he was two years ahead of her. Whenever her eyes were on him, he felt a glow; whenever he made her laugh, the glow became a fire.

Flowers didn't seem like a grand enough gesture. Instead he called the manager of The Haters, an indie-rock band from Sydney that Isla said she liked. Posing as a representative of the university, Oscar invited the band to perform at the campus refectory. Then he called the uni, pretending to be the band's manager requesting permission to perform. He printed posters and stuck them up all over campus. Presumably the ruse was discovered at some point, but by then the gig was already sold out. Oscar had bought the first two tickets, and he offered one to Isla. When she found out what he'd done, she was astonished.

Watching her dance to the frantic drums under the strobe, her face sweaty, her hair flying, he knew she was the one. That night he set up an automated fortnightly transfer into a savings account, so he could someday buy her a ring.

Three years after she graduated, they were married. Two years after that, they were pregnant. (Oscar had always scoffed at couples who said '*we* are pregnant', but when it was his turn, it really did feel like something that was happening to both of them.) He turned down a job at a consulting firm in Canberra so they could move back to Isla's home town of Warrigal, where her parents could help out with the baby.

During the birth, Isla had squeezed his hand tightly enough to cause ligament damage.

Oscar didn't think they'd held hands even once since then.

He'd heard babies were excellent mind-readers. They couldn't understand words, so they became highly attuned to body language, facial expression and tone of voice, to the point where it was impossible to trick them. That would explain why he'd never been able to settle Noah as a baby. The kid would start wailing at 12, 2 and 4 a.m. Oscar would try to feed him, but Noah refused the bottle: the kid only wanted Isla's breasts, breasts that used to be Oscar's property but which he was no longer allowed to touch. He would tuck Noah in and pat his back, and sing that fucking song over and over: 'Found a peanut, found a peanut, found a peanut just now . . .' But Noah would just keep screaming, because he could hear Oscar's thoughts: *I should have worn a condom.*

Eventually an exasperated Isla would come into the nursery, and the little shit would fall asleep in her arms immediately, sucking his thumb. She would give Oscar a look that said, *Was that so hard?* Then Oscar would go to bed alone, unable to sleep because he felt like such a failure.

There weren't many jobs in Warrigal for a guy with a political science degree, but Oscar managed to find work as a real estate agent. During the day he would stare at pre-approval forms, too tired to turn the information into knowledge. His boss, Rick, wondered aloud why Oscar's listings weren't selling, while the other agents shot him pitying looks. None of them had slept either—they'd been at Kingo's all night—but somehow their brains worked just fine. They never lost the thread of a conversation or mixed up the date of an opening.

Oscar tried the foul energy drink they were always quaffing. It gave him heart palpitations but didn't make him any more alert. He was forced to conclude it wasn't caffeine and guarana giving those other agents the edge. They were in their early twenties, still at the making-choices stage of their lives; he was almost thirty, already at the living-with-the-consequences stage.

He once suggested to Isla that her parents could look after Noah over the weekend, just so he and Isla could catch up on some sleep and start the week refreshed. She looked at him like he was insane. 'Mum and Dad are too old to look after Noah for two whole days.'

Oscar was stunned. If her parents couldn't do childminding, then why the hell had he given up his career to move to this shitty little town?

He told himself newborns were supposed to be hard. Everyone said so. Things would get better as the kid got older.

Now, though, Noah was five and still didn't sleep through. Oscar still had to get up three times a night, and change the kid's sheets every day. The house always smelled of piss and was hard to navigate because there were clothes airers everywhere. No matter how often Oscar swept the floor, there was always a sharp piece of Lego underfoot. Noah screamed at the top of his lungs if it took longer than two seconds to give him what he wanted, but whenever Oscar asked *him* to do anything—*wash your hands, get in the bath*—Noah didn't seem to hear, happily munching on a crayon. He wouldn't eat the vegetables Oscar steamed for him, but apparently crayons were A-okay. After politely asking the kid fifty or sixty times to brush his teeth, Oscar would finally snap and shout at him. Then Isla would come in, and Noah would turn into an obedient little angel, doing everything she said. And she would give Oscar that look again, like, *What the hell is wrong with you? You're pathetic.*

Late last year, Isla said she wanted another child. Oscar was floored. He'd thought they were on the same page: life with a kid was miserable, but it wouldn't last forever. But she wanted to start the whole process again.

'Why?' He kept his voice down, to avoid waking Noah. 'We can't even cope with the child we have!'

Isla looked startled. 'Since when?'

'Since he was born. We're drowning. The house is a wreck. We never sleep, we never see our friends—we barely get to talk to each other.'

'We're talking right now,' Isla said coldly, and he could already see he'd been wrong. *They* weren't drowning: *he* was.

Noah started screaming in his room.

Isla squeezed her temples. 'For fuck's sake.'

Oscar moved for the door.

'Don't.' She stormed out. Seconds later, Noah was silent.

Oscar sat down on the bed, lost for words. Noah was awful, so Oscar had done everything he could to protect Isla from him. He'd changed every nappy. He'd driven the kid around in the middle of the night so she could sleep. He'd taken Noah for endless walks during the day so she could read. Apparently this had worked too well. Isla had been living in some parallel universe where Noah was perfect and the problem was with *him*.

When she finally came back to bed, Oscar pretended to be asleep. The following day, Isla spoke to him in grunts and wouldn't make eye contact. But she spoke to Noah gushingly, adoringly. All the love she'd once felt for Oscar was going to him, the little vampire.

This continued for four months. It might not have been so bad if Oscar had someone else to confide in. But his university friends had scattered to the winds, and his family was back in Maitland. He had no one.

No wonder he'd fallen in love with Felicity.

It had started at Dom's party. Dom had been on the high school athletics team with Isla back in the day, and now worked for a finance company in Wagga. He and Isla had dated, but she refused to talk about it, perhaps because she thought Oscar would feel insecure—Dom was handsome, charming, and frequently invited people over to show off some expensive new toy. This time it was a Tesla. A few months earlier it had been a swimming pool. Before that, a stunning twenty-three-year-old wife named Felicity.

Isla didn't even seem to like Dom, but she'd accepted the invitation because Clementine would be there. Clementine was Isla's best friend. She and her husband, Cole, had been on the team, too. Both were fair-haired and muscular—Cole owned a gym, and Clementine was some kind of fitness model. They'd been married for years but were constantly touching one another, as if they were still on their honeymoon. It made Oscar sick with jealousy.

'And how old are you, Noah?' Felicity asked. 'Fourteen? Fifteen?'

Noah cackled. 'No! I'm almost six.'

You're fucking five and a half, Oscar thought.

Clementine awwed as though that was the cutest thing anyone had ever said. Cole actually teared up and escaped out onto the driveway, choking out something about wanting to hear the sound system in Dom's car.

Oscar wished he smoked, so he too would have a reason to get away from everyone. Then he decided he was past caring what anyone thought of him, and he just walked out the back door without explanation.

Dom's backyard was huge, because of course it was. In addition to the pool, it had a neatly mown lawn, fruit trees, a fire pit, a pizza oven, and four vegetable patches growing heirloom tomatoes, cucumbers and watermelons. Little tags gave the tomatoes the improbable name of 'beefsteak'.

Felicity found Oscar nursing his third beer on one of several bench seats hidden behind the four-car garage. 'Are you okay?' she asked.

It felt like a long time since he'd been asked that question—even longer since anyone had sounded like they might care about the answer.

'Living the dream,' he said.

Felicity had tangled red hair, freckles splashed across her nose, and big green eyes that seemed to miss nothing. Oscar didn't know her well—he'd met her a couple of times before the wedding but had been a sleep-deprived zombie. At the ceremony he'd been looking after Noah all night and hadn't spoken to her. Beyond wondering why rich men got young, gorgeous wives when rich women didn't seem to have young, gorgeous husbands, Oscar hadn't given Felicity much thought.

She picked up a mallet from the bench and tossed it, with impressive accuracy, into a bucket. Then she sat where it had been, so close to Oscar that the puffy sleeve of her dress brushed against his arm. Static electricity crackled between them. She took the beer from his hand, sipped it and gave it back. The intimacy of the gesture gave him a shock. He played it cool, mostly because the alcohol had dulled his reaction time to the point where he didn't seem surprised.

'I love this spot,' she said. 'People walk past the fence having all kinds of conversations. You wouldn't believe the things I overhear.'

'Like what?' he asked.

'Sorry, not telling.' She crossed her legs. 'I can keep a secret like nobody's business—except when I'm on stage.'

Oscar had heard she was a comic. 'So you won't tell anyone, but you will tell *everyone*.'

She grinned. 'Exactly.'

'Keeping secrets is a rare skill these days. People put every thought online. They don't save anything for . . .' Oscar realised he was rambling, drunkenly, to a pretty twenty-three-year-old who probably put everything online herself. He sounded so *old*. He shut his mouth.

She gestured at the house. 'You're a real estate agent, right? What do you think we'd get for this place?'

People always thought their house was worth more than it was; Oscar had learned it was safest to avoid the question. 'Thinking of selling?'

'No. I just wanted to distract you from . . . whatever's going on up there.' She reached out and poked his forehead.

He forced a smile. 'Nothing's going on.'

'You sure? I couldn't help but notice you hiding in my backyard.'

He laughed. 'You're funny.'

'Nope.' She leaned towards him, like she was sharing something confidential. 'Just honest. It turns out that if you tell the truth when it would be more polite to lie, people laugh.'

He could smell the beer on her breath—wine, too. Trying not to look down the scooping neckline of her dress, he found himself staring at his drink. She'd put her lips on the rim of the bottle; if he drank from it, that was practically the same as kissing her.

'Is it the kid?' Felicity asked. 'He's cute—like a little version of you. But he seems like he might be hard work.'

If only Isla would acknowledge that. 'I don't think she loves me anymore,' Oscar heard himself say.

It was the truth, but Felicity didn't laugh. Her theory of comedy was clearly incomplete. 'What makes you think that?' she asked.

'We haven't had sex in months,' Oscar said. The real situation was more complex, but he wasn't sober enough to explain it all. He was being *way* too honest now.

'You poor thing. You must be ready to pop.'

He sipped the beer, kissing her at one remove. 'I don't know what to do,' he said, and heard his voice crack.

'You're a beautiful man.' Felicity put a hand on his shoulder. 'If Isla doesn't want you, she's insane.'

Oscar leaned forward and kissed her.

Her lips were soft, and sticky with orange-flavoured gloss. She kissed him back—or he told himself she did. But then she pulled away, and said, 'Oi!'

He scrambled backwards as if burned. 'I'm sorry,' he stammered, but Felicity was looking past him. He turned in time to see an old man's head disappear behind the side fence.

'I see you, you nosy prick!' Felicity stood up and patted the back of her dress; Oscar realised the bench seat was dirty. 'New neighbour,' she muttered. 'Always snooping.'

'I'm sorry,' Oscar said, but he was only sorry it was over.

The corner of her mouth quirked. 'See you round, Oscar.' She slipped away towards the house.

Oscar sat there a while longer. It might be suspicious if they came back in at the same time, particularly if he had a visible erection.

When he eventually re-entered the house, no one looked at him. At first he was terrified that Felicity had told everyone what happened. But soon he realised no one had even noticed he was missing.

That night, Isla rolled over in bed behind him. She traced a fingernail from his throat down to his navel, nibbling the back of his neck. Relief washed over him. Their rough patch was over. She still loved him after all.

And then came the guilt. He'd kissed another woman— a friend's wife, no less. *Forsaking all others, till death do us part.* He had given up on those vows after only a few sexless months.

Turning around in bed, he kissed Isla. Hungrily. Desperately. He would make it up to her. He would be the husband of her dreams.

But as he climbed onto her and parted her knees, something stopped him. 'Are you back on the pill?'

She smiled seductively in the dark. 'Nope.'

Nothing had changed, Oscar realised. She didn't love *him*: she loved the baby, this new baby who didn't even exist outside her imagination.

The despair was crushing. He couldn't stay hard, which Isla seemed to take as an insult. He collapsed back into bed and blamed the alcohol.

There were two more months of frosty silences after that.

Now, as they headed up the pebbled driveway towards Ken and Ray's place, Oscar realised he'd forgotten the sunscreen. Shit. He'd have a quiet word with Cole when they got to the rental, explain the situation. Cole was Mr Organised—he probably had a spare tube.

Ken was Isla's brother. Oscar had helped him and his husband buy a handsome two-storey brick house that dated back to the nineteenth century, with pomegranate trees out the front and a bull-nose veranda that shielded the windows from the sun. The two men both worked and had no kids, so they could afford a place like this. They kept it scrupulously clean because they were trying to adopt; the agency might send someone to inspect without much notice.

When Isla rang the bell, Ken called out, 'Who could that be?' in a singsong voice that made Noah giggle. Then Ken opened the door and said, 'Look at that! It's Noah!' and swept the boy up in his tattooed arms, ignoring Oscar and Isla.

Noah shrieked, grinning as he dangled upside down in Ken's grip.

Oscar watched with wonder. Who were these men who *liked* children? How could he become one of them?

When Isla was pregnant, other parents had warned him that having a child *changed everything*. But after she gave birth, the problem wasn't that things had changed—the problem was that Oscar hadn't. He enjoyed the same activities: watching the cricket, playing video games and sleeping in on weekends, all of which were now impossible most of the time. And while he'd expected to transform into a devoted father the moment he saw his child, he found himself simply staring. Probing around the edges of the dark void where the love was supposed to be.

'We'll be back on Monday afternoon,' Isla was saying. 'I reckon around three, but it could be as late as four.'

'No rush.' Ken beamed at Noah.

Oscar and Isla each hugged Noah goodbye. He stiffened in Oscar's grip, as always—scared of his own father.

Then Oscar and Isla drove away in chilly silence. He told himself that after this weekend, things would be different. This weekend, Felicity would be his.

Felicity

'This place has hardly changed in twenty years,' Dom said wistfully.

Felicity looked around at the fluffy pollen blanketing the deserted car park. She knew her husband suffered from hay fever. 'You must have spent most of your time sneezing.'

'Yep. Back then, I couldn't afford the good antihistamines. But now . . .' Dom took a deep breath through his nose. 'Ta-da!'

'Bravo,' Felicity said drily.

Dom was always talking about the things he owned. When they first met, Felicity had assumed he was bragging: *I came from nothing, now I have everything, look how great I am.* She'd actually found it attractive, the way he wasn't embarrassed by his wealth. It helped that he was attractive in every other way, too. Thick brown hair, deep blue eyes. A head taller than her and square-jawed, with a heavy brow and broad shoulders. Today he was wearing a buttoned Hugo Boss shirt, but he still looked a bit like a sexy caveman.

She understood him better now. Bragging was designed to impress other people, and Dom didn't care what other people thought—he was just expressing gratitude. He was that rare kind of man who appreciated what he had, instead of always wishing for something better.

Felicity wrapped her coat more tightly around her body. 'Why are we meeting here?'

'Old times' sake.'

'We look pretty shady, adults hanging around a high school. We might get in trouble with the cops.'

He leered at her. 'You could pass for a high school student.'

She tried to look affronted. 'Well then, you'd be in even bigger trouble, wouldn't you?'

'I'm sure you could get me off.'

She laughed. 'Oi! No funny business. That's my job.'

Dom winked. 'Just providing extra material, sweetheart.'

She often made fun of him during her set. 'I've discovered a life hack,' she'd whisper into the mic, then pause, luring the audience in. 'It turns out, being a wife is *way* easier than being a hooker.' A single awkward chuckle from the darkness beyond the stage. 'For starters, you only have the one client. It's very easy to remember his name. I get it right, like, eight times out of ten.' Laughter, from more people, a little more comfortable now. 'And his fetishes,' she'd continue. 'No more wondering, *Is this the guy who likes being spanked, or is it the guy who's into feet?* Now I know straight away: it's both! It's *always* both. "You want me to kick you in the arse, honey? Just like last night, and the night before? Okey-dokey, you're the client—I mean, husband!"'

Like all the best bits, this had a sprinkle of truth but was completely deniable. She'd never been a sex worker, but in high school she'd charged a boy twenty bucks to touch her boob. She had accidentally said 'James' when she meant 'Dom', but only once. And Dom was indifferent to spanking, but he did love her feet; she got a lot of massages.

While she mimed a mixture of kicking and mock-sexy dancing on the stage, Dom would be in the crowd, laughing uproariously alongside all the uncomfortable-looking friends for whom he'd bought tickets. That was the other thing she loved about him: he didn't mind being the butt of a joke.

Now, in the car park, she got out her journal and scribbled

a note. *Butt of a joke.* She was sure she could work that into the spank-fetish routine.

'If the cops handcuffed us,' Dom was saying, 'could you use your old circus skills to get us out?'

'I was a clown,' she reminded him.

'Yeah, but . . .' He trailed off. This car park was adjacent to the high school campus, close enough that the buildings were visible through the fence. Dom was frowning at some kids lounging under an awning, hypnotised by their phones. 'What are primary school students doing here?'

'Oh, sweetie.' She put her hand on his arm. 'Those are high school students.'

'What?' He squinted. 'No way. Those children are ten at the most.'

'They *look* ten to you, because you're an old, old, old . . .'

He swiped at her, and she leaped out of reach.

'. . . old, old, old man,' she finished, laughing.

He chuckled. 'Okay, give me a break.'

She wrapped her arms around his waist, tilted her chin and kissed him on his stubbly cheek. 'Never.'

A dented hatchback turned into the car park. Isla and Oscar were here. Felicity felt her good mood slip away, like the sun disappearing behind a cloud.

There were two types of sexiness, in her experience—the type that needed you, and the type that didn't. Dom had the second type. He was a rugged, independent man who loved Felicity but nevertheless gave the impression he'd be just fine without her. They'd first met two years ago, after she'd quit the circus and found a job as a sales assistant at a Wagga Wagga car dealership. Dom asked her out just after buying a Jaguar from her. 'Maybe you could take *me* for a test drive sometime,' he said, spinning the key on one finger. It was the sort of line that Felicity usually rolled her eyes at, but he made it work. His smile seemed to suggest that if she turned him down, it would be her loss.

They'd really clicked, and Dom proposed after only

four months of dating. His family hadn't liked her much, particularly his grumpy old father, but that seemed to work in Felicity's favour—Dom became her defender, her champion. It was them against the world. They got married at a vineyard in the Hunter Valley, honeymooned in the Maldives, and came home to Dom's beautiful house in Warrigal. After a senior partner at his company had a stroke, Dom got promoted, and suddenly they had even more money. Felicity quit her job to focus on comedy. Dom showered her with gifts on Valentine's Day, her birthday, their anniversary, Christmas, and sometimes for no reason at all. She had never been so happy.

Soon Dom got bored with the Jaguar and went out to buy a Tesla. Felicity waited outside the dealership, while he went in to sign the paperwork. When she glanced up from her phone, she saw him talking to the pretty young woman behind the counter. The woman was laughing. Felicity wondered if it was just the Jaguar Dom was getting tired of.

That night, at the party, she told him she was going out the back to check on Oscar. She made sure to take a suspiciously long time. She talked loudly, hoping to lure Dom out. She wanted him to see them together, to realise what he had, and what he might lose.

Oscar was so pathetic that it was almost a turn-on. He had the other kind of sexiness, the kind that was desperate, hungry. Manipulating him was unexpectedly thrilling. Some well-chosen words, some seemingly innocent body language, and then, bam! This total stranger was in love with her. Kissing her. *Betraying his wife* with her. Why couldn't she seduce her own husband as easily as someone else's?

Dom hadn't come out into the backyard. Felicity had left Oscar there. She'd expected him to forget about the kiss once he'd sobered up; instead, he'd become obsessed. He liked every single one of her posts on social media. He texted her in the middle of the night. She deleted the messages and blocked his number, but the more she retreated, the more desperate he became. She seemed to be the fulcrum on which his whole world was balanced. He sent emails. Turned up at her shows. Once he even came to the house with a bunch of flowers, in the middle of the day when Dom was at work. Felicity had pretended not to be home and Oscar had gone away, but not before her nosy neighbour spotted him.

Oscar wasn't sexy anymore. He was like a drowning man who would grab hold of anyone who got too close and take them down with him.

She hadn't told Dom about the kiss, because she didn't want to admit she'd been trying to make him jealous. She couldn't allow herself to seem needy. But the longer she waited, the more impossible it became. If he found out now, he would surely wonder if she'd led Oscar on, not just that night but in the months since. What's more, Dom might start looking more closely at her background. He might figure out why she'd left Warrigal to join the circus, all those years ago.

She remembered how fast things fell apart with James, the boy she'd dated in her late teens. She couldn't let the same thing happen with Dom. But it would be hard to keep him if he thought she had cheated. He was rich, handsome and childless: he could find a new wife in a heartbeat.

Felicity had been lost before she'd found Dom. Nothing she did felt meaningful. She'd told outrageous lies out of boredom. She had friends and boyfriends but only pretended to like them, and never thought of them when they weren't around. At school, she used to think that if the Rapture happened and her friends vanished, she would shrug it off. She wondered if she was even capable of love.

Now she knew she was—and she refused to give it up.

Isla got out of the car first. 'Hi, guys!' she called. As usual, she wore clothes that concealed her body from head to toe: a baseball cap, a high-neck long-sleeve top that covered not only her wrists but also the heels of her palms, and loose pants that hung over closed-toe shoes. Perhaps she was sensitive to the sun, despite her dark skin.

She hugged Felicity, squeezing tight enough to make her ribs creak. Isla had represented Warrigal High School in the state athletics championship, along with Dom, Cole and Clementine. None of them seemed to know their own strength.

'I like your hair,' Isla said.

Felicity touched the back of her head. 'Thanks.' She'd cut her red locks to shoulder-length and straightened them in preparation for this weekend.

Isla hugged Dom next, but not as tightly or for as long. Her affection looked forced, although Dom didn't seem to notice. There had always been something off about that relationship. When Felicity queried it, Dom had said he dated Isla 'very, very briefly' in high school. Felicity had asked others, who'd confirmed this, but no one would explain the undercurrent of tension, the one Dom didn't seem to notice. She went through his old social media posts, but he hadn't joined Facebook until 2011, so there was nothing from high school. All Isla's profiles were set to private; after Felicity's friend requests were accepted, she found that the woman hadn't posted anything prior to 2009—or had deleted her old posts. Even now, she seemed camera-shy: all her photos were of Noah, not herself.

Oscar came over. He always looked a bit drawn, with dark hollows under his grey eyes, a permanent slouch in his lean body, curly ginger hair often stuck to his forehead. Now his hair was neater, but in his tattered, stained green coat, he still looked like he should be holding a cardboard sign that said THE END IS NIGH.

'Ozzie, Ozzie, Ozzie,' Dom said cheerfully, extending a hand.

Oscar shook it stiffly, then opened his arms to hug Felicity. She couldn't avoid it without arousing suspicion, so she forced a smile and spread her arms.

'It's good to see you,' he whispered, his face buried in her hair.

She slipped out of his grip, skin crawling, and patted the envelope in her pocket. *Two more days*, she thought. *Then he'll be out of my life forever.*

Cole

Cole hit the brakes too hard, so he and Clementine jolted against their seatbelts. The car came to a stop at a slight angle, not quite parallel to his best friend's Tesla.

'Are you all right?' Cole asked anxiously.

Clementine brushed her blonde hair out of her eyes. 'Are *you*?'

He forced a laugh. 'Yeah, sorry. Just excited.'

She squeezed his thigh. 'It's okay. Me too.'

Cole was a careful driver. He'd aced his driving test on the first go and never once received an infringement notice. But with his old high school friends watching, he was self-conscious. And the leather bag on the back seat was distracting him. The contents of the side pocket were like a magnet, messing with his internal compass.

Even in an almost-empty car park, Cole couldn't bring himself to leave the car crooked. He reversed slowly, giving the Tesla a wide berth.

It was ridiculous, in Cole's opinion, for Dom to have bought an electric car when there were no charging stations in Warrigal. But Dom was like that. He'd drop thousands of dollars on something just to show that he could.

Cole looked out the window. Dom was wrapped in an expensive-looking sports jacket. Felicity had her arm around him. She'd straightened her curly hair, and wore a T-shirt and cut-off jeans despite the cold. Isla looked elegant as always, even though she was dressed like a nun, almost every centimetre of her flawless brown skin covered. Oscar was gaunt and hunched, his grey eyes flicking left and right. He'd changed his hair, too: it was short at the back and the sides, like Cole's. Cole suspected the similarity was deliberate.

'You think this will be the last time we're all together?' Clementine asked suddenly.

He glanced over. 'Why?'

'Because . . .' She trailed off, like she didn't want to jinx anything.

He got it now. 'Could be,' he said, and smiled. 'We'll be a bit busy next year.'

Clementine smiled too, absently rubbing her abdomen. After several rounds of IVF, she'd gained a little weight in her breasts and belly, like she was carrying already. But Cole wasn't holding his breath—they'd been disappointed so many times.

He found it hard to picture her pregnant. In high school she'd been thin and pale, and even when she started building muscle for her career as a fitness model, she still *felt* small. After their wedding, he carried her into the honeymoon suite without breaking a sweat. When they made love he always held back, afraid of hurting her. Even her wispy blonde hair broke easily.

Sometimes he worried this was why they couldn't conceive. 'Your swimmers aren't quite strong enough,' the fertility specialist had said. But maybe Cole's sperm weren't weak— they were reluctant. They could sense he thought of his wife as fragile and were waiting for a sturdier vessel.

He got out of the car and opened the door for Clementine. 'Howdy,' he said to the others, as though he'd been transformed into a cowboy.

Clementine squealed and hugged Isla like they hadn't seen each other in years, even though they'd had brunch together twice that week. Clementine hugged Felicity too, then Oscar, then Dom, who also got a peck on the cheek.

Clementine was the lynchpin of the group—the one who organised activities in the group chat. River swims on sunny days, hikes when it was cold, board games when it rained. Once they had a baby, Cole realised, they wouldn't just leave the group: they'd shatter it.

He didn't hug or kiss anybody; he just fist-bumped Oscar and Dom. He was pleased to see them, but it wasn't manly to say so.

'This place is exactly the same,' Clementine said, looking around with wonder.

'I was just saying that!' Dom exclaimed.

'Remember that time we cling-wrapped Mr Heinrich's car?' Clementine peered through the fence at the school. 'It was stuck here for hours before he could get the doors open.'

'I remember that!' Isla said, guffawing.

So did Cole. It hadn't seemed very funny at the time—kind of mean, actually. But fifteen years later, he found himself laughing along, not because it was clever but because it was a shared memory. The past was like that, tragedy becoming comedy. Sometimes he heard a song from his youth on the radio, and even though he'd hated it back then, he'd sing along. The act of remembering gave him joy.

'What took you guys so long?' Isla lowered her aviators and raised a thick eyebrow at Clementine.

Felicity made an O with her thumb and forefinger, then jabbed her other forefinger into the hole. Dom, Isla and Oscar laughed, and Cole felt himself start to blush. He avoided Isla's gaze. *Funny*, he thought, *how taking thirty-somethings back to their old school makes them act like teenagers.*

Clementine's hands flew to her mouth. She gave them all a mock-scandalised look.

'Sorry, I was just making sure I put everything in,' Cole said, a bit defensively. He thought again of the bag, its side pocket.

'I'll bet,' Felicity said.

He blushed even harder. 'I meant I was packing.'

'You sure are.' She glanced at his crotch.

He dared not say anything else in case she twisted his words again.

She held up her palms. 'Hey, you're adults. You're allowed to have sex.'

'We *weren't* having—' Cole decided to change the subject. 'Are you sure the electric car will make it up the mountain?'

'I would have brought the Jag,' Dom said. 'But my wife had other ideas.'

Felicity rolled her eyes. 'It's a scratch.'

'It's a *dent*.'

'I had right of way. That bollard should have been watching where it was going.'

Oscar laughed, too loudly.

Clementine was stretching, as usual. 'You'll all fit in our Tarago,' she said, hands under her toes. 'But will your cars be safe here over the weekend?'

As Dom explained about the Tesla's fancy security system, Cole jogged ahead and unlocked the minibus. He quickly moved the leather bag to the storage compartment under the back row of seats. When everyone else came over, he piled their backpacks and suitcases on top of it.

'Wish our car had this much room,' Isla said as she climbed in. 'You'd be amazed how much stuff you need to travel with a kid.'

Cole winced. That was why they'd chosen the Tarago. They'd joked about having quintuplets, filling every seat. They didn't make jokes like that anymore.

Cole had bought the car just *before* profits from the gym started to slip. At first it had only been a couple of quitters, not worth worrying Clementine over. Then a few more members left, and no one showed up to replace them. Two of the treadmills broke and needed repairs. The dip became a dive.

He tried to focus on preparing for the baby. After eight months without success, Clementine wanted to try IVF.

Cole said, 'Great idea.' If she wanted it, he would make it happen, a policy that had served him well throughout their marriage.

They researched the process, learning words like 'zygote' and 'oocyte'. After some tests, they discovered he was the problem, not her. This meant they needed ICSI, the manual injection of sperm into the egg, which was more complicated than conventional IVF. They ended up at a private clinic. Cole hadn't thought much about what all this would cost until the credit card statement arrived, and suddenly the shortfall of gym memberships seemed more significant.

But still he didn't tell Clementine. The specialist had said stress might be a factor in whether or not the pregnancy took hold. Cole told himself he could handle it.

The first round of treatment failed: no embryos. He hid his disappointment—Clementine was the one who'd taken the medication and endured the headaches, the blurred vision, the fatigue. Despite this, she wanted to try again. He said, 'Great idea.'

When the second round failed, she wanted to try a third. He agreed again. Even with the Medicare rebates, he felt like he was sinking into quicksand.

The doctor suggested they use donor sperm, which was even more expensive. Clementine misread Cole's reluctance, and tried to convince him that he would still be the father in every way that mattered. He didn't know how to tell her that he was only worried about the cost.

The third round resulted in an embryo that implanted in the uterus. They were overjoyed. Cole bought a pram and a cot. But eight weeks later, Clementine started cramping. There were spots of blood in her underwear, and soon their specialist confirmed the miscarriage. Their baby had vanished. Cole held Clementine while she wept, trying to keep it together for her sake, wondering what their child would have been like.

The following day, they were scheduled to attend a party at Dom and Felicity's place. With heartbreaking optimism,

Clementine said they should still go. 'Who knows how many more parties we'll have before we need a babysitter?'

So Cole found himself on Dom's leather couch, watching as everyone else cooed over Oscar and Isla's kid. He couldn't bear it—he asked Dom to show him the sound system in the new Tesla. Dom eagerly led him out to the driveway and climbed into the driver's seat. Cole got in the passenger side as Dom switched on the music. The car automatically connected to his phone and started playing a song he'd presumably been halfway through. The singer was wailing, 'Baby, baby, baby . . .'

Cole burst into tears.

He found himself telling Dom everything. How emasculating it was to be running a failing business *and* to have subpar sperm. How much he hated the little room at the clinic, where he'd had to grimly jerk off into a sample jar, surrounded by ancient, vanilla porn magazines. How painful it was to see Clementine suffer through all the drugs and side effects and mood swings—and have nothing to show for it. How badly he wanted to be a father.

'Another round of treatment will be ten thousand dollars once you add up all the out-of-pocket costs,' he said. 'That's on top of the twenty we already took out of the mortgage. We've nearly maxed out what we can borrow—we'll be paying this off for years. Which I can live with, if we have a kid, but what if we don't? What if it's just the two of us and a debt that reminds us of that, for the rest of our lives? What if the gym goes under and we have no way of paying it all back? Clem has no idea how bad it is, and I can't figure out how to tell her.' He wiped his eyes. 'I don't know what to do.'

Dom nodded sympathetically. 'Ten thousand dollars, you said?'

Cole stiffened in his seat. 'Are you offering to loan—?'

'Loan?!' Dom said indignantly. 'I'm not *loaning* you anything.' Cole felt horribly ashamed, but before he could apologise, Dom added, 'I'll just *give* you the money. Text me your account details, and it'll be done by close of business.'

Dom said this even though it was a Saturday night. He was like that.

Stunned, Cole said, 'I can't let you pay for this.'

'Sure you can! You'd do the same for me, if our positions were reversed.' Dom gestured around at the car, as if to indicate what his position was.

'But—'

'I'm not great at emotional support. But financial support? *That* I can do.' He cleared his throat. 'Come on, mate, we've been friends forever. You were best man at my wedding, for God's sake. Let me help. It'll be just between us.'

Cole's voice faltered. 'I'll pay you back when—'

'Nonsense. Then you're no better off than you were before. I won't let you.'

'Dom, I don't know how to thank you.'

'Well, I think Dominic is a great name for a baby boy,' Dom said cheerfully. 'Dominica is nice, too.'

Cole dried his tears, and they went back into the house. He felt vaguely shell-shocked. As soon as he and Clementine got home, his phone dinged. Ten thousand dollars had appeared, like magic. He wanted to tell her how incredibly generous their friend was, but he couldn't— not without revealing how bad their financial situation had been.

Hiding bad news from his wife hadn't felt disloyal; for some reason, hiding good news did. Clementine seemed to sense that something was bothering him, but he told her he was just tired.

The fourth round of treatment didn't produce any embryos. The specialist was mystified. As Cole and Clementine held each other on the roof of their house, overlooking the sparse lights of the town, Clementine blew her nose into a tissue and sobbed, 'Can we even afford this?'

It was the first time she'd asked. Cole said, 'We'll make it work.' Taking the credit for Dom's money, and hating himself for it.

'Maybe we could have a break?' Clementine's voice wobbled. 'Go back to trying the old-fashioned way?'

'Of course,' Cole said, knowing it wouldn't work.

Over the next month, they had sex constantly. It was exhausting. Each time, they couldn't stop until Cole reached orgasm, or there would be no point. But the pressure made it difficult to lose himself. His usual fantasies didn't help. His thoughts kept straying to Dom.

The money had been a gift, not a loan, but Cole nevertheless felt indebted. More so, actually—if the money had been a loan, he could eventually have paid it back, and they would have been square. But because it was a gift, Cole felt like he would *always* owe it. Over the next few months he found himself indulging Dom's every whim, as though that would get him out from under the debt. But he remembered what his friend had said: *I won't let you.*

At yet another party, Dom interrupted the demonstration of his new wall-mounted speakers to say, 'Cole, can you grab me a beer?'

Cole said, 'Sure.' He got up off his chair, went to the fridge and brought back a can of BentSpoke IPA.

It wasn't until Clementine gave both of them a strange look that Cole realised how odd that was. Dom had been closer to the fridge; he could have got the drink himself. Instead he'd asked Cole, as though sending a dog to fetch a pair of slippers.

Paradoxically, Cole began to resent his old friend for giving him something he could never return.

Then, out of the blue, Oscar turned up at the gym with an idea. It sounded insane, at first. But the more Cole thought about it, the more he realised it might solve all his problems. He couldn't stop thinking about it.

Now, he climbed into the driver's seat of the Tarago and

started the engine. Dom sat next to him. Seatbelts clacked all around. Soon they were cruising out of the parking lot, leaving the high school behind.

'Woo!' Clementine yelled.

'Party time,' Felicity agreed.

From the front passenger seat, Dom said, 'Cole, can you put the radio on?' even though he could reach.

'Sure.' Cole hit the button. 'Affirmation' by Savage Garden buzzed through the speakers. The singer crooned over the pulsing beat.

'What *is* this?' Felicity asked.

Isla took off the baseball cap and shook out her beautiful black hair. '*God*, you're young.'

Cole had hated this song when it came out. Now he turned it way up and sang along.

NOW

Kiara

'Anyone with relevant information should call Crime Stoppers,' Kiara finishes, and recites the number. 'I'll take questions now.'

Warrigal Police Station doesn't have a room for media conferences, so the city reporters are huddled together between puddles in the car park. The rain has petered to a drizzle, but they've kept their umbrellas up to protect their phones, clutched before them like talismans. Kiara wishes she had a lectern—something to put between herself and the journalists, and hide the dog hair on her shins. Also, she wishes Sergeant Rohan wasn't standing so close behind her. Kiara is a respectable 160 centimetres tall, but Rohan stands at more than two metres; in the pictures, it's going to look like bring-your-daughter-to-work day.

Media briefings are a tightrope. Kiara needs to make the story interesting so it will be circulated widely, prompting witnesses to come forward. But she doesn't want to create a panic, reveal anything that may compromise the investigation, or get any of the facts wrong. If she makes the NSW Police look bad, her career as a detective will be over before it starts.

She knows the killer may be watching. Ideally, she'll goad them into making a mistake without helping them foresee lines of enquiry. As she looks down the barrel of one camera, she thinks, *I'm coming for you*. Then she points to a journalist with a hand up. 'Yes.'

'What were the names of the people at the house?' the woman asks.

'You know the rules,' Kiara says. 'Only age and gender until the victims' families have all been notified. Next.' She points again.

This journo says, 'Of the six holidaymakers, two are dead—do you have any suspects other than the three survivors and the missing woman?'

Actually, there is one more suspect, but it's too soon to reveal that. 'We're keeping all lines of enquiry open at this stage. Now you.' Kiara points to a journo with frameless glasses and grey whiskers.

He says, 'Do you think Ms Madden is still alive?'

Madden is the missing woman. Kiara can withhold as many names as she likes, but it won't stop journalists from digging them up. 'I'm not going to speculate on that,' she says, 'but the State Emergency Service is assisting the police in the search. Next.'

Madden was last seen on Sunday night, and it's now Thursday morning. There's no evidence that she has a vehicle, food, water or any wilderness survival experience. It's not looking good.

A reporter's pen quivers over her notepad. 'Did the victims die *during* the sex?' she asks.

Kiara's heart sinks. She hasn't mentioned this aspect of the investigation, not wanting the story to be sensationalised. Evidently this reporter has a source close to the case.

Upon hearing the word 'sex', several other journos suddenly look more interested, as though sensing all the extra clicks.

'We're still trying to establish a timeline,' Kiara says. 'But we know the first victim died at approximately 9 p.m. on Saturday, and the second at 10 p.m. on Sunday.'

Gregor has finished the autopsies, but they didn't tell her much she didn't already know. The statements of Ms Dubois and the two Kellys are consistent on every detail except one: the identity of the killer.

'Next.' Kiara points.

The journo clears his throat. 'Could the swingers have kidnapped the two victims?'

So this guy has a source, too. Kiara wishes people would talk to the police as readily as they talked to journalists. 'It appears that everyone went to the house willingly. And please don't call them "swingers". They were just regular people who decided to try something new, and unfortunately two of them came to grief.'

'Are you saying that swingers aren't regular people?' the same journo asks.

Shit, Kiara thinks. 'I'm absolutely not saying that. Next question.' She points at a guy on the other side of the group.

His voice is smug and reedy. 'Is this your first case as lead detective?'

'That's correct,' Kiara says, looking around for someone else to call on.

'There have been *eight* shocking murders in Warrigal since this time last year,' the man continues.

'Well, that depends on how you define shocking.' Kiara regrets the words immediately.

Questions flood in from all sides: 'How many more deaths have there been?' 'Are you saying murder *isn't* shocking?' 'Why are the police incapable of keeping this community safe?'

Kiara shouts over the top of them: 'Again, the public can help by calling Crime Stoppers with relevant information. That's all the time I have.'

She closes her notebook and hurries back into the station, trying not to look like she's fleeing.

Elise

The ATM spits out Elise's card. She returns it to her wallet and waits for the cash. She's nervous, taking out so much money. She's never heard of anyone getting mugged in broad daylight in Warrigal—it would be a stupid move in such a small town, where the victim would likely recognise the perpetrator—but that doesn't mean it won't happen to her. Thankfully, this is the last instalment.

As she's looking around for stupid muggers, she sees a police car turning the corner. She's relieved, until she recognises Kiara behind the wheel.

Shit. Elise pulls up the hood of her jacket and turns away from the approaching car. It won't help much. She's wearing shorts despite the cold, and if Kiara looks over, she'll recognise Elise's bare legs and faded runners.

With a whirr, a rattle and a clunk, the ATM finally ejects a bundle of fifties and starts beeping loudly, announcing to any nearby thieves that the person in front of it is cashed up. Elise snatches the notes from the slot and walks as swiftly as she dares towards the nearest business: a real estate agency, sandwiched between a jewellery store and a cafe. The closed door is recessed far enough back that Elise can duck out of sight.

It turns out to be the worst hiding place she could have chosen. Kiara pulls into a 45-degree angle spot right across the street—exactly where she would park if she were about to visit the real estate agency. As soon as she leaves the car, she'll see Elise.

Elise frantically tries to think of a plausible excuse to be here, on Edward Street, in casual clothes, when Kiara thinks she's at the hospital on call. She can't think of one.

Just in time, Kiara's phone goes off—Elise can hear the jangly ringtone even from across the street. Kiara checks the screen, then puts the phone to her ear, staying in the car.

Elise slips out of the doorway and hurries towards the cafe, the cash bundled into a fist in her pocket. She makes her way between some outdoor tables and umbrellas, then darts through the door.

There are no shouts, no approaching footsteps. Kiara must not have seen her.

'What do you want?' The barista, in his forties, is the only other person in the cafe. He doesn't feel the need to be friendly to his lone customer: not when the customer is Elise Glyk. A woman who's known for attracting trouble.

She takes a deep breath, pushing away the paranoia, and smiles with too many teeth. 'Medium cappuccino,' she says. 'To take away.'

Kiara

As Kiara crosses the street, she looks at the spot on the asphalt where Anton Rabbek died a month ago. She was never able to charge anyone for the hit-and-run. Unsolved killings are nothing new, but this one haunts her, because she was there in Anton's final moments.

She's just gotten off the phone with the deputy commissioner. Apparently her dismal performance at the press conference—discriminating against swingers and implying that murder wasn't shocking—was strike two. He wants this case wrapped up, fast. It would be easier to do that without him breathing down her neck, but Kiara was smart enough not to say so.

She approaches the real estate agency, carrying her notebook under one arm. By now it has six profiles. Dominic, the financial adviser. His wife, Felicity, the stand-up comic. Clementine, the fitness model, married to Cole, the gym owner. Isla, the full-time mum, and her husband, Oscar, the real estate agent. Dominic, Clementine, Cole and Isla were all on the athletics team at Warrigal High School. Felicity grew up in Warrigal too, but she's a few years younger than the others and went to school across the river at St Clare's. Oscar is the outsider: a little older than the rest of them and not a local; he moved here seven years ago.

Kiara has gone through their social media profiles, search histories, emails, bank records. She knows Dominic paid Cole and Clementine ten thousand dollars a few months ago. She knows Cole's gym is struggling, that the IVF is costing a fortune, and that Clementine hadn't mentioned their financial problems to Isla, even though they exchanged memes and messages almost daily. She knows Isla, Clementine and Cole often visited porn sites on their phones. She knows Oscar often tapped 'like' on Felicity's Instagram photos. But she can't turn any of that into a coherent motive for murder.

When Kiara pushes the door open, the agency is dark inside, the listings stuck to the windows blotting out the daylight.

'Detective Lui,' the agent says. He's stout and balding, with watery eyes and a pinstripe suit that has seen better days.

Kiara is surprised. 'Have we met?'

'Rick Basking. I knew your dad.' The agent extends a hand.

Kiara shakes it, warily. Her father, a Wiradjuri man, took personal pride in protecting land from developers. She doubts he was popular among real estate agents.

'Are you here about the murder house?' Basking asks, sounding oddly hopeful.

'Right,' Kiara says.

'That listing has been a pain since I got it. No one ever wants to stay for more than a couple of nights, and it takes me almost two hours each way to drive out and inspect the place afterwards. Costs a fortune in heating and cooling too, so the owner's always pushing to charge more than people will pay. I've told him to just put some insulation in the walls and the roof cavity, but he's a tight old fart. You want a cuppa?'

'No, thank you.'

Basking eases down into a chair that sighs under his weight. His desk is covered with merch—coffee mugs, pens and fridge-magnet calendars that all say *Basking Real Estate*.

On the calendars, Kiara can see Basking grinning from ear to ear, alongside several other agents, including Oscar.

'I already talked to some of your colleagues,' Basking says.

'I know.' Kiara sits opposite him. 'Got a minute to go over some things again with me?'

He gestures ruefully at the empty office. 'Shoot. But if the phone rings, I can't afford not to answer, not with the market being what it is right now.'

He opens a folder to reveal photos of the house on the mountain. When it's not full of corpses, the place looks luxurious. King parrots sit in the lush garden. Sunlight falls through huge windows onto soft-looking carpet in spacious bedrooms. In one photo, a leather ottoman is set up in front of the fireplace, waiting for some weary rich person to put their feet up. The text boasts that there are two bathrooms, a barbecue and a self-cleaning oven.

'Who rented the house?' Kiara asks.

'Bloke named Dominic,' Basking says. 'Nice guy. Bought a place from me a few years back. I tried to convince him to buy another one, but he didn't seem interested in getting on the ladder.'

'How much was it?'

'The seller wanted seven ninety, but I told them—'

Kiara stops him. 'Not the house you tried to sell him. The one he rented.'

'Oh, right. Sorry.' A nervous chuckle. 'He took the luxury package—sixteen fifty for three nights, with food and drinks included. Now that it's a murder house, I'll have to slash that price by half.' He winces, possibly regretting the choice of words. Kiara remembers the throat of the first corpse, burst like a cheap sausage.

'Dominic paid for it all himself?' she asks.

'Yup. He may have split the cost with his mates after the fact, I don't know, but the booking was in his name, and it was his credit card. His wife picked up the keys—pretty young thing. Foul-mouthed, though.'

Kiara writes this down. 'Really? What did she say?'

'Nothing, at the time. But Dominic gave me a ticket to one of her shows. I took the missus, not realising it would be so full-on.' He sipped thoughtfully from one of the mugs. 'She loved it, but.'

Kiara spots Oscar's desk—it has a Toblerone-shaped sign with his name on it. She goes over to take a look. No personal touches, not even a photo of Isla and Noah, just a computer and a jar of pens. She takes one with a gloved hand, for an extra fingerprint comparison.

'Dominic didn't mention Oscar would be at the house with him?' she asks.

Basking looks uneasy. 'No.'

'Seems odd. If I was mates with a real estate agent, and I was going on holiday with that agent, and I was renting a house for the holiday from the agency he worked at, I'd ask him to handle it. Wouldn't you?'

She can tell this has occurred to Basking, but he just shrugs. 'What can I say? I'm not Dom Pérignon—' Basking cringes, embarrassed. 'Sorry. Oscar called him that once, and the name caught on around the office.'

Kiara writes that down.

Basking adds, 'Because of his money, you see.'

'Yeah, I get it.'

She sees something on the other side of the street. It's just a split second of movement, glimpsed between the listings on the window, but that's enough for Kiara to recognise her partner's silhouette. Elise was an athlete once, and she still has a runner's body. She also favours one leg after getting kicked in the knee during her ordeal last year.

Paramedics often suffer from occupational burnout, particularly if they've been assaulted, as Elise has. The symptoms include anxiety, irritability, trouble sleeping, exhaustion—check, check, check and check. But something more sinister is going on. Elise told Kiara she'd be at work today, not out and about. Kiara thinks again of how withdrawn her partner has seemed lately; of the way she leaves the room to answer the phone. Someone must be harassing her, but she refuses to talk about it . . .

Kiara's gaze falls on the photos of the house: the fireplace, the hot tub, the double shower, the king-size bed. 'No phone reception up there, right?'

'That's right. For some people that's a deal breaker, but others seem to like it. You know, these days people feel obliged to answer emails after hours unless—'

'Can I rent the house this weekend?'

Basking's eyebrows shoot up. 'The murder house?'

'Yeah,' Kiara says. 'Unless someone else has already booked it?'

'No, I haven't re-listed it. I only got the keys back yesterday, and passed them straight on to Chantelle.'

Kiara has already interviewed Chantelle Slattery, Basking's harried cleaner. She hadn't known anything useful, and had been in a rush to get to her next job.

'If you want to take a look around, you don't have to rent the place,' Basking says. 'I can just—'

'I'd like to spend a couple of nights there. It'll help me get inside the heads of the suspects, and the victims. And you never know, I might spot something forensics missed.'

This is particularly likely, knowing Jennings, but it's not the real reason Kiara wants to go. Elise needs a break from work, and from the town in general. This luxurious house, with its beautiful surroundings, would be perfect.

'Well, okay,' Basking says.

'How much?'

'On the house.' He chortles nervously.

Kiara reluctantly shakes her head. 'I can't accept that. Against the code of conduct.'

He looks relieved. 'In that case, five fifty for two nights. That's the discounted rate—not discounted because you're a police officer,' he adds hastily. 'Discounted because of the bad publicity. That's the price I was going to re-list it at.'

'Thanks.' She gets out her wallet.

Basking digs a payment terminal out of a drawer and switches it on.

As they wait for the machine to load, Kiara says, 'Oscar never mentioned he was going on holiday with Dom?'

'No.'

'Was he there when Felicity turned up to collect the house keys?'

'No. Wait . . .' Basking puts a finger to his nose and wiggles it from left to right. 'He *was* there, actually. I remember him looking at her.'

'Looking how?'

Basking winces. 'I shouldn't speak out of turn. And I could be wrong.'

'Noted. How did he look?'

'He was—what's the word? Lascivious. You know how a man will sometimes glance down at a woman's cleavage, then back up at her eyes real quick so she doesn't notice?'

'We always notice,' Kiara says.

Basking reddens. 'Well, anyway, he didn't do that. He didn't seem to care if she saw him looking.'

'Like they were having an affair?'

'No, that's the thing. *He* acted like they were having an affair. But she ignored him, and left as fast as she could—practically ran out the door.'

When Kiara emerges from the agency, house keys in hand, the light is already fading. Elise and her little Suzuki Swift are nowhere to be seen, just dark windows and papers blowing along the deep gutters. The street looks like the set of an old Western, waiting for a new sheriff or a group of bandits to ride in. Kiara had intended to visit her mother, who owns a Vietnamese bakery a block away, but she will have gone home by now. Kiara tries not to feel relieved.

A woman is staring at the window display of the jewellery store next door. It's Ms Dubois, the one who fled down the mountain. She must see Kiara's reflection in the glass as she approaches, but the woman doesn't turn. 'Detective Lui.'

'Hi,' Kiara says. 'How are you feeling?'

'My feet are still sore,' the woman says. In the police interview room she was all dressed up, but now she wears tracksuit pants and Ugg boots, no makeup. Her hair is a tangled mess. Even her silver crucifix looks greasy.

Kiara tries to sound casual. 'Must make it hard to run your errands . . .?'

Dubois ignores the *What-are-you-doing-here?* subtext, looking in the shopfront window. 'My husband bought my engagement ring from this shop.'

'I've been asking around,' Kiara says. 'Sounds like he was a good bloke.'

Dubois nods solemnly. 'You know how they make a ring smaller?'

'No. How?'

'I watched the jeweller do it. He cut a little chunk out of the band, then bent the rest of it into shape and soldered the join. It's just like getting married. You lose a bit of yourself, but that's okay. Because you get a comfortable fit.' A tear rolls down her cheek. 'But now I've lost the thing I fit with.'

'I'm very sorry.' Kiara doesn't remember saying this earlier; she wishes it didn't sound so trite.

'Yeah.' Dubois wipes her eyes with the heel of her palm. 'Me too.' She starts walking up the street.

'Need a lift anywhere?' Kiara calls.

The woman doesn't seem to hear, shuffling away with her head bowed. Kiara guesses she's going to the pub, but a minute later she plods past it—on her way home, perhaps. She lives only five or six blocks away.

Kiara gets back in her patrol car but doesn't start the engine. She looks down at her notepad, thinking. Then she calls her sergeant.

He answers on the second ring. 'Rohan.'

'Do you know Rick Basking?' Kiara asks, without preamble.

'The real estate agent? Sure. Why?'

'He doesn't have a record.' Kiara already checked this. 'But I was wondering if you'd heard anything that might not have been reported.'

'Well, I remember a friend of Jodie's rented a house from him and had various complaints. A missing keyring . . . There were supposed to be two sets of keys, but he only provided one. And the house hadn't been cleaned properly—rubbish left behind, or something. That help?'

'Not really. When he asked if I was there to talk about the murders, he sounded . . . hopeful. Like he was worried I'd come to ask about something else.'

'Oh.' Rohan's chair squeaks. 'That'd be his son, Seb.'

Kiara writes down the name. 'How old?'

'Fifteen. Never charged with anything, but a bit of a troublemaker. Been caught skipping school, shoplifting, drinking, smoking—'

'Tobacco?'

'Among other things. He's got one of those zippy electric bikes, so he can bother people all over town. If you've ever seen *eight equals D* spray-painted on any fences, that's him.'

Kiara wonders if Basking was trying to bribe her with the free house rental after all. 'Is his mum in the picture?'

'Died of breast cancer, Christmas before last.'

'Hmm.' Kiara chews her lip. That explained why Seb had never been charged. Anyone in a position to report anything probably felt sorry for him. She changed the subject: 'Basking made it sound like something was going on between Oscar and Felicity, but I've been through their phones, and they didn't exchange any calls or texts.'

'None at all? That's suspicious.'

'Exactly my thinking. Can you get someone from cybercrime to look at the phones? See if anything's been deleted?'

'Sure.' She hears Rohan scribble a note.

'Thanks,' she says. 'Anything from search and rescue?'

'No sign of Ms Madden. They've cleared a thirty-kilometre

radius around the LKP, but the further out they get, the slower they go. You know how it is.'

Kiara does. Partly it's basic geometry—each concentric ring around the Last Known Point is much, much bigger than the one inside it—but there are other factors. The longer the search takes, the more volunteers drop out, and the more likely they're looking for someone who doesn't want to be found, which is almost impossible—or for a body, which isn't much easier. The Australian bush swallows people and doesn't always spit them back out.

'By the way.' She tries to sound casual. 'I rented the house for the weekend.'

'You did?' Rohan's voice is hard to read.

'Yeah. Elise needs a break. It's a great house, and Basking discounted it—not because I'm a cop, just because of the bad publicity. You reckon that's okay?'

'Usually I'd discourage my officers from going on holiday in the middle of a case,' Rohan says sternly. After a beat he adds, 'But I guess staying at the house overnight might help you spot inconsistencies in the statements of the suspects . . . It's just for the weekend?'

'Two nights. I don't need any time off.'

'You'll be back at work on Monday?'

'Nine a.m. sharp.'

'All right. Elise won't mind staying at a crime scene?'

Kiara hesitates. She'd wondered if it was ethical, but not how Elise might take it. 'I . . . I don't *think* so, she says hesitantly. 'I mean, every hotel room in the world has been a crime scene at one point or another. Elise knows that.'

'Well, I wish I'd thought of it. Jodie would love a minibreak.'

Kiara shrugs. 'I'll give you first dibs at the next murder house.'

'I hear you've been kink-shaming swingers,' Elise says, coming in the front door of the granny flat. Guppy barks and runs up to her, claws skittering on the tiles.

Kiara sighs and rolls over in bed, squinting at the giant glow-in-the-dark hands of her father's clock. It's almost 3 a.m. 'I was not.'

Elise's bag rattles as she puts it on the counter. She enters the bedroom, Guppy prancing around her legs. 'They aren't normal people, apparently.'

Kiara and Elise moved into the granny flat a few weeks ago so the house could be fumigated, and then never moved back in—Elise seems more comfortable in a building that isn't visible from the street, and Kiara doesn't mind staying. Her father spent his last few years out here, and she can still feel a comforting presence. Sometimes she turns a corner and gets a faintly bitter whiff of his aftershave.

When she came out as gay in her mid-teens, her strict Catholic mother advised her not to tell anyone else, because she'd probably change her mind—then immediately got on the phone tree to Kiara's aunties and grandparents. The betrayal still stings, and Kiara keeps that half of her family at a distance.

When she said she wanted to become a police officer, she lost the other half. Dad's siblings and cousins and parents, people who'd been friendly her whole life, started speaking to her stiffly, or not at all. To them, police meant danger, not safety.

But Dad himself didn't bat an eyelid at either revelation. 'Brave girl,' he said, both times, and hugged her.

He died last September. She misses him terribly.

'I was trying to say that *actual* swingers have rules, practices and social norms around communication and consent,' she says now. 'They're not just people who get drunk and fuck each other's spouses.'

'Rules, practices and social norms,' Elise repeats. 'You seem to know a lot about this.'

'Ha, ha.' Kiara doesn't admit that she spent the evening googling swinger lifestyle facts to avoid another faux pas at the next media briefing.

She watches as Elise pulls off the ambulance scrubs in the semi-darkness. She loves Elise's body. Muscular legs, narrow hips, taut stomach. A long neck that Kiara loves to kiss. She can't imagine sharing Elise with anybody.

'How was your shift?' she asks.

'Not too bad.' Elise disappears into the bathroom and turns on the shower. She shouts: 'There was a dad who was worried that his kid had meningococcal, so they got a ride to Emergency. I reckon it was the flu. A car was T-boned on Flinders Avenue, but everyone's okay, though one woman will be in a neck brace for a while. I picked up an old guy with an inguinal hernia, which was a bit interesting.'

'What's that?'

'It's when your intestines bulge into your groin, and—'

'Stop! I don't want to know. But will he be okay?'

'Yep. Embarrassed, mostly.'

When the water stops hissing, Kiara says, 'Guess what?'

'What?'

'I booked a holiday for us.'

Elise comes out of the bathroom with a towel wrapped around her torso and another around her hair. She looks puzzled but pleased. 'A holiday?'

Kiara smiles. 'I visited a real estate agent today and rented a house. It's beautiful—you'll love it. And I called Rafa to get the weekend off for you.'

Elise pauses halfway through pulling on her pyjamas. 'How expensive is this house? If you cancelled my shifts, I don't think we can afford—'

'Don't worry. The house is really cheap. I got a great deal.'

Elise laughs. 'Why is it so cheap? It's not a crime scene, is it?'

Kiara coughs.

Elise's eyes widen. 'It *is*?'

'Well, it *was*, but—'

'Wait, were you visiting the real estate agent in a professional capacity?' Elise is starting to sound shrill. 'Is this the murder house from last weekend?'

This isn't going as well as Kiara had hoped. Elise is a paramedic—surely she's not afraid of an empty building . . .?

'It's been cleaned,' Kiara says. 'Don't you think it would be nice to leave town for a bit?'

'I don't know about you, but the main thing *I* dislike about Warrigal is the violence. You want to take a break by going to a place where there was a very recent double homicide?'

Kiara tries to make a joke of it. 'What are the odds of that happening two weekends in a row?'

Elise doesn't laugh. In the shadows of the bedroom, her eyes are black wells from which nothing escapes. 'What are you hoping to get out of this?'

'I thought you needed a break.' *From whoever is making those phone calls*, Kiara doesn't say.

'You can't fix me, K.'

'I'm not trying to.'

Guppy watches them, puzzled by Kiara's tone and body language. Her dad's clock ticks too loudly on the wall.

'Where did you go today?' she hears herself ask.

'What?'

'When I was with the real estate agent,' says Kiara, trying to sound natural, not suspicious, 'I saw you through the window.'

Elise hesitates a beat too long. 'Oh. I just went to the cafe next door. Before my shift.'

Just stop, Kiara tells herself, but she can't. 'With anyone?'

'For fuck's sake.' Elise leaves the room, satin pyjama shorts flapping.

'Elise, wait.' Kiara rolls out of bed and reaches for her dressing-gown.

But Elise is already back from the kitchenette. She's holding a disposable coffee cup smudged with Vegemite—she must have retrieved it from the bin. She reads the scrawl on the side: 'Takeaway for Elise. Cappuccino, no sugar.' In her other hand, she holds up a receipt. 'Medium coffee *times one*. Four dollars fifty. Subtotal: four dollars fifty. Total: four dollars fifty.'

'I'm sorry,' Kiara says, though she thinks Elise is overreacting. Kiara didn't accuse her of anything, just asked if she was with anyone. That's a normal question to ask your partner, isn't it?

There's always an undercurrent of anger with Elise. Kiara secretly likes it—she doesn't want to be in a relationship with a dishrag. But this is something else. She barely recognises the jittery, furious woman in front of her.

Elise and Kiara hardly ever fight, at least not compared to the straight couples they know. Kiara often thinks those people try too hard to imitate the relationships they see on TV. There is no obvious template for what she and Elise have, so they're free to do what's best for themselves and each other. But now Kiara can feel the foundations sinking.

She changes tack. 'Look, I need your help.'

This takes Elise by surprise. 'With what?'

'The case,' Kiara says, like it's obvious. 'I can't get inside the heads of the suspects, or figure out their relationships to the victims.'

'I don't know them.'

'Four of the six were on the same high school athletics team—that's what brought them together. They're all sporty types, like you. I was hoping you could . . .'

Elise glares at her. 'You're patronising me.'

'Am I? Sorry.' Kiara smiles sheepishly.

Elise takes a deep breath, then sits beside Kiara on the bed. Kiara squeezes her hand, and Elise squeezes back. Finally she says, 'The house has been cleaned, right?'

Kiara is a bit offended. 'Of course.'

'There won't be little yellow evidence tags everywhere? Blood on the ceiling . . .?'

'It will be spotless.'

'Okay,' Elise says. 'We'll go.'

Kiara wraps her arms around her. 'Yay,' she whispers.

They lie down together. Guppy leaps up onto the bed and curls up on Kiara's feet. Elise strokes her hair. Kiara closes her eyes, wondering if Elise washed her hands after going through the bin.

The mechanic is a small, bearded man with matted hair and thick glasses. He wipes his hands on a rag, balls it up, then tosses it towards a bucket four or five metres away. The rag goes in without touching the sides.

'Bill shoots, he scores,' Kiara says.

'Detective Lui! I am not worthy.' The mechanic makes a little bow. 'What can I do for you?'

Bill trained alongside Kiara at the police academy in Goulburn. He'd signed up to get away from his aggressive stepfather, and was an enthusiastic recruit. But once he was a probationary constable, it became evident that he had no real passion for justice. He lasted only four months and now seems much happier wielding a spanner than a badge.

The dimly lit garage smells of sugar soap. A poster bolted to the corrugated wall reminds *all staff to use protective gloves at all times*, even though the only employee is Bill, who isn't wearing them. A Jaguar, gleaming but dented, is raised up on a steel platform. Even the undercarriage is shiny—maybe Bill's washed it.

'Hoping to book in a service,' Kiara says.

'For one of the police cruisers, or your Navara?'

She points back over her shoulder at her ute.

Bill leans sideways, eyeing the vehicle. 'What's wrong with it?'

'Nothing, I hope. But I thought it would be a good idea to get it checked before I go up the mountain.'

'Taking Elise for a drive?' Bill sounds a bit too interested.

'Yep. Can you fit me in?'

He squints. 'Dunno—I'm pretty busy.'

Kiara looks around at the garage. There are no other

customers and no vehicles other than the Jaguar. 'Doing what?'

'I'll have you know that my schedule fills up weeks in advance these days,' Bill says, affronted. 'This little beauty was booked in a month ago.' He gestures to the car on the platform.

Kiara finds this very unlikely. Bill may be the only mechanic in town, but there's not much demand. Warrigal is full of old people who can service their own equally old cars. So can Kiara, but she needs to spend the day printing out evidence photos for her case file.

Bill is still talking about the Jaguar. 'She'll take me the rest of the day, easy.'

'How about tomorrow?'

He scratches his chin. 'I've got a bit on.'

Kiara doubts this. 'Okay. Thanks anyway.' She sighs theatrically. 'Elise was really looking forward to a romantic getaway, you know?'

Bill's too-interested look returns. 'Well . . . I suppose I could rearrange some things. Let me check the calendar.'

Kiara can see it from here: the plate number from the Jaguar is scribbled on a square representing last Monday; the rest of the month is blank. 'You do that,' she says.

LAST FRIDAY

Isla

Isla climbed out of the Tarago and staggered over to the bushes near the edge of the driveway, feeling like she might throw up. The air conditioner had blown a plasticky smell onto her face throughout the long drive, which included some alarming hairpin bends with sheer drops just beyond them. *If you were out here in the dark*, she thought, *you'd be likely to walk off a cliff.*

As a kid, Isla had never been afraid of heights. She would climb the scrap heap near her parents' house every weekend, wobbling on rusted wheels and old freezers, and was one of the few who dared to leap off the top. She'd come home bruised, scratched, and grinning all over her dirty face.

She and Oscar had honeymooned in the Daintree Rainforest, at a resort surrounded by scenic trails. One night, while he was in the shower, she switched on the news. In Colorado, a climber had fallen to her death when the rock she was clinging to broke off the cliff face. For some reason, Isla couldn't get the image out of her head. She didn't sleep at all that night, and the following day, when they hiked up to a lookout, she wasn't able to go close enough to the edge to take a good selfie.

Oscar asked if something was wrong. She said no, and he believed her.

That was the moment Isla realised her mistake. She loved

Oscar partly because he hadn't gone to Warrigal High. With him, she could pretend to be the person she wished she was. But now she was married to a man who didn't know her.

Every night for the rest of the trip, she dreamed she was scaling a wall of red stone, Oscar waiting for her at the top. She would reach for his hand, and he for hers, but just as their fingers were about to touch, she'd lose her footing and plummet into the endless dark.

Dom and Cole were unpacking the back of the Tarago while Felicity stood nearby, breathing on her gloved hands for warmth. Oscar and Clementine were surveying the house. The quiet up here was eerie. A small town like Warrigal still had some level of background noise: dogs, traffic, a neighbour's radio. This far from civilisation, even the birds seemed reluctant to break the silence.

Isla turned to face the bushes and bent over, putting her hands on her thighs and willing herself not to vomit. She took deep breaths, counting the leaves on the dirt driveway between her feet—six, seven, eight . . . When she ran out of leaves, she counted the tyre tracks from cars and mountain bikes. She tried to imagine what kind of fruit loop would ride a bike all the way to the top of this mountain.

'You okay?' Cole asked behind her, making her jump.

She straightened and forced a smile back at him. 'Just a bit car sick.'

Cole owned a gym and looked the part. His muscular arms were always exposed by a short-sleeved shirt, a fitness band gleaming on his wrist, and his close-cropped hair highlighted the bulges on either side of his neck. His short blond beard often twinkled with sweat. But he was soft-spoken and gentle. Isla had once watched him lift an injured bird into a cardboard box, and she'd wondered—out of nowhere—if he held Clementine as tenderly as that.

'Try standing up straight,' he said. 'Watch the horizon. Give the fluid in your inner ear some time to stabilise.'

From Dom, Isla would have found this annoying. *I'll*

look wherever I want, thank you. But she followed Cole's advice, squinting in the midday sun as she gazed out across the endless bush.

He rested a strong hand on her back. 'Is it working?'

The moment felt familiar. Isla remembered hiding behind the science block as a teenager, her guts churning, face burning. Cole's arms around her, and his gentle voice: *don't worry. You'll be okay.*

She exhaled, banishing the memory. 'Maybe,' she said.

'Just a sec.' Cole hurried to the boot and unzipped a leather bag. He kept his back to her as he did it. When he turned around, he was holding a blister pack. 'I packed ginger tablets.'

Isla wasn't surprised. Cole was perpetually—almost pathologically—organised. He never forgot anyone's birthday and was always the designated driver. A while ago, Isla had noticed that his shoelaces usually matched the colour of his shirt, so either he had a lot of shoes or he regularly changed the laces. Even his body was tidy: no freckles on his tanned skin, no veins visible in his blue eyes.

Isla realised she was staring. Averting her gaze, she found herself looking at Clementine. She was blonde, like Cole, and equally partial to activewear. When she and Cole were side by side, with their matching serious expressions, they looked like the creepy telepathic kids from a sci-fi novel she'd discovered as a girl.

'*The Midwich Cuckoos,*' Isla once whispered to Oscar, pointing at Cole and Clementine.

Oscar had frowned. 'Huh?' He hadn't picked up a book since university.

She tried the title of the movie. 'You know—*Village of the Damned.*'

'Oh, right,' he replied, with no idea what she was talking about.

This made her realise she was making fun of Cole and Clementine, her oldest friends, because she envied them.

She'd expected to have a marriage like theirs, where two people seemed to fuse into a single organism, with the same opinions and goals. Instead, Oscar had somehow forced her into the role of the wet-blanket sitcom wife, casting himself as the beleaguered husband. If she asked him to unpack the dishwasher or get his clothes off the bathroom floor, she was *nagging*. If she did it herself, she was *being passive aggressive*. If she didn't, she was *lazy*.

When they first met, Oscar had loved the way she talked about big ideas rather than the meaningless day-to-day gossip that enthralled the other students— or so he claimed. Isla was starting to wonder if that was just something he'd said to get laid: *you're not like other girls. You're interested in serious things.* Because now she wasn't allowed to be anything other than his wife and Noah's mother. If she wanted to go to a job interview, she was *leaving him to pick up the slack*; if she tried to keep track of politics, she was *spending all her time on Twitter*. She could only imagine what he'd say if he caught her on Pornhub—particularly if he saw what she was looking at.

At that thought, her hand twitched towards the phone in her pocket. She stopped herself.

'Aren't these for sea sickness?' she asked, taking the ginger tablets from Cole.

'I think they're mostly a placebo,' he said. 'So why wouldn't they be just as effective on land?'

She laughed. 'I don't think placebos work if you tell the patient they're placebos.'

'Oh. My bad. Maybe there's some real evidence? Hang on.' He got out his phone.

'Are you going to pretend to find something, just so I feel better?'

Cole was squinting at the screen. '"Ginger tablets have been shown to cure car sickness in clinical trials."'

'Really?'

'No.' Cole showed her the screen. 'No reception up here.'

'What carrier are you with?'

'Optus.'

Isla was with Telstra. She checked her own phone: no bars.

Dom was walking past, carrying a suitcase in each of his big hands. There were sweat patches under the arms of his Hugo Boss shirt. 'This is supposed to be an unplugged weekend! A digital detox.'

'A what?' Cole asked.

Felicity, who had been rummaging through her backpack nearby, also paused when she heard this. 'There's wi-fi, right?'

'Nope,' Dom said. 'Just us and nature.'

'You're kidding.' Felicity was twenty-four—she'd probably never been without wi-fi in her whole life.

Isla thought she saw something flicker across Dom's expression—nervousness? But she couldn't think of anything he might be nervous about. Everything always turned out just fine for him.

After high school, she'd never wanted to see Dom again. But then her best friend, Clementine, had married Dom's best friend, Cole. That connection, indirect as it was, often put them all in the same room. She always acted friendly to avoid ruining everyone else's night, then went home burning with self-disgust. Now that she was thirty, her supply of fake smiles was running low.

'I don't remember signing up for a digital detox,' Isla said.

'The house has a landline,' said Dom. 'Relax.'

'A landline,' Felicity marvelled. 'Could come in handy if we need to call a phrenologist, or a blacksmith.' She resumed searching her backpack.

Isla hated being told to relax, especially by Dom. 'Whatever,' she said as she grabbed her suitcase.

The house towered over the landscape, even taller than it had looked in the photos. Metal cut-outs shaped like birds were mounted on the exterior walls. Garden chairs with weatherproof cushions were scattered around the porch, safe from thieves and vandals out here in the middle of nowhere.

Isla could hear Clementine and Oscar talking inside. She felt tense whenever her husband was alone with someone she'd gone to high school with—which, on this trip, was everyone except Felicity. But it sounded like they were just admiring the decor. Isla told herself everything would be fine.

'Here's your key,' Felicity said, handing Isla an envelope before immediately snatching it back. 'Oh, hang on—I'm supposed to give the key to Oscar.'

'I can give it to him,' Isla said, confused, but Felicity was already flouncing towards the house. Isla suddenly noticed how much the younger woman's new haircut resembled her own. She wondered if Dom had suggested the style; if he was training his wife to look like her.

Why did Oscar get a key while she didn't? She resolved to make him give it to her later, on principle.

'Can I carry your bag?' Cole offered.

'No,' she said, not wanting to be dismissed as helpless. She hauled the suitcase inside.

The living room was modern, full of sharp-edged tables, glass-doored cabinets, and other things they couldn't have at home because of Noah. There was an industrial-sized oven, in case they wanted to cook twelve pizzas at once. Huge windows overlooked the terrifying slope they'd just driven up.

'There's a hot tub,' Oscar called from the deck.

'Dibs on the upstairs bedroom!' Clementine called from somewhere else in the house.

As the others staked their claims, Isla opened the fridge. There was butter and mayo, but nothing substantial. She hadn't brought any groceries—Oscar had said Dom had paid for the luxury package, with food and drinks included.

'Are we supposed to hunt and kill our own dinner?' she asked. It was a joke, but she found herself picturing it. *Catastrophising*, her psychologist would have said. She imagined herself whittling a spear that was too blunt, stumbling through the bush looking for something to stab, then twisting her ankle in a wombat hole and freezing to death.

Dom appeared at her shoulder. 'There should be . . .' He frowned at the empty fridge. 'The agent said there would be food here.'

Isla felt a perverse joy at seeing something go wrong for Dom. She would gladly starve, if it made him look bad in front of the others. She opened the cupboards: also empty. 'No cereal either,' she said loudly.

Glowering, Dom pulled out his phone, presumably to call the agent. He pushed some buttons, and then swore under his breath.

'Digital detox,' Isla said smugly.

But Dom's anger quickly evaporated. 'No problem. Hey, Cole?'

Isla watched him jog along the hall towards the stairs, infuriated by his fake cheerfulness. When he didn't come back right away, she decided to check out the bedrooms.

Felicity and Dom had claimed the west bedroom, closest to the kitchen. One of Dom's expensive suits was laid out on the bed, and a bag had been left unzipped in the corner. Isla could see some brand-new bushwalking clothes, probably Felicity's. Isla closed the door.

Next there was a bathroom, then another door, slightly ajar. Isla could see carpet through the gap.

She thought she heard a scuffle.

She knocked. 'You decent?'

When no one replied, she pushed the door the rest of the way open. Another bedroom, and it was empty. The sound must have come from upstairs. Oscar's suitcase was under the bed. Isla's own bag was on the mattress, open. That was odd—it wasn't like her husband to start unpacking for her.

Oscar's phone was on the bed. She woke up the screen, just to check if he had reception—he was with Vodafone. But there was nothing.

This bedroom had an exterior door leading to the deck. Isla closed and locked it. When she turned around, she saw Dom hovering in the hall. 'Sorted,' he said. 'Cole's going to drive to town and bring back some food.'

He'd sent his oldest friend 130 kilometres away, like a king dispatching a knight on a quest.

Look at that, Isla thought. *Things work out for Dom, yet again.*

Dom

'You're a maniac!' laughed Felicity.

Dom was in his board shorts on the deck, trying to drag the lid off the hot tub. He was also trying not to look as cold as he felt, but the freezing wind made the hairs stand up all over his body. He wasn't as skinny as he used to be, but he didn't have nearly enough padding to withstand temperatures like this.

'Are you going to join me?' he asked, through chattering teeth.

'It's the middle of winter!' Felicity said.

'It's a *hot* tub.'

His wife looked at him like he was crazy. He liked that. It made him feel like he was in high school again, impressing a girl by doing something dumb.

And *what* a girl. No matter what she wore—right now it was the wool cardigan that had shrunk a little when he used the wrong wash cycle—Felicity was always beautiful. Whenever those cool green eyes landed on him, Dom would do anything to keep them there.

Finally the lid of the hot tub came off. He dipped a hand into the water. He'd switched it on an hour ago, but it was still tepid.

'How is it?' Felicity asked doubtfully.

'Divine,' he pronounced. 'I packed your bikini and goggles—go change!'

'Who wears goggles in a hot tub?'

'Someone planning to put her head under the water.'

Felicity smirked. 'Honey, I think your optimism might be a new source of renewable energy. Scientists could use you to power whole cities.'

Clementine emerged onto the deck, holding a yoga mat under one arm. *Another girl to impress*, Dom thought. He'd always suspected she had a bit of a crush on him. It was the way she threw back her head when she laughed at his jokes, showing off her blonde mane. Felicity had noticed this too, but seemed secure enough not to mind.

'I was going to do a workout,' Clementine said. 'Would anyone like to . . .?' She looked at Dom's board shorts, then his naked chest. 'Uh, what's going on?'

Felicity jerked a thumb at him. 'Ask Mr Freeze over here.'

'We're on holiday, and we paid for a hot tub,' Dom said. 'Are you all seriously not going to use it?'

'Wasn't planning on it,' Clementine said.

'Dom,' said Felicity, 'during the course of your work as a finance bro, have you heard of the *sunk cost fallacy*?'

Oscar came out of the house, holding a bottle of sparkling wine and two champagne flutes. 'Would anyone like a drink?'

'Please,' Felicity said.

Clementine declined with a wave. Dom wondered if she was pregnant already.

He'd been flabbergasted when Cole asked him to help out with the pregnancy. Once he realised Cole wanted his money, not his sperm, he was so relieved and embarrassed that he agreed immediately. He would have paid any amount just to get out of the conversation, like when he met charity door-knockers.

He still didn't understand why Cole wanted a baby. Having children was perhaps the most adult thing you could do, and Dom still thought of them all—himself included—as kids. None of his other friends had reproduced yet—except for Isla, who'd always been a bit of a . . . well, Dom considered himself too classy to use the word *slut*, but she certainly hadn't taken much convincing, back when she was with him. She was bound to get knocked up eventually.

Oscar filled Felicity's glass right to the top, then his own. As he handed hers over, he made a *cheers* motion. Dom's eyes narrowed.

Everyone thought Dom was an idiot, and he only had himself to blame. In high school, he'd been too busy playing sport to study, leaving him with shoddy grades in everything except PE. So he had a reputation as a dumb jock, which he leaned into. He would tell funny stories about mistakes he'd made, and he'd pretend to misunderstand things. People were laughing *at* him, but at least they were laughing, which meant they liked having him around. But as an adult he'd found this reputation hard to shake off. He'd played the fool for so long that he'd been typecast.

Dom had seen the texts on Felicity's phone. He'd talked to his neighbour, who had seen a man matching Oscar's description leaving the house in the middle of the day. He had seen the way Oscar looked at Felicity. And no wonder: she was beautiful. Dom didn't mind being envied by other men. That was half the point of having cool stuff. But this was different—Oscar thought he could take her, and he thought Dom was a big dumb Neanderthal who wouldn't see it coming.

Dom had always been lucky. Sure, he'd made mistakes along the way, like the incident with Isla, but they hadn't stuck. He'd made some investments that had turned out well. When a senior partner had a stroke after swallowing a prodigious amount of cocaine, Dom found himself promoted beyond his comfort zone, but he'd hit the ground running. He knew his life was better than he deserved, but he wasn't going to let Oscar steal it—he had a plan.

He climbed up onto the safety rail around the deck.

Clementine's brow creased with worry. 'Whoa, Dom!'

'What are you doing?!' Felicity demanded.

He was pleased to notice he had all her attention now. Oscar had been forgotten.

Dom wobbled on the rail. The edge of the hot tub was about a metre away; behind him was a five-metre drop to the woodpile and the garden beds. But he wasn't scared. Being surrounded by his old friends made him feel sixteen again, and invincible. 'You think I should try a backflip?'

'I think you should climb down, carefully and immediately,' said Felicity.

'Silence, woman!' He laughed. His core twitched, keeping him vertical.

Isla emerged from the house. Now the sun was going down, she'd taken off the aviators and was holding a paperback. She didn't look as concerned as the others; maybe she had more confidence in his balance.

The front door slammed. The wind must have blown it shut. Startled by the noise, Dom lost his balance. He leaned too far forward, then over-corrected backward, his arms windmilling.

Felicity and Clementine edged closer, their arms out, but neither tried to grab him. Perhaps they were worried about accidentally pushing him off the rail.

He stabilised, his heart racing.

'Honey?' Felicity said. 'I really, really think you should come down from there.'

He smiled and made an elaborate bow. Everyone gasped.

'Your wish is my command,' he said. 'Cannonball!' He leaped forward, hugging his knees.

Barely clearing the edge of the hot tub, he crashed down into the lukewarm water, which was nowhere near deep enough for diving. His tailbone thumped painfully against the hard plastic floor. His ears filled with the blunt roar of the jets, and the chlorine stung his nose. He burst out and took a breath, blinking water out of his eyes. Everyone was yelling at him, drenched from the splash. Tub water had displaced half the champagne in Oscar and Felicity's glasses.

Dom grinned at his dripping friends. 'Hop in, otherwise you'll freeze to death!'

Clementine

Clementine was in shavasana, or corpse pose, when she heard the Tarago rumbling back up the hill. Cole had returned from his three-and-a-half-hour grocery run. 'Namaste,' she whispered, palms together and touching her thumbs to her forehead. She hadn't used the yoga mat, which was still damp from Dom's stunt on the deck, so there was nothing to pack away.

She jogged downstairs in time to see her husband enter, laden with shopping bags.

'I missed you,' she said.

'Missed *you*,' he said, and kissed her.

He'd bought enough food for the three-day trip, including milk, bread, eggs, bacon, sauces, plus Clementine's preferred brands of rolled oats and yoghurt. For tonight, he'd bought a rack of lamb plus enough carrots and potatoes to half-fill the huge oven, and a pavlova for dessert. He'd even found some tea lights.

Clementine was proud, but she noticed that no one else thanked him for driving all that way. They didn't offer money towards the shopping, either. She supposed she and Cole could afford it—the gym seemed very profitable lately—but she was annoyed by the rudeness.

She was starving by the time Cole had cooked everything and was plating up. Dom connected his phone to the giant

Bluetooth speaker he'd brought, and strains of soft jazz filled the air. He opened one of the six bottles of red wine that Cole had acquired.

'This is amazing,' Isla said, resting her book on the arm of the couch as Cole placed the lamb in the centre of the table.

'Like a medieval banquet.' Felicity glanced at Cole. 'You're not fattening us up to eat us, are you?'

They all laughed, but Clementine felt disappointment creep in. Felicity had reminded her that while this all looked delicious, she couldn't eat much of it. She casually took a seat next to Dom.

Clementine's modelling career had started fast and ended slow. She'd sent some test shots to an agent when she was in high school and got very lucky—she was in a Target catalogue by the end of that year. Soon she was flying around the country, doing shoots for Lorna Jane and Running Bare. She had to turn down work to make room for other work. She thought she could live like this forever.

After a couple of years her schedule was merely full rather than overflowing, but she didn't notice right away. Not until she was asked to drive to Sydney for a job, rather than being flown business class with sparkling wine and warm towels. The fee would barely cover the cost of the petrol. She looked for more appealing gigs and discovered there were none. Soon even the unappealing ones grew thin on the ground. As her bank balance shrank, she called her agent, who was sympathetic but not helpful. He had other clients to look after—younger ones. The women shopping for activewear didn't just want to get fit: they wanted to look youthful. Clementine had been over the hill at twenty-six.

She avoided carbs, used moisturiser and worked out every day but never in the sun. It didn't help. The brands got smaller and the jobs less frequent, while her photos shrank in the catalogues. A small activewear company called Moray still hired her once per season, but she knew that wouldn't last forever.

Having a baby was supposed to be her way out. She could

tell herself the industry wasn't abandoning her—she was leaving it by choice, to become a mother. But getting pregnant wasn't as easy as her sex-ed teacher had warned. She was thirty now and still trying—and still dieting. To maximise their chances of conceiving, she had to make sure she got enough potassium, folate and monounsaturated fats, and she had to avoid sugar, red meat, preservatives and anything with a high glycaemic index. She definitely couldn't sample any of the wine or soft cheeses on the table.

'You okay?' Cole asked her.

'Fine.' She stroked his back as he sat down on the other side of her. 'You always deliver the goods.'

He smiled. 'My love.' He drizzled gravy on her potatoes. It was made from powder, but she didn't have the heart to stop him.

'Give it a rest!' Isla was sitting opposite them. 'We get it—you're perfect.'

Clementine could tell she was joking but not joking.

'We're far from perfect,' Cole said. 'Just this morning I brewed a cup of tea and then forgot to drink it.'

'I, too, have a shameful flaw,' Clementine said. 'I only floss once per day.'

Isla scrunched up a napkin and threw it at them. They both laughed.

'I'm kind of a hypochondriac,' Oscar said, apparently missing the point of the game. 'Last week I was shaving, and I noticed my face didn't seem symmetrical. I thought maybe I had a brain tumour. I spent two hours freaking out, before I realised my new haircut was just a bit lopsided.'

Isla seemed surprised to hear this. Had Oscar not told her? Clementine wondered what kind of husband didn't tell his wife he was worried about a brain tumour. What was the point of being married, if not to share your secrets?

'Does a tumour show on your face?' Felicity wondered.

'Poe had one,' Isla said. 'If you look at him when he was young, compared to—'

'Po from *Kung Fu Panda*?' Oscar interrupted.

Isla sighed. 'Poe from Boston.'

This struck Clementine as cruel. If Isla had said Edgar Allan Poe, Oscar might have clicked. As it was, he was stuck pretending.

'Oh, of course.' He nodded vigorously.

'Anyway, his face got more and more saggy on one side,' Isla said. 'Years after his death, someone exhumed him and found the tumour in his skull. His stories got really twisted as he got older—I always wondered if it was the tumour coming up with the ideas, rather than him.'

'They found the tumour *years* later? It didn't rot?' Felicity sounded fascinated.

'This lamb is *delicious*, Cole,' Clementine said, trying to redirect the discussion.

There were *hmms* of agreement all around.

'How's the gym going, Cole?' Dom asked. He'd taken a spot at the head of the table, like a king.

Cole looked inexplicably wary. 'Fine.'

Dom beamed. 'That's the spirit!'

'He's being modest,' Clementine said. 'We're raking it in, for once.'

Not long ago Clementine had been waiting in line at her local cafe and had checked her bank balance on her phone. It had been ten thousand dollars larger than she expected—her husband had presumably given himself a well-deserved bonus. And yet, he still acted like the gym was struggling, constantly opening an app to see how often members visited, and how his Google ads were performing.

Now Cole was cringing, but she wasn't sure why.

'Did you always want to run your own business?' Felicity was asking.

Cole's eyebrows went up. 'Me? No!'

'He was going to be a vet.' Clementine put her hand over her husband's. 'He's always been good with animals.'

'Weird,' Felicity said, as though they'd said Cole played

the accordion, or collected egg timers. 'What changed?'

'I spent a lot of time at that gym,' he said. 'So I was the first to hear about it when the owner decided to sell up and move to Port Douglas. The business seemed profitable, and I had ideas to make it even better—I thought I did, anyway.' He gulped his wine. 'The profits were going to put me through the veterinary medicine course. But running the business didn't leave much time for study, and . . .'

When Cole trailed off, Felicity turned to Clementine. 'How about you? Did you always plan to be a fitness model?'

Clementine smiled. 'I wanted to be an athlete. I was the fastest in my event at Warrigal High, then the fastest again in the regionals, but when I got to the state level, I came dead last.'

'You looked great doing it, though,' Cole said.

She smiled ruefully. 'Well, that's what one of the photographers thought. She offered to take some test shots that I could send to modelling agencies. Now I work for Moray. Well, sometimes.'

Felicity's eyes widened. 'I love Moray!' She lifted her shirt to reveal her sports bra, as though that was a normal thing to do.

Dom rolled his eyes. 'Put 'em away, babe.'

'I can probably get you some free matching undies,' Clementine offered. 'Just let me know your size.'

She had meant later, in private, but Felicity said immediately, 'Size twelve.'

'Okay, great. I'll ask as soon as we get back home. I don't . . .' Clementine was reluctant to reveal this, but the tea lights gave the table the feel of a confessional. 'I don't know how much longer the modelling work will last.'

'Because you're trying to get pregnant?'

A shocked silence spread around the table.

Felicity looked around. 'Ooh, I know that sound. That's the sound of me crossing a line.'

Clementine forced a smile, but her heart rate had spiked. 'It's okay—it was just a remarkably good guess.'

'Well, it wasn't really a—' Felicity looked to Dom, who raised an eyebrow. 'I mean, it just makes sense. You guys have been together how long?'

'Thirteen years,' Cole said uncomfortably.

'You're going to make great parents.' Isla reached across the table and squeezed Clementine's hand. She'd been saying things like this for months, never seeming to doubt that it would someday be the truth.

'Yeah,' Oscar said, less enthusiastically.

'Thirteen years?' Felicity was aghast. 'So you've been together since you were . . .'

'Seventeen,' Clementine said, saving her from the maths.

'So you've never been with anyone else?'

'No,' Clementine said.

'I mean sexually,' Felicity added.

After a beat, Dom said, 'There's that sound again.'

'Sorry,' Felicity said. 'It's just . . . you must have wondered.'

'Wondered?' Clementine repeated.

Cole flushed bright red.

'What it would be like,' Felicity said. 'With other people.'

Clementine had the unnerving sense that Felicity could see into her brain. Clementine sometimes regretted meeting the perfect man so early, before she'd had the chance to try out some imperfect ones. This might be why she'd secretly watched the video of Dom and Isla together.

She quickly changed the subject. 'You've done some modelling too, right?'

Felicity looked mystified. 'I have?'

'Dom said you were a Target Girl when you were younger.'

Felicity burst out laughing. 'Oh! That wasn't modelling. I was in the circus.'

It was Clementine's turn to be confused. 'The circus?'

'She was a clown,' Dom said.

'I was promoted to clown when the old clown left,' Felicity said, 'but before that I was a target girl. Meaning I'd stand with my back against a target, and the knife thrower would—'

'Holy shit,' Isla said.

'She's kidding,' Cole said. 'Right?'

'It's not as dangerous as it looks,' Felicity said. 'Ever played darts? Throwing a knife is actually easier, because a knife is heavier—a stray air current doesn't send it off course. Being a clown was probably more dangerous. The old clown's unicycle had been assembled wrong, and it fell apart, mid-routine. He broke his spine.'

Clementine wasn't sure whether to laugh. Surely this was a joke—a clown with a broken spine was exactly the surreal, morbid humour Felicity favoured.

Felicity's eyes twinkled mischievously in the candlelight. 'I read this article about religious couples,' she said. 'Hard-line, not-until-we're-married couples. Apparently the divorce rate is higher than you'd think, because they're so sexually inexperienced that neither of them enjoys the act all that much.'

'Not an issue for us,' Cole said firmly, but Clementine wondered if he was telling the truth. He seemed most comfortable in a servile role, doing whatever she wanted—which was great, except that what she wanted was to make *him* happy. He was reluctant to articulate his own needs, in the bedroom or anywhere else, which sometimes made Clementine worry she wasn't meeting them.

There was a flash outside the window.

Clementine leaped up so fast her chair fell over, hitting the tiles with a sharp *crack*.

Cole bumped his glass, spilling red wine across the table. 'What?'

Clementine was still staring. 'Did anyone else see that?'

'See *what*?'

She jabbed a finger at the glass. 'Something moved.'

They all got up and approached the window. But it was so dark they couldn't even see the trees, just their own reflections.

'I don't see anything,' Isla said.

'Could have been a 'roo,' Cole put in.

'No. It was like a . . .' Clementine already felt uncertain. 'A bright flash.'

Felicity looked horrified. 'Like a camera?'

'Or a torch, maybe,' Clementine said.

Felicity made her hands into binoculars and held them to the glass. 'How far away?'

'A long way.' Clementine squinted into the night. 'Just a tiny flicker.'

'Probably just car headlights on the highway,' Dom said.

Cole frowned. 'Can't see the highway from here.'

'Can't see *anything* from here,' Oscar muttered.

Dom pointed back at the giant, spaceship-like oven. 'It could have been a reflection from one of those blinking lights.'

Clementine doubted that, but she said, 'I suppose.'

Oscar laughed nervously. 'Well, nice to have a bit of excitement.'

'Hmm.' Felicity gave Clementine a thoughtful stare.

'I'm not making it up,' Clementine said.

'Of course not!' Cole sounded shocked. 'No one's thinking that.'

But Felicity was. Clementine could tell.

Dom clapped his hands together. 'Cole—did I see you put a pavlova in the fridge?'

For the rest of the night, no one mentioned what Clementine had seen. Thankfully, they didn't bring up her sexual history either, or the lack of it.

After the drinking, the dessert, the drinking, the clearing of plates, the drinking, the loading of the dishwasher, and the extra drinking, Clementine announced, 'I'm going to bed.'

'Already?' Dom said, his voice too loud in the room, like the alcohol had half-deafened him.

'Yes. We only have three days here—I don't want to be tired the whole time.'

Cole squeezed her hand. 'I'll be up in a minute.'

She kissed the top of his head, then walked out.

'I'm going to the bathroom,' she heard Felicity say, then the younger woman followed her into the corridor.

Clementine walked a little faster. Felicity breezed past the bathroom and caught up to her at the bottom of the stairs.

'Wait up,' she said.

Clementine sighed. 'I don't want to talk about this.'

Felicity lowered her voice. 'You could borrow him.'

Something prickled at the back of Clementine's neck. 'Sorry?'

'My husband,' Felicity said. 'You can't keep him. But if you wanted to try him out for a night, he'd be keen. And I wouldn't mind.'

She turned away and strutted towards the bathroom. Clementine gaped after her.

Felicity looked back, and winked. 'Everyone should try a man like that, at least once,' she said, and slipped through the doorway, out of sight.

NOW

Kiara

It's Saturday morning. Elise has thrown some clothes into a battered suitcase with no apparent consideration for the weather, and left to take Guppy to the kennel. Kiara stands in front of the wardrobe, a hanger in each hand.

This was supposed to be a relaxing minibreak, so she'd like to take her hiking clothes and walking shoes. But she'll need at least one suit, because she'll have to drive straight to work after dropping Elise off on Monday morning. And Elise made it clear that visiting a crime scene isn't her idea of a holiday. She only agreed to come because Kiara needed help with the case. That makes it a work trip, so she should *only* pack suits. Sighing, Kiara puts the walking clothes back in the closet—then changes her mind and packs them into the suitcase. Defiantly, she adds an avocado-green scarf. She still can't find her lucky ring, but she puts on a couple of silver bangles for extra sparkle.

Kiara makes a cup of tea while she waits for Elise to return. As the kettle hisses, she picks up an Aldi catalogue off the bench, then tells herself she doesn't need a standing desk or an electric bike and tosses the catalogue into the bin.

Moving the catalogue has revealed one of Elise's bank statements on the bench. Elise is like that: she leaves jumpers on the couch, reading glasses on piles of books, and coffee mugs everywhere. This isn't always unpleasant—even when she's not here, Kiara feels surrounded by her.

As the rumble of the kettle becomes a roar, Kiara's gaze falls on a particular line. *Cash withdrawal. $800.* That's the largest sum Elise's bank will dispense from an ATM in a single transaction.

On a hunch, Kiara turns the page and sees another eight-hundred-dollar withdrawal from the previous week. And then another, the week before that. Has someone stolen Elise's card? But no—the other transactions are legit. There's her hairdresser, and the pet store, and the meal they shared at Kingo's.

Kiara remembers seeing Elise walk past the real estate agency when she was supposed to be at the hospital. There's an ATM nearby.

She thinks of the mysterious calls to Elise's phone. Kiara has been assuming it's the sort of harassment Elise is often subjected to, but what if it's not? What if someone in town is blackmailing her?

Kiara checks Elise's account balance. She had less than four thousand left in savings when this statement was printed. In Kiara's experience, blackmailers ask for more and more until their victim is cleaned out. Elise isn't far off.

The door opens. Kiara drops the statement and snatches up the kettle, so fast she burns the pad of her thumb.

'Hey, babe.' Elise comes in, brandishing a running magazine. 'Got some holiday reading. Are you good to go?'

Kiara looks for signs that Elise has been somewhere other than the kennel and the newsagency. She seems out of breath—why, if she drove? The newsagency and the kennel are in opposite directions, so maybe she dropped Guppy off, brought the car back and then ran to get the magazine. That would fit with the amount of time she's been gone, but what about her sore knee? And why did she go to the newsagency before they left for the mountain, instead of making a stop on the way?

'What's up?' Elise asks.

Kiara realises she's been looking at her partner the same way she looks at suspects. She can't go on like this.

'Nothing.' She pours the hot water into the travel mug. 'Let's go.'

The mountain is formidable—Elise's little Suzuki is unlikely to make it to the top. Kiara asks Elise to drop her off at the mechanic's, waving as her partner zooms off to park behind the railway station where the car will be safe over the weekend. Or, at least, that's where she says she's going.

'How's my Navara, Bill?' Kiara asks as she walks in.

He holds out her key with oil-blackened fingers. 'I have good news and bad news.'

She isn't sure she can handle any more bad news. 'Go on.'

'The bad news is that the Blu Tack didn't hold.'

'What Blu Tack?'

Bill peers over his glasses at her. 'Or chewing gum. Whatever it was you used to plug the hole in your coolant tank. It's completely dry.'

'I didn't try to fix my car with Blu Tack, Bill,' Kiara says.

'Well, whichever clown you hired last time did. Next time, come to me, eh?'

'What hole are you talking about?'

'There was a crack at the bottom of the coolant tank. Could have happened a while ago, I suppose—you wouldn't notice it if you were just driving to the shops and back. But I'll tell you what, you wouldn't have made it up that mountain.'

Kiara's heart sinks. 'How did it happen, the crack?'

'Beats me. You weren't mucking around in there with a screwdriver, were you?'

'No. Can you fix it?'

'A part like that has to be replaced rather than fixed, and usually you'd be waiting a couple of weeks to get one. But that's the good news—I had a spare tank on hand from a Nissan that was written off last Tuesday. It's installed, filled, and ready to go.'

'Wow. Thanks, Bill.'

He looks pleased with himself. 'No worries.'

'How much do I owe you?'

He smiles. 'Nothing. Just promise me you ladies will have a nice time.'

She opens her mouth to tell him she can't accept that, because she's a cop—and because it's creepy. Then she hesitates. 'You ever seen a cracked coolant tank before?'

'After a crash, sure. But not in an undamaged vehicle. Why?'

'And your first thought was that someone might have done it with a screwdriver? And then tried to fix it with Blu Tack?'

'Well, yeah. That's what it looked like.'

'Can you show me the crack?'

He leads her to a blue wheelie bin at the back of the garage. Rummaging through blackened paper towels, he eventually pulls out a plastic cylinder that reminds Kiara of the vaporiser her dad used to set up in her room whenever she had a cold.

'See?' Bill points to the crack at the bottom.

She examines it. There are scratches on either side, as though someone stabbed it a few times before breaking through. 'What's right next to the coolant tank?'

'The brake fluid reservoir. Why?'

A chill runs down her spine. 'Show me that.'

He pops open the bonnet of the Navara, and points. The reservoir looks a lot like her new coolant tank. She can easily imagine someone trying to sabotage her brakes and wrecking the tank instead, particularly if they were working in the dark. But why would they try to fix it afterwards?

Bill's police training finally comes back to him. 'You're not thinking someone did this on purpose?'

'That's exactly what I'm thinking.' Kiara is already running a mental list of recently paroled criminals. The home addresses of police officers are kept secret, but Warrigal is a small town. Her house wouldn't be hard to find, and the Navara is usually in the driveway, unguarded.

'Well, for starters,' says Bill, 'that would never work in real life. You'd notice the brakes weren't working as soon as you backed out—you'd crash into your own letterbox at about two kilometres per hour, and that would be it. No one could kill you that way.'

'Maybe it was a warning, then.' Kiara peers into the engine, as though it's a criminal's brain. 'Someone trying to scare me off a lead.'

'Is there much mafia activity in Warrigal?' Bill asks doubtfully. 'Because unless you're a major organised crime group, threatening a cop just gets you arrested quicker. It's a dumb plan.'

'Well, I know some dumb crooks.' As Kiara turns back to the broken coolant tank, something else occurs to her. 'If they'd punctured the brake fluid rather than the coolant—'

'They didn't,' Bill says.

'Say they did. Would the Blu Tack have held?'

'Not for long. We're talking about a lot of pressure. If you were going slow and tapped the brakes you'd probably be okay, but . . .' He seems to realise what he's saying.

'But if I was going fast, and braked hard?'

Bill has gone pale. 'You should call this in.'

'Hi, Bill.' Elise strolls into the garage, back from the railway station. She puts her arm around Kiara's waist. 'Call what in?'

'Your girlfriend's car,' Bill tells her. 'It's been—'

'Fixed,' Kiara interrupts, slamming the bonnet. 'Thanks, Bill.'

Bill looks at the two of them. 'But shouldn't we—'

'No.' Ignoring Elise's suspicious look, Kiara gets out a credit card. 'How much do I owe you?'

'Nicer than I expected,' Elise says, getting out of the Navara.

'What were you expecting?' Kiara asks.

'Dunno. Broken windows, cobwebs, maybe a weather-vane. A haunted mansion vibe.'

Kiara is a little offended that Elise thinks she'd invite her to a place like that. Then again, 'murder house' would conjure that image for most civilians. Police know homicides happen more often than not in well-lit, friendly-looking dwellings.

Kiara can't get the ATM withdrawals out of her head, but can't ask Elise about them without implying she's hiding something. Kiara spent the whole car ride up the mountain talking warmly about other things, hoping Elise might open up. But Elise seemed distracted, staring through the windscreen at the forbidding peaks ahead.

'Guess we should take a look inside?' Elise says.

'Guess so.'

Kiara slips past her to get in first. It's cold in the hallway. One of the doors leading to the back deck has been left ajar, maybe to help flush out the odour. It hasn't worked—Kiara can still smell death in the place. Maybe she's imagining it. She switches on the extractor fan in the kitchen and runs to check the bedrooms. They're clean, thank God. Jennings has collected all the evidence tags, and there's no blood or fingerprint powder anywhere. The crime scene scrubbers did their job.

Elise enters behind her, looking amused. 'Clearing the rooms for me, Officer Lui?'

Kiara smiles. 'Of course, Madam President.' She opens some windows to flush out the bad air.

Elise crosses her arms. 'Are you crazy? It's freezing out there.'

'It's mountain air. It's good for us.'

'Even Canberra wasn't as bad as this.'

'Okay, okay.' Kiara closes the windows.

She paid for the same luxury package Dom did, so Basking's cleaner was supposed to leave a welcome hamper on the kitchen bench, with crackers, olives and quince paste. But the bench is bare. Kiara pulls out her phone to call Basking about the missing hamper, then remembers there's no coverage up here.

'Do you have reception?' she asks Elise, who's with a different carrier.

Elise checks. 'Nope.'

So Kiara can't complain to Basking about his cleaner. She would feel bad about doing that anyway—during the interview, Chantelle seemed overworked, underpaid and exhausted. At least the black spot means Elise can't be harassed over the phone, which was the point of the trip.

They walk through the house together, Elise checking out the two downstairs bedrooms and the bathroom in between. A rat or a possum is scratching inside the walls. Kiara pretends not to hear, hoping Elise won't notice.

When they go upstairs, Kiara sees the door she kicked in has been fixed so perfectly that it's as if she's gone back in time. She has the surreal feeling that when she opens it, she'll find Mrs Kelly pointing a knife at her husband.

She goes in. The room is empty.

On the night of their argument, Kiara realised that coming here might upset Elise rather than relax her. It's only now dawning on Kiara that it might mess with her own head, too.

She notices a faint whistling from the ceiling. Looking up, she spots the hole she thought was from a champagne cork. Now she sees a trailing wire—a light fitting must have been removed. Luckily, the big windows brighten the room.

Elise admires the view. 'Wow. How much of this is part of the property?' She gestures at the endless expanse of trees.

'A little over twenty thousand acres. You could get very, very lost.'

'You think that's what happened to the missing woman? Madden?'

A wedge-tailed eagle wheels through the grey sky.

'Maybe,' Kiara says, looking into the bushland. 'But

Ms Dubois managed to follow the trail all the way to the road, at night.'

'So if Madden got lost . . .'

'Then she probably did it on purpose,' Kiara finishes. 'The search party has cleared a forty-kilometre radius around the house. It's been a week, so they're probably—' Kiara stops herself from saying, *looking for a body* '—not going to find anything.'

'Hard to survive out there.' Elise's eyes are fixed on the eagle.

Kiara agrees. Even with a torch, a sleeping bag, a tent, a phone and a box of matches, the prospect would be daunting. Still, her ancestors managed just fine.

'Shall we take this bedroom?' Kiara asks. 'It's the biggest.'

Elise is looking at the bed. 'The first victim died at 9 p.m. last Saturday, and you found him in the bed—'

'Not this bed,' Kiara says quickly. 'That was downstairs. The west bedroom, closest to the kitchen.'

'But up here there was . . .?' Elise makes a stabbing motion, like the famous scene in *Psycho*.

'Right,' Kiara says, feeling gloomier by the minute. This was a terrible idea. 'How about the east bedroom, with the door to the deck? No dead bodies in there.'

'Ooh, romantic,' Elise says. She's clearly joking, but Kiara is hurt.

Downstairs, they unpack their things in silence. Kiara notices that the sheets in this room are rumpled—hopefully because they were changed inexpertly, rather than because they haven't been changed at all. She surreptitiously smooths them out.

She wants to ask Elise, *Who's blackmailing you? What do they know? How much money have you given them?* The longer she holds the questions in, the more uncomfortable they become, like coughs.

Elise finally speaks. 'I've never been on a holiday like this.'

'A murder house holiday?'

'A house holiday. My family usually went camping.'

'Mine too,' Kiara says. 'Always Dad's idea. Mum wasn't a fan. She said if she'd wanted to bathe in a river, she would have stayed in Haiphong.'

'There's a lot to be said for plumbing,' Elise agrees. She meets Kiara's gaze.

It strikes Kiara that Elise doesn't often do this. She's willing to make eye contact with people she doesn't like—she'll shout at them, get right up in their faces—but with her friends and family, she gets uncomfortable.

'Anyway, thank you,' Elise says.

'For what?'

'For taking me on my first house holiday.'

Kiara forces a smile. 'You're welcome.' But it's hard to quiet the storm in her gut.

They get the fire going, though it doesn't warm the house much. Remembering what the agent said about heating costs, Kiara raps her knuckles on the walls. They sound hollow—no insulation. If the fire dies, the heat will leak out soon after.

There was supposed to be food in the fridge, but there isn't. Luckily, Kiara brought bread, cheese, ham and relish, thinking they'd have a picnic lunch tomorrow. She still doesn't like the faint ammonia smell in the kitchen, so she assembles the sandwiches at the dining table.

'Who decided that sandwiches had to be a lunch food?' she asks as she sits down.

'The rules are oddly strict.' Elise takes one of the triangular slices. 'Cereal for breakfast, sandwiches for lunch, pasta for dinner. If you mess with the order, people think you're a maniac.'

'Mum sometimes reheated a stir-fry for our breakfast. I loved it. But when I started having sleepovers with friends, they thought it was weird, and I got embarrassed. After that I refused.' Kiara takes a bite. She hasn't thought about this for twenty years. She can see it from Mum's perspective now, and she feels a prickle of guilt.

'I like your bangles,' Elise says.

Kiara rattles them. 'Thanks. I couldn't find my ring, so I brought these instead—you haven't seen it, have you?'

Elise already seems distracted again. 'Seen what?'

'My mum's ring,' Kiara says impatiently. 'The one with the opal.'

Elise lowers her gaze. 'No, sorry.'

Silence falls. This was what Kiara wanted—just the two of them, no distractions. Why does it feel like she's wading through treacle?

'I'm sorry about the sandwiches,' Kiara says. 'I tried to buy you a hamper.'

Elise looks surprised. 'You did?'

'Yeah. I ordered figs, and goat's cheese, and fancy olives. There was supposed to be food in the fridge, too. But the real estate agent's cleaner must have forgotten to leave it for us.'

'You did well to pull this together, then.' Elise gestures at the sandwiches. 'Maybe the hamper will turn up tomorrow.'

Kiara sighs. 'I wouldn't count on it. Seems to be a habit with this agent—according to the suspects, the fridge was supposed to be fully stocked when they rented the place, but it was empty then, too. Cole, the gym owner, had to drive back into town for groceries on the first day.'

Elise stares at her.

'What?' Kiara asks.

'Nothing,' Elise says, but her eyes are wide. 'Anyway, what are we going to do tomorrow?'

'I've been looking at a map of the walking trails in the area,' Kiara says, 'but given the weather . . .'

Elise dips a finger into the jar of relish.

Kiara laughs. 'What are you doing?'

Elise's face is grim. She uses the relish to trace a message on the tabletop.

'Well, whatever we do, I'm sure it will be nice,' Elise says, her voice loud but a little shaky.

She's written: *are we alone?*

A chill creeps from Kiara's tailbone to the top of her head. She thinks of the missing food, and the rumpled sheets in the downstairs bedroom.

They both look at the ceiling when they hear a distinct *thump*.

LAST SATURDAY

Oscar

'Morning,' Cole said.

Oscar flinched guiltily. 'Just waiting for the shower,' he said, pointing a thumb at the door of the downstairs bathroom.

The truth was, he'd been *listening* to the shower because he knew Felicity was inside. He could hear the water drizzling off her fingertips and the faint slapping of her bare feet.

'How'd you sleep?' Cole jogged on the spot, as though his body would melt if given even a second of rest.

'Like a baby,' Oscar said, which was true. In his experience, babies didn't sleep at all, and he'd been awake most of the night, knowing Felicity was in the other downstairs bedroom. He'd imagined her sneaking in at midnight. Slipping into bed with him while Isla snored, oblivious. Climbing atop him and leaning down for a kiss, her red hair a curtain on either side of his head.

'You want a coffee?' Cole asked.

'Sounds good,' Oscar said.

'White with one?'

'That's it.'

As Cole was turning away, Oscar said quietly, 'You ready for tonight?'

Cole just grunted, not meeting Oscar's eye. Oscar told himself that was a *yes*, in the language of masculine fitness junkies.

Soon after, the bathroom door opened. Oscar's smile froze as he found himself face to face—well, face to chest—with Dom, who was naked except for a towel around his waist. He smiled, revealing the slight gap between his front teeth. 'Oscar. How'd you pull up this morning?'

'Not bad.' Oscar leaned sideways, checking that Felicity wasn't also in the bathroom. 'You?'

'I'm okay. That fourth drink might have been a mistake, though.'

'Really? I'd have thought a big fella like you could handle it—though you are light-footed.'

'Light-footed?' Dom's eyes seemed to radiate superiority and disgust, as though Oscar was naked in front of him, not the other way around.

'Graceful,' Oscar said. 'You don't sound as big as you are, walking around.'

'You're a funny man, Oscar.' Dom squeezed past, wafting aftershave and steaming skin, and walked to his room, his feet making exaggerated thumps.

'Learned it from your wife,' Oscar muttered under his breath. He told himself he'd imagined the menace in Dom's voice. Dom didn't know anything. Did he?

When Oscar got to the dining room, the breakfast table was heaped with toast, eggs, spinach, bacon and mushrooms. Isla was already there, dark glasses on, a cup of tea in one hand. Cole had put Oscar's coffee next to her. Without looking at her, Oscar moved the coffee and sat next to Clementine. 'Do you and Cole eat like this all the time?' he asked her, gesturing at the feast on the table.

She nibbled at a mushroom. 'I'm usually a bit more careful. But yeah, he spoils me.'

Oscar wondered what 'careful' meant for her, if mushrooms on dry toast were risky.

'I used to hate cooking,' Cole called from the kitchen, where he was loading hash browns onto paper towels. 'I used to fantasise about having enough money that I'd never need to do it again. But now it's my favourite part of the day.'

'What changed?' Isla spooned spinach and eggs onto her toast, neglecting the bacon. She'd recently become vegetarian as part of her ongoing campaign to make Oscar's life difficult.

'We started getting one of those meal delivery services,' Clementine said. 'You know, where they send you the recipes and a box of all the ingredients each week?'

'Ooh, maybe I should get Oscar on to that,' said Isla.

Oscar said nothing, stunned by how easily she could turn any conversation into an opportunity to belittle him.

Felicity walked into the dining area, still towelling off her beautiful red hair. 'Morning, all!'

A chorus of grunts and mumbles.

'Yikes,' she said. 'We've already reached that stage of the holiday, have we?'

Clementine laughed. 'Yup. Yesterday we regressed to high school, this morning we've made it all the way back to Neanderthal.'

Isla's face lit up. 'Hey, I just read something interesting about Neanderthals.'

'Here we go.' Oscar sighed, his exhausted brain letting part of his inner monologue escape.

On a sitcom, everyone would have ignored it; in real life, an appalled silence fell. Everyone became suddenly fascinated by their food, avoiding eye contact with one another.

Clementine was the first to speak. 'What did you read, Isla?'

'Never mind. It's not really a suitable story for mealtimes.' Isla stood up, half her breakfast still on her plate.

'I have a strong stomach,' Clementine offered, but Isla was gone.

Oscar could feel everyone glaring at him. He stared down into the immaculate latte Cole had made, his face reddening.

'So,' Felicity said finally, 'anyone up for a bushwalk?'

Felicity

Truth be told, Felicity wasn't much of a bushwalker. She got enthusiastic about it every couple of years, but her interest usually dried up once she'd bought new hiking shoes, quick-dry pants and a moisture-wicking shirt. Dom had said she was more of a bush shopper.

But Felicity wanted everyone to be laughing, flirting, having fun, getting along. Cole clearly hadn't told Clementine about his failing gym or the money from Dom, who seemed to be watching Oscar with great suspicion. Oscar and Isla were basically at each other's throats—could Isla have found out about the kiss? No, because she didn't seem angry with Felicity. Either way, the house was full of tension. The obvious solution was to get everyone out of the house.

It hadn't quite worked. Isla had stayed behind to read a book, and Cole had said he wanted to start prepping lunch; the guy sure liked cooking. But at least Dom, Clementine and Oscar were following Felicity down the hill.

She'd pretended to choose the trail at random. Only Clementine seemed suspicious.

Twigs cracked and leaves crunched beneath their boots. The terrain was difficult. The trail was narrow and winding, the sort used by animals rather than humans. But occasionally she saw tyre tracks in the dirt, as though mountain bikers had come this way. She stamped because she'd heard that heavy footfalls would alert snakes up ahead and make them retreat; then again, maybe the reptiles were hibernating and the stomping would wake them up.

The winter sun filtered through the trees, igniting flecks in the air that could have been snow. After an hour of walking, the cold was burning the back of Felicity's throat, even as sweat poured from her armpits. Occasionally the trail turned a bend and a gap between the trees exposed the spectacular mountain range lining the horizon like a giant's molars.

Clementine was right behind her. 'I know what you're doing,' she said.

'How can you talk?' Felicity wheezed. 'I can hardly breathe.'

'We're just walking,' Clementine said, not sounding even slightly puffed.

'There's walking,' Felicity gasped, 'and there's *walking*.'

For about a year, she'd been telling herself that stand-up was all the exercise she needed—she'd worn a Fitbit onstage once, and it had tracked an impressive number of steps over the course of her set. But she now realised the difference between pacing back and forth across a flat surface and *this*: marching downhill on rocks and lumpy dirt. Coming back up would be even tougher.

'You're trying to work out if I was telling the truth about the light,' Clementine said.

Felicity feigned confusion. 'What light?'

'The light I spotted out the window last night.'

'Oh. The light that very conveniently changed the topic away from your sexual history?'

'The light I saw coming from exactly this direction.'

Felicity looked around as though that hadn't occurred to her. 'Really? Are you sure? Because I don't see anything that would create a light around here. The highway isn't visible, there are no other buildings, there's no—'

'You've made your point,' Clementine said. 'Maybe, *maybe* I imagined it. But that's not the same thing as making it up.'

'You ladies okay down there?' Dom's voice was distant. He and Oscar had fallen behind.

Unease burbled in Felicity's gut—she didn't like the two of them being alone together.

'Fine!' she and Clementine called in unison.

'Listen.' Clementine lowered her voice. 'I've been thinking about what you said.'

'I say a lot of things,' Felicity said, but hope fluttered in her chest.

'About borrowing.'

'Oh, that.' She shrugged, as though she offered to lend out her husband all the time.

'Are you sure Dom would be comfortable with it?'

'It was his idea.'

Clementine looked startled. 'Really?'

'We talk about you quite a lot. Sometimes he asks me to wear a blonde wig.'

'You're joking.' Clementine blushed furiously.

'I wish.' Felicity wasn't joking so much as lying—the line was always fuzzy. She knew Dom was attracted to other women, but he'd never expressed interest in Clementine specifically. If Felicity admitted that though, she thought Clementine would be reluctant to participate in tonight's entertainment.

Before Clementine could respond, they rounded a corner and found themselves facing a pile of garbage.

Felicity's hand flew to her nose. 'Urgh, gross.'

The semi-transparent plastic bags were stacked in a pyramid, like someone was building a temple to wastefulness. There had to be fifty bags or more. Some were stuffed with food scraps, while others held old clothes and blankets. A broken folding chair and a battered bike lay nearby, surrounded by apple cores, soiled wet wipes and crumpled wrappers.

'So much for virgin wilderness,' Felicity said.

'Why here?' Clementine looked around. 'It's a crazy place to dump anything.'

'Looks like garbage from the house.' Felicity stooped to examine an empty packet of sliced ham. The use-by date was still days away.

'You think the cleaner left it here?' Clementine wondered.

'Right. Just out of sight from the back deck.'

'That's ridiculous. Why wouldn't they drive it back down the hill when they left?'

'The broken bike wouldn't fit in the car?' Felicity guessed. 'Or they were saving money. People have to pay to dump stuff at the tip. Cheaper to leave it up here.'

'But they must have known someone would find it. Bushwalkers would rent this house all the time.'

'The odds of them taking this particular trail are low.' Felicity gave Clementine some side-eye. 'Unless they spot mysterious lights in the dark.'

Oscar and Dom caught up. 'What the hell?' Dom said, looking at the garbage.

'Don't worry, we've already solved the case,' Felicity said. 'It was the cleaner, on the mountainside, with the garbage bags.'

Oscar stared at the pile. 'You think the cleaner just chucked all this here?'

'Seems so,' Clementine said.

Dom hugged Felicity, as though she might be traumatised by seeing garbage. 'I'm so sorry.'

'I'll live,' Felicity said.

'You know I don't like giving anything less than a five-star review . . .'

She squeezed him back. 'You can do it, baby. I believe in you.'

Oscar looked uncomfortable, and Felicity remembered he worked for the real estate agency. 'Chantelle's never done this before,' he said.

'That you know about.' Dom raised an eyebrow. 'There could be secret garbage piles hidden near *all* your properties.'

Oscar's brow furrowed. He reached for his phone, then paused, probably remembering there was no reception.

'Shall we keep going?' Clementine asked.

'Nah,' Felicity said. 'All this sleuthing has made me hungry. Let's head back. By now your husband has probably plucked a pheasant for lunch and roasted it in that giant oven.'

As they walked back up the hill, Felicity glanced back. It felt ominous, this pile of stuff left behind by other couples who had rented the house: the grubbiest parts of their lives, festering just out of sight.

As they hiked back up the hill, Clementine seemed to fall behind, even though she was the fittest of the bunch. Taking the hint, Felicity fell back as well. Soon there was enough of a gap between them and the men that they wouldn't be overheard.

'Borrowing,' Felicity prompted.

Clementine took a deep breath. 'Right,' she said. 'Let's talk logistics.'

Isla

'You were gone a long time.' Isla tried not to sound suspicious, but wasn't sure she'd pulled it off. She compensated by not looking up from her book, as though she couldn't care less that her husband had gone into the bush with two women and come back in the door sweating, laughing and generally seeming happier than he had in years.

Oscar would never cheat on her, because there was no way to do that passive aggressively. But taking pleasure from the company of other women was a kind of infidelity, wasn't it?

He waved off her remark. 'We didn't even make it halfway down the hill.'

'Maybe it seemed like a long time because life's so boring without us,' Felicity put in.

Isla turned a page without reading it. 'Hmm. That must be it.'

Her psychologist would have said she was *projecting*, because she'd enjoyed being alone with Cole. Other than the blond hair and the beard, he looked a lot like her husband, yet he was somehow much more attractive. Without being asked, he'd left a cup of tea by her side while she was reading. The tea was steeped to exactly the right strength and came with a little biscuit on an entirely unnecessary plate. She felt like the Queen. She'd read amusing passages aloud while he cleaned the kitchen, and delighted in that soft chuckle of his. She'd relaxed in a way she'd forgotten was possible. Glancing over at him now, watching the veins in his arms and the intent look on his face as he polished the kitchen bench, she found herself thinking, *Why didn't I marry* you?

She knew the answer: timing. In high school, she'd heard Cole had a thing for her, but she'd already been dating Dom. By the time that relationship fell apart—exploded, actually—Cole was with Clementine, Isla's best friend.

I'm so screwed up, she thought. She couldn't just let herself enjoy a couple of hours with a gentle, gorgeous man; she had to ruin it by thinking about all the ways she wished her life were different. And then she had to find reasons to be suspicious of her husband to beat back the guilt.

She missed Noah. Her relationship with him wasn't complicated. Making him happy made her happy, and it was usually as straightforward as buying him a doughnut or a water pistol.

She closed her book and rubbed her eyes.

'Drink?' Dom asked, already pouring her a glass of white wine.

'It's twelve-thirty,' Isla said. She *did* want a drink—but not from him.

For lunch they had wraps filled with roast chicken, rocket, cherry tomatoes and shaved parmesan. Cole had fried some haloumi to replace the chicken for Isla and whipped up a seeded mustard mayo to go with it. She found herself closing her eyes as she ate.

'Cole, these wraps are better than sex,' Oscar said.

'Sounds like you're doing sex wrong,' Felicity replied.

As the others laughed, Oscar glanced at Isla. Too late, she realised he expected her to defend him.

'You're fine at sex, honey,' she said.

Dom guffawed. '"Fine."'

Isla poured herself the glass of wine she'd refused earlier.

'It must be different,' Clementine said carefully, 'since the baby?'

'You got that right,' Oscar grumbled.

'Noah's five years old,' Isla said. 'My body is in tip-top shape these days, thank you very much. It's just hard to find the time.'

Actually, her pelvic floor had never quite recovered from the birth. She could jog, but couldn't sprint without leaking. Whenever she looked in the mirror on her way to the shower, her breasts seemed unwilling to meet her gaze, one hanging a little lower than the other. But she wasn't about to say any of that in front of three men, or in front of Clementine, who was trying to get pregnant.

'Nothing but time up here . . .' Felicity said.

'Yeah.' Isla tried not to sound gloomy. She'd noticed that Oscar had packed condoms, but the thought of it was exhausting.

Clementine didn't seem reassured by any of this. She coughed, then sipped her water.

'Don't worry.' Isla touched her wrist. 'You and Cole will be fine. I'm sure you'll find him as irresistible as he is now.'

Cole's ears went pink.

Clementine looked amused. 'Cole is "irresistible"?'

Panic squeezed Isla's chest. 'I said *you'd* find him irresistible! I didn't say *I*—' She looked at Cole. 'I mean, not that you're *not*, I just—'

'Oh, God.' Felicity rolled her eyes. 'Would you all just fuck each other already?'

Awkward laughter around the table. To Isla's horror, Felicity kept talking: 'Just get it out of your systems! Isla and Oscar clearly need to mix things up a bit. Clementine needs to find out what she's missing—or maybe prove to herself she's not missing anything. Cole, *no one* puts this much effort into cooking unless they're trying to get laid. And as for us—'

'That's enough, babe,' Dom said, and she fell silent. Everyone seemed to reach for their drinks at the same time, sipping instead of speaking.

Isla had always thought alcohol's main function was as a smokescreen. People only pretended to like the taste. What they really wanted was the freedom to do crazy things and then blame it on the booze: to pretend they hadn't always secretly fantasised about dancing like that, kissing that guy, voicing that dangerous opinion. *It wasn't me—it was the shots.* Deniability, paid for by a failing liver.

Clementine broke the silence. 'What are we going to do this afternoon?'

Felicity opened her mouth, probably to make a crude suggestion, but Oscar got in first. 'I brought Settlers of Catan,' he offered.

Everyone groaned.

'Charades?' Dom said.

Even louder groans.

Felicity's smile turned impish. 'How about truth or dare?'

'We went to high school together,' Dom objected. 'We all know one another's secrets.'

'Mutually assured destruction,' Clementine agreed.

'I wasn't there,' Felicity said. 'Nor was Oscar.'

While the others discussed this, Isla glanced at Cole. She knew Felicity had been kidding. But just for a moment, she allowed herself to imagine it.

He looked at her, and she wondered if he was imagining it, too.

Clementine

'Dare,' Oscar said.

They were all sprawled on the couches, the windows darkening. A mixture of full and empty glasses covered the coffee table, along with cheese, crackers and grapes. Dom's Bluetooth speaker crooned in the corner. Oscar had chopped some wood, and now the fire was crackling. The scrunched-up newspapers under the logs looked like black roses. The flickering light felt faintly magical. Anything could happen.

Clementine sat between Oscar and Dom, nibbling on a dry cracker, wondering if the whole weekend would pass like this—everyone gorging themselves on food she shouldn't have and alcohol she couldn't drink, just in case there had been a miracle and she was pregnant. Being the only sober person at a party was tiresome. She supposed she'd have to get used to it.

Felicity looked thoughtful for a moment, then said, 'I dare you to give Clementine a foot massage.'

Oscar looked at her for permission. She laughed despite herself and rested her feet on his lap. He got to it, working his thumbs deep into her arches. She let out a hum of pleasure. 'Good dare,' she murmured.

Cole's eyebrows went up. 'Sounds like you got skills, bro.'

Oscar wasn't bad-looking, in this light. Clementine

supposed most men would be more attractive while rubbing her feet. But tonight his deep-set eyes, which normally seemed haunted, instead looked soulful. Between that and the five o'clock shadow, he had the aura of a poet—though Isla claimed he didn't even read, much less write.

Yes, Clementine thought. *If I don't get Dom tonight, Oscar wouldn't be too bad.*

'My turn to ask someone now, right?' Oscar said, compressing Clementine's heels.

Dom leaned back on the couch, taking up far too much of it with his spread arms and legs. 'That's the rule.'

'Cole,' Oscar said. 'Truth or dare?'

Cole smiled warily. 'Truth.'

Oscar's face was grave. 'Do you . . . pee in the shower?'

Everyone laughed, especially Clementine, who knew he absolutely did.

'It's more efficient,' Cole said defensively, which only made them laugh harder.

'I'm with you, buddy,' Felicity said. 'Why waste a flush? Save the planet.' She let Cole think she was on his side for a moment, then added, 'Where do you do number twos? The sink?'

'Okay, give me a break.' Cole cracked his knuckles in an ominous way. 'Truth or dare, Isla?'

She tucked her dark hair behind her ears and leaned forward. 'Truth.'

'Who was your first celebrity crush?'

Looking relieved, she cleared her throat. 'Tristan Bancks, from *Home and Away*.'

'He was cute,' Clementine agreed.

'Before my time,' Felicity said mildly.

The reminder of Felicity's youth was grating. Clementine found herself touching the edges of her eyes, feeling for crows' feet. Her mother had gone grey at thirty-five. If she didn't get pregnant soon, she'd look like a grandma when she took the child to the playground.

'My turn,' Isla said. 'Dom—truth or dare?'

The corner of Dom's mouth twitched. 'Dare.'

'Give Oscar a lap dance.'

Oscar's hands stiffened around Clementine's feet. Dom looked so taken aback that Clementine couldn't help but laugh.

'Well, I'm giving a foot massage right now . . .' Oscar began.

Clementine snatched her feet away. 'Oh, don't let me stand in the way.'

Cole was guffawing, but Clementine noticed that Felicity, usually the wildest of the bunch, looked tense.

'Relax,' Isla said. 'If either of you is too chickenshit, you just have to take a drink instead. That's the rules, right?'

Cole looked down at his mostly empty glass. 'Wait, am I only supposed to be drinking when I refuse a dare?'

'I'm not chickenshit.' Dom sounded uncomfortable, but as usual he covered it with braggadocio. 'I'm just not sure Oscar can handle me.'

'I've never had a lap dance,' Oscar said. 'But it's my understanding that all I have to do is sit there.'

'That's all you're *allowed* to do,' Cole said.

Clementine raised an eyebrow at him.

'At least in the movies,' he added hurriedly, and everyone else laughed.

Isla had been Clementine's maid of honour and had organised a stripper for her hen's night. The guy had been older, thinner and grosser than she'd expected—definitely more of a McConaughey than a Tatum. Clementine couldn't remember whether she'd been instructed not to touch him, but it was a moot point, because she hadn't wanted to. His bronzed skin had left orange stains on the table. Clementine and Isla had giggled at his sparkly little thong, but afterwards Clementine had felt a twinge of disappointment that her last night out as a single woman hadn't been sexier.

The laughter had broken the tension and seemed to give Dom confidence. He stood up. 'All right, Oscar. Brace yourself for all this.' He shimmied, rubbing his hands down the sides of his body.

Isla scooped up Dom's phone and started swiping through songs he'd downloaded. She stopped at 'Need You Tonight' by INXS. Clementine and Cole chortled, while Felicity watched on, still looking wary.

Dom strutted slowly over to Oscar, catwalk-style, taking the long way around the coffee table.

'Quit stalling,' Isla said.

When Dom reached Oscar he turned his back on him, put his hands in the air and lowered himself into a crouch, hips rolling the whole way down. Though he was hamming it up, he was clearly a better dancer now than he'd been in school. Clementine found she couldn't look away.

Placing his palms on the floor, Dom straightened his legs and waggled his arse in Oscar's face. 'How long do I have to dance for?' he asked.

'The whole song, I reckon,' Isla said.

'I'll get you for this.'

She smirked.

Oscar tried hard to cover his discomfort. 'Has anyone got five dollars? To tuck into Dom's belt.'

'On the house for you, big boy,' Dom purred. He turned and straddled Oscar, pushing his chest forward into Oscar's face.

Isla screamed with laughter. It seemed funny to Clementine, too, but other emotions started to creep in. Beneath the mock-seductiveness, Dom's moves felt aggressive and predatory. He wasn't just giving Oscar a lap dance—Dom was threatening. The way one male dog might hump another, showing the pack who's boss.

This unsettled Clementine but also fascinated her. A dormant seed, finally watered, sprouted inside her brain. She'd never been with a Dom.

Soon the song was over. 'You can stop thrusting now, mate,' Cole said.

Dom climbed off, wiping his forehead with his sleeve. 'Strippers must be in pretty good shape,' he puffed, as though this had never occurred to him before.

'I wouldn't know,' Cole said quickly.

Dom didn't go back to his seat. He stared down at Oscar. 'Truth or dare?'

Oscar hesitated. The pause felt loaded, in a way Clementine didn't quite understand.

'Truth,' Oscar said finally.

'Have you ever cheated on anyone?' Dom's voice was flat, the playfulness gone.

The firelight dimmed. The room seemed to grow colder.

'No,' Oscar said, without breaking eye contact.

For a second, Clementine thought Dom was going to interrogate Oscar about his answer. The silence grew tense. But then Dom shrugged and sat down. 'Well, that was a waste of a turn.'

Clementine felt Oscar relax into the couch beside her. 'My go again,' he said. 'Felicity—truth or dare?'

No one had asked Clementine anything yet. She decided not to point this out.

'Truth,' Felicity said.

Oscar hesitated. Maybe he'd expected her to pick dare. 'What's the worst break-up you've ever had?'

'That would be with James,' Felicity said.

'What went wrong?'

Dom squeezed his wife's arm. 'You don't have to talk about this. It's just a game.'

'It's okay.' Felicity took a deep breath. 'He died.'

Clementine almost laughed—a reflex, since Felicity was usually kidding. The sombre look on the woman's face stopped her.

'Oh my God!' Isla put her hands to her mouth. 'What happened?'

'Technically we were already kind of broken up,' Felicity said. 'I'd gotten sick of him. He was older than me and a bit clingy. He got into drugs and started hanging out with dodgy people. I went back to his flat for some clothes I'd left behind, and he . . . well, the point is, he was shot. By a police officer, pretty much right in front of me.'

Cole's jaw dropped. 'Shit, really?'

'Yep,' Felicity said. 'But the whole experience—maybe this is a horrible thing to say, and his family definitely wouldn't approve, but it was a blessing in disguise. Someone I met at the funeral later offered me a job at a car yard, and years later, that was where I met Dom.'

Dom smiled sadly. He'd clearly heard this story before.

'I'm so sorry,' Clementine said.

'Because I'd had a shitty boyfriend,' Felicity continued, 'I could tell what a good catch Dom was. And because I'd seen someone die, I really, deeply understood how short life is. How if you want something, you shouldn't wait. You should take it while the chance is there.' She glanced at Clementine.

'Rough way to learn that lesson,' Oscar said.

'No kidding. But I like who I am—who it turned me into. So, it's hard to wish anything had been different.' She took another sip of her wine. 'Anyway. How's that for truth?'

Dom patted her knee. 'I don't think anyone will be able to top it.'

'Let's see,' Felicity said. 'My turn, right?'

The others nodded.

'Clementine,' Felicity said, and Clementine's breath caught in her throat. 'Truth or dare?'

She hesitated, picturing herself doing a lap dance, then panicked. 'Truth.'

Felicity smirked. 'If you could have sex with anyone here other than your husband, who would it be?'

Clementine felt the colour rising to her cheeks. This wasn't what they'd discussed. She glanced at Cole, expecting him to tell her she didn't have to answer, the way Dom had stuck up for Felicity.

'It's okay, Clem,' Cole said instead. 'I won't be offended.'

'It's just . . . hard to picture myself with anyone but you,' Clementine lied, glancing from Oscar to Dom like she didn't already know the answer; like she hadn't watched that video of Dom and Isla, over and over.

Her husband had always been cautious, even timid. He would put on a seatbelt just to move the car from one parking spot to another. He would stay up late frowning worriedly at spreadsheets, even though it seemed to be raining money at the gym lately. During sex, he kept asking her if she was okay.

Whereas she thought Dom would just take what he wanted.

'I assume it doesn't have to be a man,' Isla put in.

'Ooh, hello.' Felicity raised an eyebrow.

'I think it does,' Clementine said quickly. She looked at Oscar and Dom again. 'But, I mean, I don't know what either of them is like in bed.'

'Confident,' Dom said immediately.

'Generous,' Oscar countered.

Everyone laughed, no one meeting anyone else's eye.

'Isla, is that true?' Felicity asked.

Isla tilted her hand from side to side. 'Meh.'

Everyone laughed again, except Oscar.

'Well, Dom then, I guess,' Clementine said. She risked a brief glance at him. Part of her still couldn't believe what Felicity had said: that he wanted to try her out, and he'd asked his wife to make it happen. Clementine was surprised to see a shy smile on his face. He looked more vulnerable than she'd ever seen him.

'For the record,' Oscar said, 'you're missing out.'

'Maybe we should have a dare, then,' Felicity said.

'It's not your turn,' Isla pointed out. 'It's Clementine's.'

'Shouldn't Oscar get a chance to prove himself?' Felicity said.

Isla looked alarmed. 'How?'

Felicity spread her palms wide. 'Well . . .'

Isla

Isla could feel herself losing control of this situation, if she'd had any to begin with. Was Felicity seriously proposing that Oscar—Isla's husband—have sex with Clementine—Isla's best friend?

Felicity was joking . . . obviously. She told jokes for a living. But Isla saw a glance pass between Clementine and Cole, like she was seeking his permission.

Holy shit, Isla thought. *She's seriously considering this.* The betrayal was like a sip of acid, burning all the way down.

Oscar was giving Isla a similar look, trying to gauge her reaction.

'We've all had a bit much to drink,' Isla said, pointedly lowering her glass to the table.

'Or just the right amount.' Felicity winked.

'Very funny. I'm not loaning my husband out for sex with another woman.' Isla gave Clementine a pointed look. 'Not even my oldest friend.'

Oscar's lip curled. She could guess what he was thinking: *if you won't sleep with me, why can't I have sex with someone else?*

'What if you got something in return?' Felicity wondered aloud, giving Cole a sidelong look.

His cheeks reddened, and Isla's heart fluttered. But no—she couldn't do this.

She found herself looking to Dom, of all people, for support. But he was smiling. It infuriated her, the way nothing got under his skin.

He acted like high school was a long time ago. They all did. *Remember this? Remember that?* Isla didn't have to remember: at any time, she could search *Isla kneels before me* on Pornhub. And there she would be, seventeen years old. The camera of Dom's iPhone had been blurry, but it was still recognisably her.

She always clicked *report*, but it was like pulling up weeds. The video would disappear for a while and then be reuploaded by some other hoarder who had saved it to his hard drive and saw himself as a librarian rather than a pervert. The internet was full of sociopaths who had decided that *any* man was entitled to see the body of *every* woman, and who considered it their solemn duty to make this possible. Never mind that it was a crime.

Every time she thought about this, her hand twitched towards her phone. Searching for the video had become a compulsion. But there was no reception up here. It felt as though she'd left the stove on. What if copies of the video were silently proliferating, with her unable to thin the herd?

That first day back at school, everyone seemed to be either looking at her or avoiding her eyes. Some boys made lewd gestures; others were suddenly too friendly, buzzing around her like mosquitoes. The girls stopped inviting her to events, like she was contagious.

It was Cole who told her the bad news, behind the science block. She wanted to throw up. He held her while she cried.

Dom said he hadn't shown the video to anyone. He'd 'only told one person' that it existed. They must have stolen his phone out of his bag and slipped it back in after—

'Why did you tell *anyone*?' Isla screamed.

'I know, it was stupid. I'm sorry, okay?' He tried to hug her.

She punched him in the solar plexus, so hard that he couldn't talk for an hour. She wished the damage was permanent.

Dom grovelled for a month. Long enough that all the other students seemed to think Isla was being petty. After all, wasn't she partly responsible? She had done the deed and let him film it. And while his face wasn't visible in the video, his naked body was exposed, and everyone knew it was him. Isla, meanwhile, was fully clothed. Wasn't Dom the real victim of this unnamed, video-sharing phone thief?

But Dom's reputation was only enhanced. While Isla frantically tried to make sure her parents and teachers didn't find out, Dom was the envy of the school for weeks. Then everyone seemed to forget about his role. Now he was a successful financial planner, charging a fortune to tell people to put more money into their super.

For Isla, this would never be over. She eventually caved to the social pressure and pretended to forgive him, but the shame still burned inside her. Her parents wondered why she'd become so withdrawn. After she graduated, she screwed up one job interview after another. She would stammer and sweat as she looked at the recruiter, wondering if they'd somehow seen the video and recognised her.

Oscar missed all this, having gone to high school in Maitland. Meeting him had been an opportunity to reinvent herself. But every time he gave her a strange look, she wondered if he'd finally found out.

Now, Isla saw that Dom wasn't just unruffled by the prospect of partner swapping: he looked satisfied. *He orchestrated this*, she realised. *He* told *Felicity to bring this up*.

Isla put her drink down and stood. The world spun woozily. 'We've all been friends for a long time,' she said. 'Let's not ruin it. It would be very hard to look someone in the eye after you've cheated with them, don't you think?'

'It's not really cheating if you have permission,' Clementine mused, running a finger around the rim of her water glass. She was the only sober person in the room, and even she seemed to be on board with this. Isla felt like her best friend had been replaced with a body-snatcher.

'We could turn out the lights,' Oscar suggested.

'I don't follow,' Isla said coldly.

'I mean, if we swapped partners in the dark, no one would know for sure who they've been with—easier to look them in the eye afterwards then.'

'Like a game of heads down, bums up,' Felicity said.

'That's not what the game is called,' Isla said through gritted teeth. 'You think we can't tell each other apart with the lights out?'

'I mean, Dom would need a haircut,' Oscar said. 'Cole would have to shave off his beard. We'd all wear the same aftershave, or perfume, or whatever. And there'd be no talking, obviously.'

He's thought this through, Isla realised. She remembered the condoms; the fact he'd cut his hair short, like Cole's. *He knew this was coming before we left.*

A terrible rage stirred in her heart, like a dragon slowly awakening upon its pile of gold.

'Cole's taller than you,' she said. She knew Oscar was insecure about his height, and she wanted to hurt him—to *kill* him.

But he shrugged it off. 'Not lying down, he isn't.'

Isla glanced at Cole, who had gone even redder. The image slipped into her head: his naked body between the sheets. She wondered if he was picturing her, too.

'As for you three . . .' Oscar gestured at the women 'I guess Clementine's more athletic, and Felicity might be . . .'

'Fatter,' Felicity put in.

Cole laughed awkwardly.

'*Curvier*, babe,' Dom said.

'But only a little,' Oscar continued hastily, turning back to Isla. 'And you're about halfway in between. So either one of them could be you, in the dark.'

Heads were nodding all around. Isla couldn't believe it.

Her own husband was acting like she was interchangeable with two other women. But, she realised, he was pretending. They all were. If this went ahead, they would all realise who they were with, darkness or no—they just wanted to be able to act like they didn't.

'What if we end up with our own partners?' Clementine asked.

'Then *I'll* be a very lucky man,' Dom said.

'Aw.' Felicity slapped him playfully.

'In Secret Santa,' Oscar began, 'if you pull your own name out of the hat, you just redraw. Maybe any man who recognises his own wife could—'

Isla glowered at him. 'Women are not names in hats.'

While Oscar was talking, Dom whispered in his wife's ear. Isla noticed again Felicity's red hair, straightened and cut to the same length as her own. Oscar wasn't the only one who'd come prepared.

Looking around, she could imagine why the others might be keen for this. Oscar hadn't got laid in months. Clementine seemed sexually unfulfilled. Dom was just sleazy, and Felicity was desperate to please him. But for Isla, the odds were bad. There would be a two-in-three chance she'd end up in bed with a man she held in contempt: Dom or Oscar.

On the other hand, there was a one-in-three chance she'd be with Cole.

She turned to him. He was giving her a searching look. Those veiny hands, clenched around his wineglass. Was he running the same calculation, weighing up the chances he'd find himself in her arms?

Later, she'd wonder how much of her decision had been the alcohol and how much had been anger at her husband. But right then, she was only thinking about Cole and the chance to taste the life she'd missed out on.

And if she ended up with Dom, well, that was an opportunity to live out an entirely different fantasy.

Revenge.

NOW

Kiara

Elise and Kiara leap up from the table. Kiara bolts towards the front door, then realises Elise isn't following—she's running to the hall instead, *towards* the thump from upstairs.

'What are you doing?!' Kiara whispers.

Elise stops. 'What are *you* doing? We have to catch her!'

'I have to get you out of here!'

'Stuff that.' Elise resumes her sprint towards the stairs. Despite the bad knee, she's fast.

'Elise, wait!' As Kiara gives chase, she berates herself for being so foolish. She assumed Ms Madden was lost in the bush and probably dead. It never occurred to her that the missing woman might have doubled back and taken shelter in the house. And if she's been living here in secret for a week rather than trying to get back to civilisation, that could mean she's the killer.

Elise isn't a cop, and she's unarmed. She's come face to face with evil before, and survived. But she may not be so lucky this time.

Just as Elise gets to the landing at the top of the staircase and reaches for the doorhandle, Kiara manages to grab the back of her shirt. Elise stumbles, almost falling down the stairs and crushing them both. 'Let go,' she snaps.

'Stay behind me,' Kiara growls, pushing Elise aside.

The door is unlocked, and the room seems empty. Kiara

151

checks under the bed and in the ensuite. Perhaps the thump was just a possum in the roof cavity.

But Elise is leaning out the window. 'I see her!' she yells.

Kiara runs over in time to see a lithe form in dark clothes climbing down the side of the house. Night is falling, and the suspect's face is hidden by a hoodie, but Kiara is automatically memorising other identifying features: *about one-seventy tall, maybe sixty kilos. Matches Madden's description.*

The window overlooks an eight-metre drop onto a gravel path lined with garden beds. The suspect climbs down without obvious difficulty, digging gloved fingers into invisible seams, then leaps off the wall and flattens a shrub before scrambling up and sprinting towards the tree line.

Elise runs back towards the stairs, but by the time she gets out the front door and circles around to the back of the house, the suspect will have disappeared into the endless bush.

'Aw, shit,' Kiara mutters, and climbs out the window.

A cold wind attacks, trying to pluck her off the side of the house. The void below is terrifying. She dangles from the window, hips hugging the wall, the toes of her shoes slipping against the bricks, unable to find the footholds the suspect used. Kiara spots a drainpipe bolted to the wall a metre or two to her right, but her outstretched hand can't quite reach it. She'll have to jump.

She grits her teeth, swings sideways and lets go of the sill. For a heart-stopping second she's not connected to anything, five metres above the ground—then she crashes into the pipe and grabs hold. It's too thick to wrap her hands all the way around, and she finds herself sliding down, her feet scrabbling against the wall, until they find purchase on a bracket.

When she's still two metres above the gravel, she hears the front door bang. Elise is coming, ready to make a citizen's arrest.

The pipe groans. As Kiara frantically tries to shift her weight, she loses her footing on the bracket. After half a second of freefall, she hits the ground feet first and tumbles onto her side. The impact bruises her ribs and knocks the wind out of her.

As she rolls over, she sees the dark figure in the distance, running through the trees.

'Stop! Police!' Kiara scrambles to her feet and gives chase, limping from the fall. Every step in the dark risks a twisted ankle.

The fugitive seems to know the bush, following the trail even in the dark, while Kiara gets tangled at every bend. After only a few seconds, her quarry has vanished between the trees. She stops running, instead listening for the footsteps. Hopefully she can follow by ear alone.

Something crashes through the brush to her left. Kiara brings up her guard, elbows tucked, fists clenched. 'Hold it!' she yells, but the figure is already barging into her, slamming her off her feet. She hits the ground, winded again, the other woman on top of her.

'Elise!' Kiara wheezes. 'It's me!'

Elise opens her fist, lowers it. 'K?'

In her statement, Ms Dubois insisted she didn't know which man she'd slept with on Saturday night, because the lights were out. The claim no longer seems ridiculous.

Elise climbs off, and Kiara sits up dizzily.

'Sorry. I thought . . .' Elise looks around. 'Fuck me, it's dark out here.'

Away from town, the moonless night is impenetrable. They have no hope of tracking the suspect. If they hadn't left the dining-room lights on, they might not even be able to find their way back to the house.

Kiara coughs. 'I have to get you out of here.'

'No,' Elise says. 'We can backtrack. Pick up the trail.'

Kiara grabs her hand. 'You're not a cop. This isn't your job.'

'We can't just leave.'

'That's exactly what we should do.'

'I'm not running away again,' Elise snaps.

Kiara frowns. 'Again?'

Elise starts trudging back towards the house.

Kiara hurries after her. 'You didn't run away last year. You stood up to those people. You—' She stops herself from saying *killed them*. They've never talked about this. Kiara had thought, naïvely, that there was nothing to say.

Elise's gaze is on the dirt between her feet.

'Listen.' Kiara keeps her voice low, in case the suspect is close enough to overhear. 'We'll tell search and rescue to update the Last Known Point. We'll go home and come back at sunrise to help with the manhunt.'

'You can go, if you want,' Elise says. 'I'm not leaving.'

Kiara wants to shake her. *Do you know how insane you sound?*

'Okay,' she says instead. 'But we need to warn the other officers that the suspect is nearby.'

'There's no phone reception up here,' Elise objects.

'There's a landline at the house. Come on.'

Kiara has been using her cop voice, calm and firm. It works, thank God. Elise follows her around to the front door, which is standing wide open, letting in the cold.

In their statements, all three suspects agreed there had been no batteries in the cordless handset when they'd tried to call for help. Kiara brought new ones, but it looks like someone has already replaced them. When Kiara dials Warrigal police station, the phone works fine.

The acting station chief, Clive Wallworth, picks up. Kiara explains that someone, possibly Ms Madden, has been secretly living in the house and is still in the area.

'Bloody hell,' Clive says. 'I'll send a team out. You get Elise back here.'

Kiara shuts her eyes. 'We're staying.'

'You're what?'

'Send the team. We'll meet them here.'

'You have a civilian with you. This suspect may have committed a double homicide—'

'I'm technically off-duty,' Kiara says. 'You can't make me leave.'

'What am I supposed to tell Rohan if you get killed up there?' Clive complains.

'Tell him not to let Jennings investigate our deaths,' Kiara says, and ends the call.

They search the house room by room, in case the suspect doubled back. Kiara tries to focus on the places where the suspect might hide. But she keeps looking sideways at Elise, who's scanning the environment like a Terminator, arms crossed.

Kiara thinks there are two types of relationships. The first kind grows stronger under pressure, and is fuelled by time together. The second kind gets weaker under pressure, and depends on time apart. She's seen loving couples break up because they're forced to live in different cities for a few months. She's also seen marriages crumble after decades when someone retires and is suddenly exposed to their spouse's company.

Kiara always thought she and Elise had the first kind of relationship. It could endure stressful situations, but was threatened by the long hours they spent working separately. Now they're together, and it doesn't feel like they're facing this crisis as a team. For the first time in a year, Kiara allows herself to wonder: *what if we don't make it?*

LAST SATURDAY

Dom

Why was Dom nervous? He'd had sex hundreds of times. On top of that, he juggled millions of other people's dollars for a living. He drove expensive cars around sharp bends at dangerous speeds. His *appetite for risk*, as the business books put it, was high. He and Felicity had that in common. She'd tell new jokes on stage, knowing half of them would bomb. When Dom took her out for dinner, she always ordered something she'd never tried. If they were alone on a beach, she would strip naked and dive right in.

But this was different.

They'd all discussed the logistics of the partner swapping—or, as Felicity insisted on calling it, the Secret Santa Sex. The lights would be switched off. The men would spend five minutes on the deck while the three women—Felicity referred to them as Ho, Ho and Ho—each chose a bedroom to wait in. The men would come back inside, select a room and enter. Each man would sleep with whoever he found, even if he suspected she was his wife. No one had come up with a good way to avoid that possibility, and no one had dared try too hard in front of their partners.

Afterwards they would take turns in the shower, in a complicated schedule based not on name but on gender and room: East Downstairs Bedroom Man, followed by West Downstairs Bedroom Man, and so on. There would be no talking, either during the act or in the years to come—what happened on the mountain would stay on the mountain.

It was an exciting plan. But as Dom sat on the dining chair in the downstairs bathroom, letting Felicity cut his hair short to match Cole's and Oscar's, he couldn't shake off his sense of unease. 'Are you sure you're okay with this?' he asked her.

He thought he felt the clippers hesitate for just a moment before they continued buzzing up the nape of his neck. 'I think it'll be fun,' Felicity said. 'Why?'

'It could also ruin the weekend,' Dom said. 'Make everything weird and awkward.'

'That's true. But you only live once.'

He was acutely aware of this. His father died last year after taking too much warfarin. His colleague had been felled by a stroke. A neighbour had recently been killed in a hit-and-run. It felt like death was circling him.

'In one of my business books, there's a chapter about the explore–exploit trade-off,' he said. 'Apparently you should explore when you're young and exploit when you're old.'

'Those aren't business books—they're just self-help books that happen to be written by men.' She massaged his shoulders. 'Are you thinking you're too old for sexcapades?'

Dom smiled. 'Never. I'll still be trying new things with you when we're in aged care.'

'Just think how many new positions could be opened up by a walking frame,' she mused. 'Or one of those beds that tilts up and down.'

He laughed and closed his eyes, his muscles turning to butter under her fingertips.

'Is it the thought of me with someone else?' she asked, a little nervously.

Dom wanted to be the sort of man who didn't care about that. Everyone had consented. Condoms would be used. But love was indifferent to logic. He *was* uncomfortable—not that he'd ever admit it.

'Don't worry,' he said. 'I can be the bigger man.' He added a wink for good measure.

Felicity picked up a makeup brush and swept the hair off the back of his neck, then examined the results. 'Not bad. If my career as a stand-up comic slash trophy wife doesn't work out, I could do this professionally. Would I need a formal qualification?'

Dom checked the mirror. He looked good—and young. Ready to explore. 'You have the knack. But I think you'd miss comedy.'

'Oh, I wouldn't give it up. Running a barbershop would be a great opportunity to try out new material. What man would dare heckle me if I had a razor to his throat?'

Dom chuckled. 'Not me, for sure.'

Squinting at his sideburns, she picked up the blade again. 'It's not too late to back out, you know. You don't have to do this just because the opportunity has come up.'

He forced a smile. 'It's like you don't even know me.'

Felicity scraped some stubble off his cheek. 'I do, though. You'd always wonder.'

She'd touched on one of his deepest fears. Dom had always worried more about regret than remorse. Missed opportunities haunted him, particularly sexual ones. When he was nineteen, two women approached him at a bar: they seemed to want him to take *both* of them home. He demurred, not wanting them to see his crappy little apartment. He'd thought about those women every day since, cursing himself.

'Will you still love me?' he asked.

'You weren't a virgin when we met.' She sounded amused. 'I know there have been other girls.'

He cleared his throat. 'That was before, though. I . . . I just don't want to lose you.'

Dom would never have had a conversation like this with anyone else. He spent his whole life being strong. But Felicity always made him melt, in a way that he both loved and feared.

She circled around the chair and straddled him, sitting

on his thighs and draping her arms over his shoulders, then rested her forehead against his. 'I will always love you,' she said. 'No matter what happens tonight, or any other night, for the rest of our lives. You're mine, and I'm yours.'

Dom looked into her eyes. 'Forever?'

'Till death do us part,' she said, and kissed him.

Isla

Cole and Clementine had been whispering, but they fell silent as Isla entered the dining room.

'Everything okay in here?' she asked.

'Mm-hmm,' they said in unison, neither meeting her gaze.

When the others emerged, they all shared a tense dinner filled with sidelong glances and self-conscious flirting. Dom opened a bottle of 2004 Margaret River sparkling white, which loosened everyone up a bit. He made Isla's glass especially full.

She had assumed Clementine was the one he wanted—the only woman in the room he'd never slept with. But was it Isla he was after? Maybe she was the best he'd ever had.

She thanked him, smiling sweetly. If he got her tonight, he would regret it.

By eight-thirty she, Felicity and Clementine were hovering in the hall, dressed only in terrycloth robes. She still couldn't believe this was really happening. Even as they'd discussed the rules, the whole thing seemed hypothetical. Now the darkness made it feel like a dream she might wake up from at any moment.

Or a nightmare. Too soon to tell.

'I can't decide which room to take,' she whispered.

'Why not? It's random.' Felicity was already twisting a doorhandle.

'It's not, though,' Isla said. 'The boys won't be choosing randomly. They'll *think* they are, but the laziest one will grab the room closest to the kitchen. The least decisive one will take the upstairs room, because the other two will be taken by the time he's made up his mind—'

Isla couldn't see Felicity's face in the shadows, but she could hear the eye-roll in her voice. 'Well, there you go. If you don't want a lazy or indecisive lover, take East Downstairs Bedroom. Done.'

It's easy for her and Clem, Isla thought. No matter which door they picked, each of them would find themselves in bed with either a handsome man or their own loving spouse—while Isla could end up with her gloomy husband, her treacherous ex . . . or Cole.

Regardless of what the others were pretending, she was sure she'd know who she was with, whether she wanted to or not.

'Won't they be guessing which rooms *we* will pick?' she said. 'So they end up with their . . . preferred girl?'

She'd made it sound like they were in a brothel. She wondered which room Cole would expect her to choose. Hopefully he didn't think she was indecisive or lazy.

Clementine touched her elbow. 'Babe. Are you okay?'

'Fine, it's just . . . do either of you have a preference?' She wanted someone else to make the decision for her; wanted it not to be her own fault, if this turned ugly.

'For a room, or for a guy?' Clementine asked.

'Either.'

'No,' Felicity said.

'No,' Clementine repeated, too quickly.

Isla smiled wryly. 'So do I,' she said. 'Shall we toss a coin?'

'For God's sake,' Felicity muttered. She disappeared into one of the bedrooms and closed the door, leaving them to figure it out.

'I don't have a coin,' Clementine said.

She and Isla looked at each other in the gloom.

They'd been friends since kindergarten. In primary school, they spent recesses playing games they'd made up, with rules too convoluted for anyone else to follow. In high school they got the same mobile plan so they could text each other for free, all night. They did one another's makeup before the school formal. They were maids of honour at each other's weddings. Isla had never been jealous of anything Clementine owned, because it felt like she owned it, too.

But in that whispered conversation, had Cole and Clementine arranged to pick the same room? Had Clementine decided not to share?

Please, Isla thought. *You get him all the time. Let me have him for just one night.*

Out loud, she said, 'Scissors, paper, rock?'

Cole

On the deck, Cole glanced at Dom's phone for the third time. It was 8.51 p.m. There was a timer in the centre of the screen: big, clear numbers ticking down, surrounded by a purple circle. This was the longest five minutes of his life.

All three men had dressed in suits and ties, so their wives wouldn't be able to tell them apart by their clothes. Other than their hands and heads, everything was covered, whereas the women were supposed to be bare. Cole reflected on the strangeness of female desire—women seemed attracted to men who revealed less of themselves, not more.

But maybe it depended on the man, and what he was hiding.

Cole had brought his suit because Oscar told him to, and Dom had presumably done so because he never went anywhere without one. Clementine had seen Cole pack the outfit but hadn't questioned it. He wondered if the other wives had been suspicious.

The silence stretched out. Cole had always envied women's ability to talk openly to each other. Sometimes he would sit in a cafe and listen with wonder as old ladies nearby spoke of very personal things with no apparent embarrassment. With other men, he rarely mustered the courage to say anything, and whatever they said to him always sounded defensive, boastful or threatening.

Maybe men didn't bond with one another because they weren't oppressed. Or maybe women made just as many boasts and threats, but at a frequency he couldn't hear. Or perhaps it wasn't about gender at all, just about him: his own private defect.

Oscar interrupted his thoughts. 'You nervous?'

Cole forced a smile. 'Oh, you know. Little bit.' Which meant, *very*. And he knew the anxiety might make it hard to perform—which made him more anxious. He was in a death spiral. But he could never admit that, not in front of other blokes.

They seemed to sense it anyway.

'Relax.' Dom patted him on the back. 'You'll be fine.'

'Yeah, I know.' Being told to relax always had the opposite effect on Cole. He felt like he was on the deck of a ship, and everyone else was pretending not to see the iceberg.

He flashed back to a high school athletics carnival. His class had been lined up from shortest to tallest, so he and Dom were side by side. As they waited for the long jump, Cole was touching his toes, stretching his quads, rolling his shoulders back in the sunshine. Dom was reassuring him, encouraging him, as though they were team-mates rather than competitors.

But the pep talk didn't help—in fact, it stopped Cole from mentally preparing, getting into the zone. He jumped a measly four metres, while Dom managed almost five and a half.

Now Cole wondered if Dom's 'encouragement' had been deliberate sabotage.

'I'm okay,' he said, hoping Dom would stop talking.

Dom didn't. 'I like to reframe my nervousness as excitement. Whenever I'm about to make a presentation to a prospective client—'

'No offence, mate,' Oscar interrupted, 'but I think this situation is a bit different.'

Dom didn't seem offended. 'Is it? Either way, you're trying to please someone, to make a human connection with them . . .'

'But this time you can't use PowerPoint slides,' Oscar pointed out. 'You can't even talk.'

Dom's smile didn't reach his eyes. 'You think I got to where I am using PowerPoint?'

Cole glanced at the phone again: two minutes and forty-five seconds left on the clock.

'If you screw up a presentation,' he said, 'the client walks away and you never see them again. But you can try again with someone else tomorrow. Right?'

Dom ran his tongue over his teeth. 'I don't have meetings with prospective clients every day, but—'

'That's why this is different,' Cole said. 'It's a one-off, no do-overs. And the "clients" are our wives. They won't walk away.'

'Unless it goes *really* badly,' Oscar said, unhelpfully.

'Cole straightened his spine. 'Whatever happens, we have to live with the consequences.'

'You sound like you want to back out,' Dom said.

'No, he doesn't,' Oscar said.

There was so much more Cole wanted to say. He wanted to ask Oscar what Isla's turn-ons were. He wanted to beg them both to be gentle with Clementine. She was fragile. At the same time, he wanted to warn them about what she might ask them to do. But he followed the unwritten rules of male conversation. He said, 'I'm fine,' then lapsed into silence.

A minute later, Dom's phone chimed like a glockenspiel.

Oscar took a last swig of his drink, then left it on the edge of the hot tub. 'See you on the other side,' he said.

Clementine

The bedroom door opened.

Clementine lay on the bed, trying to get a sense—from just the click of the handle and creak of the hinges—of who might be coming in.

The door closed again, firmly. Perhaps a little more assertively than she was used to. But in the end, a door was a door. The man could have been anybody.

She opened her mouth to whisper hello, then remembered the no-talking rule. So she lay there, under a thin sheet, feeling faintly ridiculous.

She had never before considered just how much talking was involved in sex. She and Cole usually sustained a conversation the whole way through. Flirty remarks, encouraging sounds, sometimes even jokes. Requests to go slower, or faster, yes, no, that's it, right there, stop. How was this even supposed to work without words?

Despite how polished and graceful Hollywood made it look, sex was always a bit silly in real life. The secret, in Clementine's experience, was for both parties to acknowledge that and then embrace it, having fun with each other. Impossible, in the grim silence of this bedroom.

She'd violated one of the rules: the women were supposed to be naked, so the men wouldn't be able to guess their identities from the feel of their underwear. But Cole had never seen this soft-cup bra or these V-string knickers; she'd bought them months ago in a moment of madness, thinking that somehow he would be more fertile if he saw her in them. She'd come to her senses and hidden them in the bottom drawer—until, packing for this trip, she'd thought, *What the hell. I'll surprise him.*

She smelled something as the man approached: aftershave, expensive fabric and just a hint of sweat.

She thought about Cole's offer: *you could skip the condom.* In some ways it was perfect. She was at the most fertile part of her cycle. They could avoid the murky, unromantic world of anonymous donation.

But while using a stranger's sperm would still feel like having Cole's baby, that might not be the case if the father was Dom, or Oscar. What if she could see the resemblance? What if *they* could?

She hadn't decided what to do, and she was running out of time.

Soon the man was standing beside the bed. Clementine reached for him and found herself touching a wall of muscle behind a silk shirt. She slipped two fingers between the buttons, stroking the skin beneath his navel.

His hand felt large, or at least strong, as it found hers and held it in place. Not as timid as Cole.

Dom? she wanted to whisper. Her heart beat a little faster.

Another hand stroked her cheek. Fingers traced down her throat, her collarbone, across one nipple and over her abdomen. The man was guessing at the shape of her, trying to identify her.

She found that she wanted him to succeed. If it was Dom, she wanted him to know it was her. She rolled towards him, letting his hand stroke her hip, where there was a butterfly tattoo he couldn't see. She'd lost some modelling jobs because of the ink, even though it was so well hidden, designed to share with only those she chose.

The man's finger glided down, stroking her sheer undies. His breath hitched, and his hand vanished.

Clementine waited, her heart thumping. Should she not have shaved? She'd felt a bit foolish doing it. But men liked that, didn't they?

There was a soft rustle of carpet as the man kneeled beside the bed. It sounded like he was reaching under it, though she couldn't think why. Something rattled, perhaps his belt buckle.

Clementine made her decision. She sat up and stretched out, cupping the back of his neck with her fingers. She pulled him in so she could whisper in his ear, telling him to forget the condom.

Then a hand clamped over her mouth and a handcuff snapped closed around her wrist.

NOW

Elise

Elise is woken by a pounding on the front door.

She leaps out of bed, with a twinge of protest from her knee. It's still dark, and she has no clue what time it is. She could have slept for ten minutes or ten hours. Terror scratches at the inside of her ribs. This isn't her bedroom. Where is she?

She stumbles around until she finds a light switch. The darkness is banished. She's alone in the east bedroom of the holiday house. Not in an underground septic tank.

Elise has the nightmares almost every time she goes to bed. Whenever she wakes up, at 1, 3, 5 a.m., there's a moment of utter panic. The fear that getting rescued by Kiara was a dream, and she's still down there in the dark.

She blames her frequent awakenings on a small bladder and says she only needs a nightlight to find her way to the bathroom. But she can't hide this forever. Kiara has seen things on the job that would turn most people to jelly; she won't want to be in a relationship with someone who's terrified all the time.

Elise pokes her head out into the hallway. 'Kiara?' she whispers, as loudly as she dares.

There's another knock at the front door.

Elise slips out of the bedroom and runs towards the kitchen. She can hear a male voice from outside the front door, but can't make out the words over the droning extractor fan—Kiara left it on to clear out the ammonia smell. The tiny blue standby light on the TV provides just enough illumination for Elise to find the knife block. She draws a blade and turns back around, her heart hammering. Now she's ready to answer the door.

All the lights come on. Elise squints against the sudden glare. Kiara enters the room, followed by a police officer in his forties, with broad shoulders and ears that stick out.

'What's that smell?' he's asking.

'I hoped I was imagining it,' Kiara says.

Elise tosses the knife into the sink. Kiara and the man hear the clatter and turn to face her, looking startled—but less so than if she'd been brandishing a blade.

'Elise,' Kiara says, 'you okay?'

Elise nods warily. *Act sane*, she thinks.

Kiara gestures to the man. 'This is—'

'Constable Seamus Whitmey,' the man says. 'Sorry I woke you.'

Elise crosses her arms over her thin pyjamas. 'You have a very loud knock.'

'Occupational hazard, I'm afraid. A lot of people buy their doors online these days. Sometimes they're so thin I can feel them bending.'

Elise, still waking up, can't work out if what Whitmey just said makes sense.

'Seamus is an old friend of mine,' Kiara says. 'He's going to help me search for the suspect.'

'Help *us*,' Elise says.

Kiara and Seamus exchange uncomfortable looks.

'Help us,' Kiara confirms. 'As soon as the sun comes up.'

'You can go back to sleep,' Seamus says. 'I'll keep watch.'

Elise pours a glass of water as an excuse to stay out here, listening to their conversation. It's like being a toddler again, pretending to be thirsty to put off going to bed. Kiara leads Whitmey through the house, explaining the situation. He grunts from time to time.

After taking the glass of water to the bedroom, Elise sits on the mattress. It's going to be hard to sleep with a stranger in the house, police officer or no.

'All right,' Kiara says, when she comes in. 'Seamus is set up. We can get some rest.'

'You said he's an old friend of yours?' Elise asks.

'Friend and colleague.'

'You've never mentioned him before.'

There's a pause.

'I guess I try not to talk about work too much at home,' Kiara says. She doesn't add, *Because I don't want to set you off*. But Elise knows she's thinking it.

'Fair enough.' Elise lies down on the bed, looking at the ceiling.

'Are you okay?' Kiara asks again.

'When am I not?' She closes her eyes.

LAST SATURDAY

Isla

Isla emerged from the bedroom, heart pounding, and closed the door behind her. She looked around. The hall was empty.

The hollow internal walls hadn't muffled the sounds much. There had been moaning, whimpering, sobs of pleasure. Thumping and dragging noises, as though someone's secret kink was rearranging furniture. She'd even heard a scream from one lucky woman, or possibly a very lucky man. But now there was an eerie silence.

It's okay, Isla thought. *No one will know.* She took a second to compose herself, then made her way to the lounge room, trying to keep her face neutral. Like nothing out of the ordinary had happened.

Clementine was sitting on the floor by the fireplace, hugging her knees, her blonde hair a curtain around her face. Like Isla, she wore only a robe.

Isla opened her mouth to say hello, but the sound wouldn't come. There was a lump in her throat. She ducked back into the hall, hoping Clementine hadn't seen her.

She couldn't stay there forever—soon the men would come out. It was against the rules for her to see which bedrooms they emerged from. Then again, who cared about the rules, after what just happened?

There'd been a pond in the backyard of her parents' house, where she often sat on a warm rock and watched the dragonflies. Isla pictured herself there, looking into the still water. She took a deep breath, held it, released. Then she walked back into the living area, pretending to see Clementine for the first time.

'Hey,' she said.

Clementine didn't look away from the fire.

Isla went to pour herself a glass of sparkling, but the bottle was gone. She opened the pantry and found an open cab sav, brought back by Cole. Thoughtful Cole.

'Drink?' she asked.

No response from Clementine.

Back in the hall, a door clicked open. Isla kept her gaze on the wineglasses but listened as footsteps padded around. Another door opened, then closed. A shower hissed.

She brought the two glasses over to the fire. She sat beside Clementine and held one out. Her friend didn't take it, so Isla placed it gently on the tile next to her. There was an angry red mark around Clementine's wrist, like she'd been rubbing it.

Another door opened somewhere, but no one emerged from the hall.

Isla watched the glowing coals for a minute. The tears were threatening to come back, but the heat seemed to help, drying out her eyeballs.

The man in her bedroom had made her feel like a goddess. He had kissed every centimetre of her skin, massaged every throbbing muscle. He had escalated slowly, always sensing the moment her frustration became agony. To him, only her pleasure had seemed to matter. She'd never been with a man like that before. He had spent what seemed like hours bringing her to a climax, but then—

Well, she didn't want to think about what had happened after that.

'How was it?' she asked.

Clementine finally turned to look at her. She usually had the bright, cheerful gaze of a fit person; now, her hollow stare shocked Isla.

'Are you okay?' Isla asked, alarmed.

Clementine turned back to the fire, tears brimming.

Sympathy crowded out the envy. Isla knew exactly what Clementine was feeling, because she was feeling it too. It was okay to be sexually unfulfilled, stuck forever with a half-hearted man. You could allow yourself to forget what real love felt like and convince yourself you were happy. Until you were with someone else, when it all came rushing back—the sensations you'd denied yourself for years and might never experience again.

'It's okay.' Isla wrapped her arm around Clementine's shoulders, pulling her into a sideways hug. 'I know.'

Clementine's mouth fell open. Her voice was raspy: 'You do?'

'What's got into you two?' Felicity said from behind them.

Isla laughed, but for once, Felicity didn't appear to be joking. Her smile looked forced. She'd tied her hair back and dressed in oddly formal-looking pyjamas, with a collar and buttons.

This whole thing was a mistake, Isla thought. *It's done something to all of us.*

'Did you have fun?' she asked.

'Ask me again tomorrow,' Felicity said. 'I'm still . . . unpacking. How about you?'

'Yeah. Same.'

If anyone was willing to talk about the experience, Isla would have expected it to be Felicity. Apparently not.

Felicity cocked her head. 'Did you hear that?'

'Hear what?'

Frowning, Felicity disappeared around the corner to the front door. A key rattled, and the door creaked. A moment later she was back. 'Thought I heard something outside. Just my imagination, I guess.' She went to sit next to Isla and Clementine, then paused when she spotted the wine on the bench. She poured, her back to the others.

Isla wished she could go to bed, but the men were still in the rooms. A flaw in the plan—they all had to confront each other right after the act. A six-person walk of shame.

Isla had never experienced a comfortable silence, and she certainly wasn't experiencing one now. She always felt like it was her responsibility to speak, to keep everyone else happy and entertained—unless it was Dom she wasn't speaking to, in which case his discomfort was the point.

But what could you say to someone when you'd just slept with their husband, and they knew it? The issue was too dangerous to talk about but too big to ignore.

Isla was still trying to find a safe path through the landmines when Oscar emerged from the hall, damp from the shower. He looked years younger, his cheeks flushed, his posture erect—but his expression was vaguely mournful. Was he, too, reflecting on his experience and the fact that it would never be repeated?

An emotion halfway between anger and grief flashed through Isla. Another woman had given Oscar something he used to get from her.

He smiled at the others, but his smile faded as he sensed the mood. 'Uh, hi,' he said.

'Oscar,' Felicity acknowledged, a bit stiffly.

Isla just nodded. Clementine didn't react at all.

'Cole and Dom are still . . .?' Oscar jerked a thumb towards the hall.

'Seems so,' Isla said.

Oscar found empty glasses and started washing them in the sink, perhaps so he didn't have to make eye contact with anybody.

'There's a dishwasher,' Isla pointed out.

'Seems wasteful,' Oscar said. 'Since Cole didn't buy much powder.'

'What didn't I do?' Cole entered the room, wearing a tank top and boxer shorts.

Isla averted her eyes. The experiment was over; she no longer had permission to ogle him.

'It's all good, mate,' Oscar said. 'I was just saying I didn't want to waste the dishwasher powder you brought.'

'It's a self-cleaning oven—maybe we could put the dishes in there,' Cole joked awkwardly.

Oscar smirked. 'If we leave the door open, maybe it'll clean the whole house.'

Felicity stood up, apparently sick of the banter. 'I'm going to bed.'

'Wait,' Isla said. 'Dom's not out yet.'

'So?'

'So if you see which room he was in, you'll know whether he was your—'

'He wasn't,' Felicity said shortly.

Isla stiffened. They all looked at one another.

Felicity made a move towards the hall, but Isla stepped into her path. 'We agreed we'd wait for everyone.'

'It's almost midnight,' Felicity said. 'Aren't you tired?'

Isla was more than tired: she felt like she'd just given birth. 'I'm sure he'll be out soon.'

'Don't count on it. He usually conks out right after. If you wanted to kidnap Dom, you could use sex instead of chloroform.'

Oscar laughed. No one else did.

'I could go get him,' Cole suggested. 'I know which room he—'

'For God's sake.' Felicity stepped around Isla and walked into the hall. 'Dom! Come out! We all want to go to bed.'

Isla was about to follow but stopped herself, turning her back. She wasn't supposed to see which room Dom was in.

'Dom?' She heard Felicity opening the two doors downstairs. Footsteps on carpet. Accelerating. Hurried thumps as Felicity went up the stairs.

A minute later she came back down. Her eyes were wild. 'Where the fuck is my husband?' she demanded.

Felicity

Isla was the first to speak. 'What do you mean?'

The panic felt like a cat in Felicity's chest, shredding her heart with its claws. 'Dom's gone!'

'It's not a big house,' Cole said. 'I'll help you look.'

'I'm telling you, he's not here!' Felicity ran to the entryway and pushed the front door open. A cold wind slipped under the cuffs of her pyjama bottoms and crept up her legs. An owl hooted in the distance. She stumbled out into the front yard, scanning the darkness around her. The Tarago was still in the driveway. But no sign of her husband. 'Dom!' she screamed.

Nothing moved in the dense, forbidding bush. Her heart raced. She'd never felt this kind of fear. Not when she was on stage. Not when she was blindfolded in front of a target board, waiting for the knife thrower to take his shot. Not even when the police burst into James's apartment with their guns. Her husband was everything to her. Where was he?

She hurried back into the kitchen. She opened the pantry and the broom cupboard. She knew she looked crazy, but she didn't care. Where could he have gone?

'Dom?' Oscar yelled from the hall.

'Dom!' Isla shouted upstairs.

Clementine hadn't moved from her position by the fire. *What the hell is wrong with her?* Felicity wondered. Already a clock was ticking in her head, measuring how long it was since she'd seen her husband and how far he could have gone in that time.

Her vision tunnelled. She watched her own hands as they opened the back door, then her feet as they ran out onto the deck. She grabbed the railing and peered out at the forest, but the moon was like a spotlight, glaring directly at her and leaving the rest of the world in darkness.

Someone else came out onto the deck behind her.

'Oh, *shit*,' Isla said.

'Felicity,' Oscar said, a warning note in his voice.

'What?' She tried to turn, but he grabbed her shoulder.

'Don't look, okay?' he said. Urgent. Firm.

Splashing sounds. 'Dom?' Cole was saying. 'Dom! Wake up, mate.'

Felicity squirmed out of Oscar's grip and spun around. Isla and Cole were bent over the hot tub. Dom was sitting in the water, still wearing his suit, eyes rolled back. His hand rested on the edge, loosely curled around the stem of a champagne flute, like he didn't know the party was over.

Cole grabbed Dom by the armpits and lifted him out. As his body flopped sideways, the moonlight revealed a dent above his temple, a spiderweb of blood filling the cracks.

'How did he get out here?' Felicity heard herself ask. 'What is he doing out here?'

No one answered her question. The others were talking over the top of each other: 'He's not breathing.' 'Call an ambulance!' 'It'll take them hours to get here.' 'My phone has no reception!' 'Does he have a pulse?' 'He must have hit his head on the side of the tub . . .' 'Oh my God, oh my God.'

Felicity realised she was falling. Oscar caught her. She found herself looking up into his loving face, and a deep chill swept through her body as he lowered her down, down, down, before the night embraced her.

Oscar

Oscar squatted next to the couch where Felicity lay, her skin pale, eyes rolled back. His sleeping beauty. 'Will she be okay?' he asked.

'Will *she* be okay?' Isla sounded incredulous. 'Dom is dead!'

It was the first time any of them had said it out loud. Cole was still on the deck doing CPR, but presumably even he knew it was hopeless. You couldn't treat brain damage with chest compressions.

Clementine was still crouched like Gollum in front of the fire. Her voice was quiet: 'I heard a story about a woman who shot herself in the head and survived. She wandered off before she collapsed—'

'He's definitely dead,' Oscar said. 'We can't help him. But Felicity might be going into shock.'

Isla said, 'Now that we've got her horizontal, she'll be fine.'

Oscar had long fantasised about getting Felicity horizontal, but this wasn't what he'd had in mind. He grabbed one side of the couch. 'Help me move her closer to the fire.'

Isla gripped the other side, and they dragged the couch across the room, into the pool of warmth around the flames.

Oscar examined Felicity's cheeks, waiting for the colour to return. Even her freckles had disappeared. 'I've never seen her freak out like that,' he said.

Isla glared at him. 'Her husband just died.'

A fair point, but it troubled Oscar. If Felicity loved *him*, then why was she so upset? She should be grateful to have her husband out of the picture.

He started to wonder if he'd made a terrible mistake.

Clementine spoke without looking away from the fire: 'What do you think happened?'

'He obviously tried to jump into the tub again, and this time he hit his head on the side,' Oscar said.

'Why would he jump in wearing a suit?'

'Because he's Dom,' Oscar said.

'He *was* Dom,' Isla said.

They all let that sink in.

The sliding door opened, and Cole entered, puffing. 'I'm sorry. He's gone. I tried my best, but . . .' His voice broke, and he didn't meet anyone's eye.

Isla hugged him. 'Oh, Cole. I'm so sorry.'

It struck Oscar that it should have been Cole's wife comforting him, not Isla. But Clementine didn't even look at him. Oscar had never been good at reading a room, but this one was particularly inscrutable. He supposed it was natural for everyone else to be acting strangely. They'd all known Dom longer than he had.

Cole released Isla and wiped his eyes. 'Have you tried all the phones? Emergency calls sometimes go through. Different providers share phone towers when you dial triple zero—'

'I tried them all,' Isla said. 'Upstairs, downstairs, inside, outside. I tried the landline, but it doesn't work.'

'Well, we need to get an ambulance here somehow.'

'Two ambulances,' Clementine said softly.

'Dom is way past that point,' Isla told her.

'I know, but we have to get rid of the body.'

Everyone looked at Clementine, aghast.

'I meant, get it to the morgue,' she said. 'Obviously.'

Oscar noticed how rapidly, for her, Dom had become *it*.

'We'll have to drive down the hill,' Cole said.

'What, just go to town with a corpse strapped into one of the seats?' Isla sounded a bit hysterical.

A good husband would have put his arm around her. As usual, Oscar thought of it too late. If he did it now, it would seem staged. He looked out the window. Dom's body was still on the deck, surrounded by a puddle. It was starting to rain.

'No, no,' Cole was saying, 'one of us just needs to drive far enough to get reception and call triple zero.'

Clementine asked, 'How did Dom get out there without any of us seeing him?'

'The east downstairs bedroom has a door onto the deck,' Oscar said. 'He must have gone through that way. Or he could have climbed out the window of the other downstairs bedroom. Maybe even the upstairs window, if he was feeling especially . . .'

'Dommish,' Clementine put in. 'I guess the police will figure it out.'

A palpable fear settled over the room. Isla put their thoughts into words: 'Do we tell them about the . . .?' She gestured to the bedrooms but stopped short of miming the sex.

'I think we have to,' Oscar said, though the thought made him feel ill.

Cole looked more embarrassed than Oscar had ever seen him. 'It's not like the . . . like it had anything to do with what happened to Dom.'

'We don't know that,' Clementine said. 'Maybe he had a stroke from all the excitement. That might explain why he got in the tub with his clothes on.'

'That is pretty much how he would have wanted to go,' Oscar said. He felt Isla staring at him and realised he was stroking Felicity's hair. He quickly moved his hand to his pocket—then realised he had no pockets and found himself simply patting the side of his own leg.

Cole cringed. 'You want to tell the police that no one knows what happened to Dom because we were all . . . busy?'

'Do you really want to try to hide that from them?' Isla asked.

'But someone will tell the media,' Cole said. 'Someone always does. All of our reputations will be ruined.'

'Not as ruined as they'll be if we lie to the police,' Isla insisted. 'That will make the investigation a thousand times more complex—'

'Dom is dead, Cole,' Clementine said, 'and you're worried about our reputations?'

Her husband rubbed his face with his palm. 'You're right. I'm sorry. I'll drive down the mountain until my phone starts working, then I'll make the call.'

'I'll come with you,' Isla offered. 'So you don't have to drive and keep an eye on your phone screen at the same time.'

Oscar glanced over at Clementine, who didn't volunteer to ride with her husband.

Cole said, 'Sure, but at least one person needs to stay with Felicity.'

'I can do that,' Oscar said.

Isla shot him a suspicious look. He returned it.

'Okay,' she said finally. 'Give me a minute to get dressed.' She disappeared into the hall.

Cole went into the entryway, then came back a second later. 'Who's got the key for the Tarago?'

'You,' Oscar said.

Cole pointed towards the front door. 'I left it just there, on the hook. Who picked it up?'

Clementine and Oscar looked at each other.

'You drove to town yesterday—' Clementine began.

'Yeah, and I put the key on the hook.'

'Is the car still there?' Oscar asked. It had been in the driveway when they were searching for Dom.

Cole vanished towards the front door. There was a click, a creak, a pause, another creak, and another click. He returned. 'It's right where I parked it.'

Isla returned from the bedroom, pulling her coat over a

loose top and holding her walking shoes in one hand. 'Maybe Felicity has it?' she suggested.

'I'll check.' Clementine finally stood, apparently planning to go through the pockets of Felicity's pyjamas.

'We can ask her once she's awake,' Oscar objected.

'Sweetheart,' Isla said coldly, 'Dom is dead. There's no reception up here. Right now we can't call an ambulance, or the police, or anyone at all. Warrigal is more than a hundred kilometres away. We're trapped here without that key—'

'What key?' Felicity said.

'The one for the—' Isla broke off. 'You're awake!'

'Yeah. I must have . . .' She sat up on the couch, then collapsed again. 'What happened?'

'You fainted,' Clementine said.

Felicity gasped. 'Dom! Is he . . .?'

Oscar nodded, perhaps too eagerly.

'Are you sure?' Desperation was written across Felicity's face. 'Maybe he's just concussed, or—'

'We're sure,' Cole said.

Her eyes filled with tears. 'I thought maybe it was a nightmare.'

'It is,' said Clementine, as she sat back down next to the fire.

'Do you have the car key?' Cole asked. 'We need to get to somewhere with reception, so we can call the police.'

'I thought you had it,' Felicity said. She nevertheless turned out her pockets. Empty. 'Did you try the landline?'

'It doesn't work,' Oscar said.

Clementine spoke up. 'Dom might have the car key.'

Everyone looked out the window to where Dom's body lay sprawled alone on the deck. Then they looked at each other.

'I'll check,' Cole said.

'No.' Felicity stood up. 'I'll do it.'

Oscar hovered beside her. 'Are you sure?'

She opened the back door and stepped out into the drizzle. Oscar watched as she crouched over Dom and went through his suit pockets. She pulled out a pen, then a sleeve of business cards. No key.

'We could check his bags?' Cole murmured.

'We should let Felicity do that,' Clementine said.

'You don't have a spare key?' Isla asked them.

'It went into the washing machine a couple of weeks ago,' Cole said.

On the deck, Felicity had finished searching Dom's clothes and was gently cupping his cheeks in her hands. Tears poured down her face and dripped onto his forehead.

She whispered something to her dead husband. Then she lowered her face to his, and kissed him.

Oscar finally looked away, anger coming to a boil in his gut.

NOW

Elise

'Thirty-two-year-old financial planner Dominic Pritchard,' Kiara says. 'Lifelong Warrigal resident but works in Wagga. Married, no kids. The medical examiner, Gregor, put the time of death between six in the evening and midnight on Saturday, which is consistent with the three witness statements.'

Elise holds the coffee mug under her nose and inhales the steam, trying to get the caffeine straight to her brain. The early morning sun is doing nothing to wake her up. But it's good to be out on the back deck, despite the cold. The smell of death still seems to linger in the house.

She slept restlessly, even with Whitmey keeping watch—or perhaps because of that. At dawn, the search and rescue team arrived and started trampling the bush around the house. They'd found nothing so far, and were now out of earshot.

'I reckon Pritchard's wife did it.' Elise sips the coffee. 'Felicity.'

'This isn't a TV show,' Kiara says sharply. 'You don't start with a theory and then try to prove it. That's how wrongful convictions happen. Instead you gather as much evidence as you can, then you put it all together at the end and see what makes sense.'

'Okay, okay.' Elise walks around the deck in a slow circle—anticlockwise, so as to put less weight on her bad knee. 'What else did Gregor say?'

'Stomach contents indicate that he ate dinner about two hours before his death. Lividity suggests the body was moved from a sitting position to lying on its back; again, consistent with the statements of the three suspects. No defensive wounds—he didn't see the impact coming.'

'And they found him just sitting here?' Elise leans against the hot tub, staring down at the submerged jets.

'Right. Fully clothed, with a cracked skull.'

'I don't see any blood in the water.'

'The tub has been drained and refilled,' Kiara says. 'Chemical analysis of the original water discovered no blood but a lot of urine, which Gregor found puzzling.'

'Why?'

'Urine suggests Pritchard died in the tub, and his bladder relaxed. But apparently the head wound wouldn't have killed him instantly—you'd think he would have bled into the water for a while before his heart stopped beating.'

'Maybe someone else peed in the tub earlier,' Elise suggests. 'Or later.'

'Maybe. But there *was* blood on his pillowcase. So it's as if he was hit in the head, then died in the tub, but didn't start bleeding until his body was moved to the bed.'

Elise runs her tongue across her front teeth. 'Perhaps he had low blood pressure in general? The blood didn't go to his head until he was horizontal?'

It's a weak theory, but Kiara says, 'Good thinking.' Patronising her.

She brought Elise here to get her away from Warrigal, thinking the problem is the town rather than the tripwires tangled throughout Elise's own mind. Kiara doesn't actually think Elise can help with the case. Knowing this, Elise is determined to be useful.

'There was a full moon last weekend, right?' she says.

'That's right. At the time of death, the moon would have been about there,' Kiara points. 'And the trees aren't tall enough to block the light, so visibility would have been okay. Dominic would have seen the killer if they'd been right in front of him. So the lack of defensive wounds suggests he was attacked from behind, probably by a right-handed individual, since the damage was to the right side of his head.'

'Why was he fully dressed?'

'I'm told he was a bit of a larrikin.'

'You mean a dickhead.'

Kiara gives a slight nod.

'Was he drunk?' Elise asks.

'His blood alcohol was point oh nine per cent.'

Almost twice the limit for driving, Elise thinks. *But not so much that you don't know what you're doing.* She leans on the edge of the tub. 'Who gets his money? His wife?'

Kiara takes a deep breath. 'It's a bit complicated. From what I can tell, Dominic and Felicity signed a binding financial agreement before they tied the knot—the gist of it was that if they divorced, she wouldn't get his money.'

Elise feels a flicker of excitement. 'But they didn't get divorced. He died.' Her thoughts spin into overdrive. 'Maybe she wanted to leave him but couldn't afford it, so she—'

'Hold your horses. Yes, she'll inherit his money . . . but it turns out he didn't have very much.'

'Really?'

'Sixty thousand in savings, eighty in super.'

'Sounds like a lot to me,' Elise says.

'Well, they still owed three hundred K on their house. The interest was fixed at a low rate, so apparently Dom was in no hurry to pay it down.'

'Did Felicity know they were in dire straits financially?'

'They weren't,' Kiara says. 'Dominic was earning more than enough to make the payments. She might be in trouble now, though. I don't think stand-up comedy pays very well.'

'He was a financial planner. Surely he had life insurance?'

'You'd think so. I'm still trying to confirm. But it could be like the mechanic who never gets around to fixing his own car.'

'Or anyone else's.' Elise thinks of the snail's pace Bill works at. That dented Jaguar is probably still sitting there. 'So Felicity is either bankrupted by her husband's death or set up for life by the insurance, and we don't know which?'

'At this stage,' Kiara says.

'Is she right-handed?'

'Left.'

Elise nods, disappointed. 'What about the camper?'

According to the three suspects, there had been an unexplained light outside the window on their first night at the house. On the second day, they'd found evidence of a camp site.

'Search and rescue hadn't found any sign of them,' Kiara says. 'The story didn't sound credible. I'd think the killer made it up to cover their tracks, except . . .'

'Except *all* the suspects are saying it?'

Kiara looks troubled. 'Yeah.'

'Could the three women have been working together? Maybe it's a movement. Burn your bras. Kill your husbands.'

'Maybe,' Kiara said doubtfully. There are two more angles to consider: the ten thousand dollars Dominic transferred to Cole six weeks ago, supposedly to cover IVF treatments, and the letter we found from Oscar to Isla.'

Elise knows about the letter. Oscar had threatened to leave Isla and take their son.

'If Oscar and Isla got divorced,' Elise begins, 'who would—?'

She jumps. Whitmey is standing right next to her, having appeared as silently as a ghost. He doesn't look like a man who's been up all night keeping watch. His uniform isn't rumpled, there are no bags under his eyes and there's no body odour, just a trace of cologne.

'You're a ninja,' Elise says.

He ignores her. 'Getting some help with the case?' he asks Kiara.

She holds his gaze. 'What, you never bounce ideas off your wife?'

'I don't take her to crime scenes.'

'I'm standing right here,' Elise complains.

Whitmey looks down his nose at her. 'You are,' he says disapprovingly. 'Anyway, I'm heading off. Constable Vickers just radioed in—she's on her way. And Rohan wants you to call him.'

'Thanks, Seamus,' Kiara says. 'Can you tell Vickers to bring some food?'

'Will do.' Whitmey disappears back into the house.

'Arsehole,' Elise mutters.

'Vickers is the arsehole,' Kiara says. 'She'll report us. Seamus was trying to keep us out of trouble.'

'Right.' Elise tries not to look like she's sulking, but she wishes Kiara had taken her side. Isn't that the point of being a couple—having someone on your side even if you're wrong?

Kiara seems to sense her annoyance. 'Come on, let's get this thing solved before Vickers gets here.'

'No, I need a break.'

Elise walks back into the house and switches on the kettle. Without looking back, she goes into the hall that leads to the bedrooms. Both downstairs bedrooms have windows that are visible from the deck, so she goes upstairs instead, getting as far away from Kiara's stare as she can. She leans against the window and breathes, looking out at the endless, hostile bush.

It's not hard to see why Madden came back. Survival out there would be impossible at this time of year—which means she'll be back again.

There's something in Elise's shoe, worrying at her heel: a speck of grit, or maybe a grass seed. She sits down on the bed, intending to take the shoe off. But suddenly that seems like too much work. *Everything* seems like too much work.

Elise lies back on the bed, staring at the ceiling, thinking about the two dead men and what went so wrong with their marriages that they wanted to sleep with each other's wives. Being attracted to other people is a normal part of a healthy relationship—or at least, Elise hopes it is. She certainly notices other women. Sometimes it'll be a waitress who smells good, leaning over the table; other times it's a woman emerging from a gym, with great legs and cool hair. Although people never talk about this, she can't be the only one who feels it.

But letting those fleeting moments of attraction become fantasies, and then obsessions, and then *actions*—to Elise that implies a deep sadness, one that is probably exacerbated rather than eased by an affair.

She sighs and flops her arms out sideways on the bed, like she's making a snow angel. She finds herself looking at a small hole in the ceiling.

It takes her a moment to notice the eye staring back.

LAST SUNDAY

Clementine

Clementine compressed a raincoat in her hands, crushing all the air out of it, then stuffed it into her backpack. 'Have you seen my phone charger?' she asked Cole.

'What do you need it for?'

'To charge my phone.'

They were in the upstairs bedroom. Dom's body had been moved to his bed, and the others were gathering their belongings. Only Cole and Clementine were going down the mountain, but everyone wanted to be ready to leave as soon as the police arrived.

'We'll find some reception long before we find a power point,' Cole said reasonably. 'And it could be a long walk. We don't want any unnecessary weight.'

He was right. But Clementine hadn't asked him for advice—she had asked him where the fucking charger was. 'Have you seen it, or not?'

He opened his mouth, then closed it, before disappearing into the ensuite and coming back with the charger. Clementine took it and silently pushed it into her bag.

Last night, in bed, they had lain back to back, Clementine on the edge of the mattress as if she'd rather risk falling off than being touched by her husband. The skin of her wrists was still raw from the cuffs, and her voice was croaky from being strangled. She was desperate to tell Cole who she'd been with and what he'd done to her. But at the same time, she wanted to make sure Cole never found out, *ever*.

He hadn't asked her about the condom. Hadn't asked her anything. They'd all agreed they wouldn't talk about the sex afterwards—but even as Clementine proposed that rule, she'd assumed she and Cole would disregard it. They weren't just married, they were friends. Clementine had joined him at the gym almost every day, before fertility appointments and research filled her schedule. Neither seemed to need privacy. They never closed the toilet door. They'd installed a double-headed shower in their house; her favourite part of each day was washing her hair while they gossiped about their friends.

Now the silence was deafening. While Clementine had been getting cuffed and choked, had her husband been making love to her best friend? Or had he been with Felicity, young and fresh-faced? Either way, Clementine could make peace with it—but only if he told her.

Finally Cole spoke. 'Last night. While you were . . .' He shouldered his pack, cleared his throat and started again. 'Did you hear anything?'

Was he trying to figure out which room she'd been in?

She forced herself to meet his eye. 'Like what?'

'Anything.'

Moans and gasps from the other rooms. Her own terrified whimpers. The rattling of the cuffs.

'No,' she said. 'Did you?'

'There was a thud.'

She softened. Dom had gotten what he deserved, but her husband shouldn't have to feel guilty about it. 'You think you might have heard him slip over in the hot tub?'

Cole nodded tersely. 'If I'd gone to check it out, then maybe I could have . . . maybe he wouldn't be . . .'

'There was nothing you could have done.' Clementine thought of the cavity in Dom's skull. His brain leaking out through the cracks.

'I could have been there with him.' Cole stared at the wall, blankly. 'He died with no one.'

Again, she was torn. Part of her wanted to reach for her husband, comfort him; the rest wanted to run and hide. She turned away so he couldn't read her expression and found herself facing the bedside table. There she saw the bottle of sparkling. 'Did you put that there?'

'What?'

'The wine bottle. Did you bring that up here?'

'No,' he said. 'Did you?'

'Obviously I didn't, or I wouldn't be asking.' She lifted the bottle by the neck: empty. The base left a red ring on the tabletop. But it was white wine.

No, she thought. *This is all wrong.*

'That thud you heard,' she said. 'Could it have been more like a "thunk"?'

Isla

'What are you saying?' Isla asked. The unease felt like wet cement, slowly setting around her.

They all sat on bar stools around the kitchen bench, their bags lined up against the wall. Everyone had packed except Felicity, who was still in her pyjamas.

Cole's voice was low. 'We're not saying anything.'

'Yes, you are.' Felicity gripped the edge of the bench, knuckles whitening. 'You're saying someone killed my husband. Hit him with a wine bottle.'

'There are probably lots of ways the blood could have gotten there.' Isla's mind raced. *Do they suspect me?*

'And one of them,' Felicity said, 'is that someone clobbered Dom, dragged him down the stairs and dumped his body in the hot tub. Right?'

Isla shrivelled under Felicity's glare.

Unexpectedly, Oscar put a protective hand on Isla's knee. 'It's hard to imagine someone doing all that without any of us noticing,' he said calmly.

'It's possible, though,' Clementine said. 'We should consider it.'

'Let's work out who it was, then,' Felicity proposed. 'Who was in the upstairs bedroom?'

She looked from Isla to Clementine and back again. Neither replied.

'Come on.' Felicity balled her hands into fists. 'Let's sort this out right now. Who was in which room?'

'We said we wouldn't—' Cole began.

'For God's sake, this is going to come out. You get that, right? We'll have to give statements to the police. *Where were you all?*'

Isla's mouth was dry. If she told them where she had been, they would realise who she had been with. What she'd done.

'You think I care about your privacy?' Felicity snapped. 'You think I care about your marriages? So you'll all have to do some counselling. Boo-fucking-hoo. My husband is *dead*!' Her voice echoed through the house.

'You're right,' Isla said. 'All this is going to come out when we talk to the police. So how about we focus on getting in touch with them? That's the most important thing right now.' She reached for Felicity's hand.

Felicity shook her off. 'My husband is dead,' she said again, her voice breaking. Tears streamed down her face. 'I never get to have another conversation with him. I never get to make him laugh again. I never get to say sorry.'

Isla couldn't help but ask: 'Sorry for what?'

'I . . .' Felicity glanced at Oscar. 'I wasn't a good wife.'

Clementine spoke up. 'Yes, you were. Dom loved you so much.'

Felicity made a strangled sob.

Isla thought of Noah, whose tears were easily banished by a kiss, a bandaid and an episode of *Bluey*. If only adults were that simple. Felicity would never get over this.

'Look, Clementine and I are ready to go,' Cole said finally. 'The terrain is rough, but I reckon it'll only take us eight to ten hours to reach the road. Hopefully the weather will hold out. There might be pockets of reception on the way, but if not, we should be able to get a lift into town. Either way, expect the police to be here by sunset.'

'Assuming you make it to the road.' Felicity wiped her eyes and took a shuddering breath.

His eyes narrowed. 'Why wouldn't we?'

'Think about it. Why is the car key missing?'

'Dom must have left it somewhere,' Isla said. 'We discussed that.'

'Or,' said Felicity, 'someone doesn't want us to leave.'

Oscar scratched the back of his neck. 'What are you saying?'

She gave him a hollow look. 'Maybe this killer is just getting started,' she said.

Cole

Cole marched down the trail in silence. He had wanted it to be just him and Clementine. He'd wanted to explain himself, to tell her everything, before she found out some other way.

But no one else would agree to that. After Felicity said the killer might target the rest of them, all hell had broken loose. The others seemed to think that if Cole and Clementine were left alone, and one of them was the killer, that person would murder the other one. The idea was insane: Cole would never hurt his wife. Never, ever.

So he had volunteered to go alone. But no one would agree to that, either. Clementine didn't want to be left at the house with a murderer, and everyone else said Cole couldn't be trusted to call the police, not if he had killed Dom. Cole insisted that he hadn't, but no one was convinced, except his wife.

And possibly not even her. She didn't say she suspected him, but her sidelong glances spoke volumes. It was lucky no one knew about the money, or they might have convicted him on the spot.

He should have been relieved—he no longer needed to feel indebted to Dom. The ten-thousand-dollar gift was no longer hanging over his head. But guilt crowded out every other emotion.

He should have told Clementine everything last night. He'd

opened his mouth so many times, but the words wouldn't come.

Felicity had refused to abandon her husband's body. After some paranoid bickering, the others had agreed they would all hike down the mountain together, leaving her behind. So here they were, breathing the freezing air and trampling the dead undergrowth. Cole had suggested they take the trail rather than the driveway, since it was a more direct route.

He regretted it now. The weather had worsened after only an hour, and the rain was slowly turning the trail to mud. As the path narrowed, they fell into single file. No one wanted a potential killer right behind them, so the order revealed who trusted whom: Oscar was in the lead, followed by Cole, then Clementine, then Isla.

When the path widened again, Cole glanced sideways at Clementine and saw she was crying.

'Hey.' He put his arm around her. 'You okay?'

She stiffened at his touch.

'What's going on?' Oscar asked.

'Nothing,' Cole said. He meant, *None of your business*, but realised too late that it might sound to Clementine like her feelings didn't matter. 'I'm sorry,' he told her, forcing a nervous laugh. 'This isn't quite the relaxing holiday we needed, is it?'

'No.' She wiped her eyes and cleared her throat. 'It's been a tough year.'

'I know.' He rubbed her back. His heart ached.

'A tough *year*?' Oscar repeated.

'With the fertility treatments,' Cole said shortly. He hoped Oscar would hear his tone and stop prying.

'We get our hopes up over and over,' Clementine said. And every time, we . . . It's just demoralising. And I thought this weekend would make a difference; I don't know why. Now we have to talk to the police, then go back home, to our empty house.'

Oscar looked astonished, like he couldn't believe that making a baby was a challenge for some couples.

'We're not all as lucky as you,' Cole snapped. 'We don't all get pregnant on the first try.'

'Lucky,' Oscar echoed, a smile spreading across his face.

Cole frowned at him. 'What's so funny?'

'Let me get this straight.' Oscar let out a giggle. 'Your problem is that you *don't* have children?' His laughter grew and grew, an insane cackle that echoed through the bush.

Clementine looked stricken.

'What the hell, mate?' Cole demanded.

'I'm sorry,' Oscar wheezed. '*Not* having a kid must be so depressing. How do you even fill the time? You'd have to waste your nights *sleeping*. You'd have to spend the weekends doing . . . whatever you want, I guess?' He doubled over, laughing even harder. 'Plus, what would you do with all that spare money? No nappies to buy, no toys, no—'

Cole punched him in the side of the head, knocking him into a bush.

'Ow, fuck!' Oscar shouted.

'Cole!' Clementine cried.

He ignored her. His knuckles smarted—he'd never punched anyone before. But the violence felt good, just like it had last night. He kneeled on Oscar's chest and pushed a forearm against his neck.

Oscar gurgled. He swung his fists at Cole, but the blows were weak. Veins bulged on his forehead. He was still grinning, though. Still *laughing*.

'You son of a bitch!' Cole raised his fist again, ready to smash those smiling teeth right down Oscar's throat.

'Cole!' Clementine grabbed his wrist. 'Isla's gone.'

Cole froze. He looked around. 'Where?' he asked stupidly.

'I don't know.'

He released Oscar, who stayed on the ground, gasping.

'Isla?' Cole shouted. His voice echoed through the bush.

Some part of him noted, guiltily, that he had ignored his wife until she'd said Isla's name. Another part of him wondered if Clementine had known he would react to it and had said it for that reason.

'Isla!' Clementine screamed.

Birds chittered. Rain splashed.

Oscar clambered to his feet. 'Where's she gone?' he croaked.

'Maybe she heard you being a dickhead,' Cole muttered, 'and decided to distance herself.'

'Maybe she saw *you* turn into a total psycho, and she ran like hell.'

The words stung, even though Cole was sure they weren't true. 'You didn't see her leave?'

'I was busy getting assaulted.'

Clementine was jiggling on the spot, like she was holding a jackhammer. 'She might have left before that, she was at the back—Isla? Where are you?'

Cole scanned the bushland around them, squinting against the rain. 'Perhaps she forgot something. Went back to the house to get it.'

Oscar frowned. 'Why would she turn around without telling us?'

'Depends what it was, I guess.'

'Look!' Clementine pointed through the trees.

Cole followed her gaze. But it wasn't Isla—it looked like a pile of garbage in the distance. 'What's that?'

'The rubbish we saw yesterday,' Clementine said urgently. 'We told you about it, remember?'

'Oh. So?'

'I spotted an old bike among the junk. If it works, one of us could ride back up the trail and look for Isla.'

'Wouldn't riding uphill be harder than walking?' Cole asked.

'Only one of us would fit on it,' Oscar said at the same moment. 'We were going to stay together.'

'Yeah, but now your *wife* is missing,' Clementine said angrily. 'Don't you think that changes things?'

'Why would someone chuck out a bike way up here?' Suspicion gnawed at Cole's sanity. Before he could expand on this thought, he stepped in a puddle that turned out to be a deep hole. His leg was submerged up to the knee in a foul-smelling soup of rainwater and animal dung. 'God dammit,' he muttered, examining his shoe.

At least this time Oscar had the sense not to laugh. Violence, it turned out, was an effective way to silence people. Why had Cole wasted all those years being nice?

The others were walking towards the garbage. Cole followed, shaking drips off his leg. When Clementine described the scene to him, Cole had pictured a messy mound of rubbish with debris strewn around. Instead, the garbage bags made a neat pyramid with a plastic tarp underneath, as if someone didn't want them to get dirty.

Ground sheet: the words popped into his head.

Oscar was examining the mountain bike. 'This looks like an electric bike,' he said. 'They cost a fortune. Why would someone throw it out?'

'Maybe it's broken,' Clementine said. 'Or stolen.'

Cole circled the pile of garbage, then froze. 'Look at this.'

'What?' Clementine followed him, then covered her mouth with her hand. 'Oh my God!'

At first the pile had looked like forty or fifty garbage bags. From this side Cole could see there were only a dozen, but they'd been stacked against the wall of a one-person hiking tent. And the rubbish wasn't rubbish. It was supplies: plastic plates, old utensils, torn blankets. This was someone's camp site.

Oscar stared. 'What the hell . . .?'

'Did no one think to look at this side of the pile?' Cole demanded.

'We turned back as soon as we saw it,' Clementine said. 'Somebody has been *living* out here?'

'That's insane.' Oscar gestured to their surroundings:

nothing but tall trees, hard ground and cold wind in every direction. 'Why would anyone do that?'

'If they were wanted by the police, maybe,' Cole said, 'for something serious.'

'Like murder?' Clementine asked.

He peeled back a tent flap to find a camping mattress, a torch, dirty clothes and a battered romance novel with a moderately pornographic cover.

'In that case,' she said, 'I think the hole you just stepped in was their toilet.'

Cole grimaced and pointed to the torch. 'You think this could have been what you saw out the window on Friday night? The flashing light?'

She paled. 'You think someone was spying on us?'

Oscar was still catching up. '*How* would someone live out here? What would they eat?'

'They've been stealing food from the house,' Cole said. 'They probably live in the place, too, whenever it's empty. That explains why the fridge was cleared out on Friday—'

As he glanced at the others, he saw the ramifications dawn on them. Then they all bolted back up the trail towards the house.

Oscar

Cole and Clementine were fitter than Oscar. They quickly overtook him, pelting back up the hill so fast that he was spattered with mud in their wake.

He didn't ask them to slow down. Someone had to get back to the house and warn Felicity as soon as possible. Hopefully Isla was there too.

Oscar shivered as he ran, blinking rain out of his eyes. How could he have suspected one of his friends was a killer? It seemed obvious now that somebody else had been lurking nearby. A dangerous lunatic, living on the fringes. If they'd trusted one another more, they would have figured it out much earlier. They wouldn't have all gone marching down the trail, ready to be picked off one by one, like . . .

Oscar's blood ran cold. What if Isla *hadn't* gone back up to the house? She'd been at the back of the queue. The owner of the camp site could have slipped out of the shrubbery, grabbed her from behind and clamped a hand over her mouth. Maybe the killer had already claimed their second victim.

'Isla?' he called, voice quaking.

There was still no answer. Even Cole and Clementine were out of earshot now. Oscar was alone with the mud, the cold, the hissing rain.

His marriage was broken, maybe irreparably. But he was sick with fear at the thought of his wife getting hurt.

Please, please, please, he thought, turning around and around, scanning the trees.

A stick cracked nearby, as if answering his prayers. He squinted through the rain, but couldn't see anything.

'Isla?' he called again. 'Is that you?'

For a moment there was no answer. Then he heard a grunt of exertion from right behind him.

Oscar instinctively ducked. Air swept across the back of his neck, like a magpie swoop, and then a fucking *axe* thunked into the tree next to him.

Oscar whirled around and screamed. A hooded figure had come out of nowhere, gloved hands raised, a black raincoat flapping around mud-spattered legs. A grey ski mask hid his attacker's face. Mirrored goggles reflected Oscar's terror back at him.

His assailant wrenched the axe free from the tree trunk and swung again. Oscar's legs collapsed under him, more from terror than strategy. The blade whipped past, snagging Oscar's shirt as he crabbed backwards through the mud. When he tried to get up, his feet slid outwards and he hit the ground again, bum first.

He clawed around for a stick or a rock he could use to defend himself. His fingers closed on a garbage bag, and he flung it as hard as he could. The thin plastic tore in his grip and garbage rained down: stale breadcrusts, apple cores, carrot stumps and crumpled chocolate bar wrappers. His attacker flailed, as though being attacked by a swarm of insects.

'Help!' Oscar screamed, writhing on his back in the slippery mud. But no one else was here. Just him and the maniac. He was going to die. He pictured Isla crying at his funeral; his parents and his sister visiting his grave; Noah, growing up without a father.

This last thought brought out a primal instinct he hadn't known he possessed. As the killer recovered and raised the axe, Oscar rocked back onto his shoulder blades and kicked with both feet, aiming for centre mass.

The killer let out an explosive cough as Oscar's shoes sank deep into the solar plexus. The blade of the axe hit the mud next to Oscar's hip and he rolled sideways. The killer doubled over, wheezing, as Oscar scrambled to his feet and fled. Blinded by the rain, he lost the trail and barged into the scrub, branches scratching his outstretched hands. He ran, and ran, and ran.

When he eventually dared to look back, he could no longer see his pursuer. Nor could he see the garbage tent, or the trail, or anything else he recognised.

He was lost.

Felicity

By the time the sun was setting, Felicity was in bed with Dom, wearing the lacy bra and panty set he'd bought her for Valentine's Day, because he would have liked that. He'd be looking down from heaven at his corpse, in bed with a sexy woman, and thinking, *Still got it*.

She told him about her sleepless night on the couch, the discovery of the wine bottle upstairs, the argument about who would hike down the mountain—and her anger at the group for caring about their reputations while Dom was going cold. Then she confessed to the things that happened before he died. She told him about that moment in the backyard with Oscar. The terrible mistake she'd made. How badly she'd wanted to fix it.

'I'm so sorry,' she whispered in his ear. Her guilt was like a borehole: whenever she thought no tears were left, she dug a little deeper, and they gushed up again.

When she blinked them away, she saw that Dom was smiling.

She flinched, startled. But it was just his facial muscles stiffening in the hours after death. It would pass all too soon.

She knew about rigor mortis, lividity, decomposition bloat. As a kid, she'd been fascinated with dead bodies. She remembered asking her parents, over and over, 'But what *makes* them dead?' and never being satisfied with the answer. Some people had stopped breathing but could still be revived, and others came back after hours without a heartbeat; people with no brain activity could live for years on a ventilator. When she was ten, she feigned an illness just so she could ask her GP the question. He'd said the main difference between the living and the dead was that living people didn't decompose. But Felicity had met old people who were withered, saggy, rotten. They'd looked far more decomposed than her husband did right now.

'Please wake up,' she said.

Dom didn't move.

She ran her hand down his body. It wasn't just his facial muscles—everything was hard. She had read about that, too; they called it *angel lust*. But soon it would be over, forever. She found herself wondering which would be worse: missing one last chance to be with her husband, or taking it.

Felicity was saved from this line of thinking by a crashing noise outside. She kissed Dom on the cheek, then walked out to the back deck. She welcomed the freezing rain on her bare skin. She didn't deserve to feel good ever again.

She peered over the edge of the deck. There was no one out here. Just trees, ferns and mud.

There was an axe next to a woodpile, and a battered mountain bike lay sideways on the gravel.

The front door clicked and creaked.

Felicity went back inside. 'Hello?'

Clementine's voice rang out: 'Isla? Felicity?'

Felicity rounded the corner and saw Clementine in the hallway, dripping and shivering.

'What's going on out there?' Felicity asked.

'What's going on in *here*?' Clementine asked, her eyes widening at Felicity's underwear.

She crossed her arms. 'None of your business.'

'Is Isla back?' Clementine demanded.

'No. I thought you were all going down to the highway. Why would she be back? Why are *you* back?'

'That pile of rubbish is a camp site,' Clementine said. 'Someone else has been out here with us the whole time.'

Felicity's blood ran cold. 'Holy shit.' She pictured the heap of garbage. She could visualise a tent behind it, but wouldn't want to meet the kind of person who would live there.

'We came to warn you,' Clementine said. 'But Isla's missing.'

'Who's we?'

'Me and—' Clementine turned to face the empty doorway. The colour drained from her face. 'Cole?' she shouted.

The only sound was the pounding rain.

'I took a few wrong turns, but I'm sure he was with me,' she whispered. 'Oh Jesus. Cole.'

She tried to go back outside, but Felicity grabbed her arm. 'Don't.'

'My husband is out there!' Clementine cried.

Felicity felt for her. She sometimes found it difficult to imagine other people's pain, but in this case, she didn't have to imagine it—her own husband had been missing, just last night.

She'd always been good at strategising. No matter how bad things got, she could quickly make a plan. 'Be smart,' she told Clementine. 'If Cole was right behind you, and now he isn't, there's a reason for that. Whoever's out there will expect you to come running, calling out for him.'

'I can't just leave him,' Clementine snapped.

Felicity opened her mouth to explain the rest of her plan— and then Cole barged in. Like Clementine, he was wet and looked exhausted, his breaths ragged, his cheeks bright red. He also stank, and a dark stain covered one shoe.

Clementine threw her arms around his neck. 'Thank God!'

'It's okay, darling. I'm here.' Cole kissed the top of her head.

'I thought I'd lost you.'

'I might have done something to my ankle when I stepped in that hole. I couldn't keep up with you.' Cole looked over Clementine's shoulder at Felicity. 'Are Isla and Oscar okay?'

'They're not here,' Felicity said. 'It's just been me and Dom.'

Cole noticed the lingerie. He looked at her with a mixture of horror, pity and disgust.

'It's not like that,' Felicity snapped, though it nearly had been. 'You're telling me you lost Oscar *and* Isla?'

'Oscar must be back,' Cole said. 'The bike from the camp site is right behind the house. Someone must have ridden it up the driveway.'

They looked at each other, eyes widening.

'We have to search the house,' Clementine murmured.

'No one's here,' Felicity said. 'I would have heard them come in.'

'We have to be sure.'

Cole locked the front door, then they searched the living area, the kitchen, the laundry, the upstairs bedroom, the ensuite and the downstairs bathroom. They locked all the windows after clearing each room. They found no one, as Felicity had known they would.

They left her room until last—Clementine and Cole seemed reluctant to go in.

'I'll search this room.' Felicity didn't want them to see Dom's corpse in its current state.

'We should stay together,' Cole said again.

'It's okay. If anyone's in there, I'll scream.'

Cole and Clementine nodded.

Felicity entered the room. She checked behind the curtains, in the closet and under the bed: no axe murderer. Dom hadn't moved, but he'd gone soft. She'd missed her chance.

Felicity kissed his forehead, then walked back out. 'Clear.'

The others looked relieved.

'So, what are we thinking?' Cole asked. 'The camper rode the bike up the hill and dumped it but didn't even try the front door . . .?'

'Maybe they're lying in wait nearby,' Felicity said.

'Waiting for what?' Cole asked.

Someone pounded on the door, and they all jumped.

'Probably Jehovah's Witnesses,' Felicity whispered. She couldn't help it: the more tension in the air, the greater the urge to break it with a joke.

'What do we do?' Cole demanded.

'If we ignore it, they might break a window,' Clementine said.

A scream from outside: 'Let me in!'

Even in these circumstances, hearing Oscar's voice made Felicity's guts twist with revulsion. 'I'm going to put some clothes on,' she said, and escaped into her bedroom.

Clementine

When Clementine unlocked the front door, she saw a terrified, angry and very wet Oscar. He barged past her and slammed the door so fast she nearly lost fingers. 'Christ, Oscar.'

His eyes were wild. 'You locked me out.'

'I thought you had a key?'

'I gave it to Isla—are the doors and windows locked?'

'Yes,' Clementine said. 'You're safe.'

This didn't seem to calm him down. 'Where is she?'

'Isla? She's not here. You couldn't find her out there?'

'I was a bit busy getting attacked by an axe murderer.' He ran his hands through his wet hair, spraying the wall behind him.

Clementine's jaw dropped. 'Axe murderer?'

'Someone in a raincoat and a ski mask. They tried to chop my head off. I got away, but then I couldn't find the trail.' Oscar bent over like he was going to vomit.

'Oh my God.' It didn't sound real. Even after Dom's murder, Clementine hadn't really felt like she was living inside a horror movie until now.

Cole appeared, carrying a towel. He didn't look as shocked as Clementine felt. 'Must have been the owner of the camp site,' he said, throwing the towel to Oscar. 'Their bike is up here, too.'

'Fuck.'

225

Guilt tugged at Clementine's heart. She and Cole had left Oscar behind, knowing the camper was out there somewhere. *Forsaking all others*. Keeping her vows felt even worse than breaking them.

If only they'd spent the weekend playing Settlers of Catan. Yesterday she'd dreaded returning to her empty house; now she'd give anything to go back to Warrigal, where her biggest problem was her husband's weak sperm.

Felicity emerged from the west bedroom, wearing a puffer jacket over a T-shirt and jeans. Clementine wondered again what the hell she'd been doing, prancing around in sexy underwear. Had she been hoping to resurrect her husband somehow?

Clementine blushed, remembering her own lingerie set and her hopes it would make Cole more fertile.

'Glad you could join us,' Felicity told Oscar drily.

'Is Isla here?' he asked.

It struck Clementine then: Oscar had been in love with Felicity. She'd seen the hungry sideways looks; the way he followed her from room to room and laughed loudest at her jokes. But the love was obvious to Clementine only in its absence, when he ignored Felicity and asked about his wife.

'We thought she'd be with you,' Felicity said.

Cole went to lock the door again, but Oscar barred his way. 'If Isla's not here, she must still be out there.'

'So is an axe murderer,' Cole said. 'We can't leave the door unlocked, mate.'

'Wait,' Felicity said. 'So the person with the axe attacked Oscar, and the rest of you ran, but you and Isla got separated somehow?'

'No,' Cole said. 'Isla vanished, then we found the camp site and started running back up the hill, *then* Oscar was attacked.'

'How long was Isla missing before the killer turned up?'

'I don't know,' Oscar said. 'Why?'

Clementine wondered if Felicity was implying it had been

Isla with the axe. But that made no sense. Now that they knew someone had been camping out there, that person had to be the murderer—didn't they?

Felicity leaned against the wall. 'So, Dom's dead, Isla's missing, we still have no way to contact the outside world, and we can't leave the house because someone is hunting us. Is that about right?'

'Pretty much,' said Cole and Clementine together.

'Well, fuck this,' Felicity said. 'I'm going back to bed.'

Cole

After washing the stinking muck off his leg in the shower, Cole helped Clementine and Oscar search the house, again, for the car key. They spent hours going through pockets and drawers and the bags lined up against the wall. Cole checked his own leather bag—he didn't want anyone else seeing what was in there.

The rain grew louder, drumming on the roof and hissing against the trees. Thunder boomed in the distance. If a killer was still out there, Cole suspected they would be desperate to get into the house just to avoid being washed away.

Clementine emerged from the west bedroom. 'Felicity's asleep,' she said. 'No sign of the key.'

'She's sleeping next to a dead body . . .?' Oscar looked unsettled.

'Seems to be.'

'That's . . . odd.'

'There's no wrong way to grieve,' Clementine said. Neither she nor Cole had mentioned the lingerie.

Cole collapsed onto one of the couches in the lounge room. Before today, he'd thought he knew what exhaustion felt like, having spent hours doing squats and lunges and deadlifts. That was nothing compared to this. The adrenaline leaving his system, combined with the trek down and back up the mountain, plus the sleepless night before—it had all left him as limp as the head of a mop. He would gladly have shared a bed with a corpse, if that was what it took to get some rest.

'The killer must have taken the car key,' he said, rubbing his eyes. 'There's nowhere else they could be.'

'If the killer was in the house, why didn't they kill Oscar then?' Clementine asked.

Oscar looked alarmed. 'Pardon me?'

'They snuck in and killed Dom on Saturday night. They could have killed you—could have killed *all* of us—but they just left, and didn't attack you until today. Why?'

Silence fell. Cole couldn't get his brain into gear; his skull felt packed with cotton wool, and he couldn't see his own thoughts through it. 'There might not be much point analysing the motives of a crazy person,' he said.

'I don't care *why* they did it,' Clementine said. 'I care about what they're going to do next. Why would they go for both Dom and Oscar?'

Cole crossed his legs. 'Maybe they have a problem with men.'

'Then why not *you*? And why the fifteen-hour gap between attacks?'

'It's freezing in here,' Oscar said, out of nowhere. 'Can we start the fire?'

Cole didn't think it was that cold. 'The firewood will all be wet.'

'It's so we're scared of them,' said Felicity.

He looked up to see her in the doorway, wearing her buttoned-up pyjamas and holding a glass of water. He wondered how long she'd been listening.

'The killer could have got us all while we were bonking,' she continued. 'But there would be no fear that way, because we would have been caught by surprise. We didn't even know there was a threat. They want us to stay at the house, getting more and more frightened as they pick us off one by one.' She shrugged, as though this was no big deal. 'What—you've never seen a slasher movie?'

Clementine sank into the couch next to Cole. He put an arm around her.

'I still don't get why Dom was in the hot tub, fully dressed,' she said.

'Oscar and Isla's room has a door to the back deck,' Cole said. 'Maybe that's the room he chose on the night.'

'No,' Oscar said, at the same time as Clementine said, 'It wasn't.'

A horrified silence fell. Cole felt like he'd been punched in the heart.

Clementine stared down at her lap. 'It was me, okay? I was with Dom.' She took a breath and met Felicity's eye. 'I'm so sorry.'

Felicity's glare could cut steel.

Cole squeezed Clementine protectively. 'How do you know?' he asked her. He still wasn't certain the woman in his own room had been Isla.

She didn't look at him. 'I just do.'

'It's okay.' He rested his cheek against her hair. 'Did he tell you why he wanted to go out onto the deck?'

'He didn't say anything. Those were the rules, remember?' Clementine clamped her hands between her knees. 'Once he was finished, I left.'

Once *he* was finished. Her words made it real. Cole couldn't take this. He dragged himself up off the couch and walked over to the cordless phone.

'It doesn't work,' Oscar said.

'I know.' He picked up the handset and hefted it. It felt light. He popped off the back of the casing, revealing the inner workings. 'No batteries,' he said.

Clementine was by his side immediately. She seemed to have warmed to him again, perhaps because she'd ruled him out as a suspect. He was relieved, though he would have preferred it if she'd trusted him all along.

'You think the killer stole the batteries when they took the key?' she asked.

He nodded. 'But maybe we can find other batteries. It needs triple As.'

'Hang on.' Felicity hurried over to the coffee table, picking up the remote. Her face sagged as she examined the insides. 'No batteries here, either. Did anyone bring a vibrator?'

'Will you be serious for once?' Clementine snapped.

'I'll start searching bags,' Oscar volunteered.

'We just did that,' Cole objected.

'We weren't looking for batteries.' Oscar was making his way towards the bags.

Cole said, 'All my stuff runs off USB power—'

'It'll only take a second.' Oscar started unzipping the bags and tipping them upside down. Clothes, chargers and books spilled onto the floor.

Cole reached for his own bag, but Oscar had already grabbed it.

'Wait,' Cole said.

Oscar ignored him, tipping the bag upside down. Jeans, jumpers and a metal water bottle tumbled out.

Something rattled in the side pocket. Oscar unzipped it.

'Wait,' Cole said again.

The front door clicked unlocked.

Oscar

Oscar had helped Isla choose her wedding dress and had attended fittings, so he hadn't expected any surprises. It was a vintage gown with wrist-length sleeves and embroidered lace up to her throat. But on the day of the ceremony, when he saw her gliding down the aisle between their crying mothers, she was so beautiful that he could hardly breathe, and all his anxieties melted away.

He felt the same now, when he saw her standing in the hall, dripping and muddy, her hair smeared all over her forehead.

'Isla!' He ran up to her and hugged her fiercely. He hadn't planned it; hadn't worried she might not hug him back. One moment he was watching her walk in, the next she was in his arms. It was like his body knew how much he'd missed her and hadn't waited for his mind to make the right decision.

She was so wet that hugging her felt like standing under a waterfall. He didn't care. He never wanted to let her go.

'You're here,' he whispered.

'Oh, thank God!' Clementine barged in on the hug.

'I'm okay, Clem,' Isla said, and kissed her cheek. 'What happened to you guys?'

'We were looking for you,' Clementine said, 'and the rubbish pile turned out to be a camp site, and so we went back up the hill to warn Felicity—'

'And I was attacked,' Oscar interrupted. 'Someone showed up with an axe and tried to cut my head off.'

Isla boggled at him. 'An *axe*?'

'But they missed, and then I kicked them, and then I ran, and then I got lost, and then . . .' Tears sprang to his eyes. 'And I didn't know where you were.'

Isla frowned at the side of his head, where the bruise from Cole's punch still throbbed. 'You're hurt.'

'It doesn't matter,' Oscar said, and it didn't. The axe hadn't split his skull, but it had split the timeline of his life. Everything before—the arguments with Isla, his problems with Noah, the thing with Felicity—seemed unimportant, like it had all happened to a different person.

'Where did you go?' Clementine demanded.

Isla opened her mouth to speak, then hesitated. Oscar realised that Felicity and Cole were hovering behind him, waiting for Isla's answer.

'Give her some space,' he growled.

They backed off, but only a little.

'I saw someone in the bush,' Isla said. 'A man, or maybe a teenage boy—he looked shorter than either of you.' She gestured to Oscar and Cole.

The killer hadn't seemed especially short to Oscar, towering over him with the axe.

'Was he wearing a mask?' Oscar asked. 'Goggles?'

'Couldn't tell. He was a long way away, and it was raining. I would have called out to you, but I didn't want him to know I'd seen him. So I let myself fall behind, and then hid behind some trees. When I heard him moving again, I followed him.'

'Why?' Oscar demanded, horrified by the risk she'd taken.

'I was trying to figure out who he was and why he was sneaking around,' Isla said. 'Soon he started heading back up the mountain towards the house.'

'Maybe he realised you were following you,' Felicity said.

'Or he counted us,' Clementine said quietly.

Cole glanced sharply at her. 'What do you mean?'

'I mean he knew there were five of us left alive but only saw four people going down the hill. He might have seen an opportunity to get one of us alone.'

Felicity wrapped her arms around her body. 'Jesus.'

'Anyway, I lost him,' said Isla. 'So I started going back down the trail—and then I heard yelling in the distance.'

'That was me,' Oscar said. 'The guy must have doubled back.'

'Guess so. I ran towards the noise, but I couldn't find you, and I didn't want to call out in case the guy was still around. I kept going down the trail, hoping I'd catch up to you, but eventually I reached this massive tree that had fallen across the path. It would have been easy enough to climb over, and I could tell you hadn't done that, because it was covered with spiderwebs.'

'I'm not afraid of spiders,' Oscar said, insulted.

Isla looked amused. 'I meant the spiderwebs would have been scraped off if anyone had climbed over.'

'Oh. Sorry.' In his newfound clarity, he realised how often he took offence to something banal. Isla *didn't* belittle him all the time—he belittled himself, and projected it onto her.

He remembered the beautiful girl in the huge purple jumper, sitting next to him at Chili's. He'd *married* that girl. They had a healthy son, a home, food to eat. How could he have been so miserable?

No more, he promised himself. Once they were out of here, he would never forget how lucky he was.

'So then I spent the next few hours walking all the way back *up* the mountain . . .' Isla flopped down onto the couch. A dark stain spread across the cushions as the water soaked in. '. . . and now here I am.'

Oscar sat next to her and took her hand. He had the feeling that if he didn't maintain contact, she might vanish again.

'You're shivering,' she said.

'It's freezing in here,' he replied.

'No, it isn't.' When she put a hand to his forehead, it felt like years since she'd touched him so tenderly. 'It doesn't feel as though you have a temperature . . .'

'I punched him,' Cole said quietly.

Isla's eyebrows shot up. 'You did what?'

Oscar cleared his throat. 'It's okay. I was being a dick.'

'Jesus, Cole,' Isla snapped. 'What's the matter with you?'

'I'm sorry.' He looked at his feet. 'I overreacted. The stress of this whole situation—but that's no excuse. The point is, a head injury can mess with your sense of hot and cold. I fell on a treadmill once, hit my temple on the bar. Felt cold for hours afterwards, even though the thermometer said I was fine.'

Isla held up two fingers in front of Oscar's face. 'How many fingers?'

'Two,' he said.

'Are you confused?'

He looked into his wife's rich brown eyes. 'No.'

'We're glad you made it back,' Felicity told Isla. Her face was hard to read, but Oscar got the feeling she didn't believe Isla's story. He hugged his wife a little tighter; he wasn't going to let anyone call her a liar.

But Felicity didn't make any accusations. 'We'll need to sleep in shifts,' she went on. 'Someone needs to be awake at all times, watching for axe murderers. I only just woke up, so I can take the first three hours.'

Oscar's eyes burned with exhaustion, but he knew she was right. 'I'll take the second shift.'

'Geez, all right,' Cole said. 'Third.'

'Fourth,' Clementine muttered.

'Guess I'm last,' Isla said. 'But what about tomorrow? How do we get out of here?'

'Someone will notice when I don't come to work on Tuesday,' Oscar said, hoping it was the truth. He wasn't especially valuable to the company—Rick Basking might be pleased if he stopped showing up.

'Ken will know something's wrong when we don't pick up Noah tomorrow,' Isla reminded him.

Oscar tried to picture her brother's reaction, but couldn't. He'd never seen Ken in a stressful situation. 'Will he call the police?'

'Not straight away. He'll probably try to call the rest of you first. Then he might drive up here himself to see what's going on. He might even bring Noah.'

Oscar's heart clenched as he pictured Ken driving up to the house with the little boy, unaware that a lunatic was waiting in the bush. 'We've got to warn him.'

'Yeah,' Isla said. 'But how?'

'The killer took the batteries from the landline phone.' Oscar went back over to the bags. 'We were just looking for some spares.'

Cole leaped up. 'Oscar, don't.'

He was already emptying the side pocket of Cole's bag. A wallet came out, along with a phone charger . . .

And a pair of handcuffs.

NOW

Elise

Elise screams.

The eyeball quickly disappears from the hole in the ceiling above her head. There's a flurry of scratching and scuffling: shoes, knees and hands on wooden beams.

Elise leaps off the bed and grabs the nearest solid object—a tall bedside lamp with a heavy brass base—and pulls the cord so hard the power point is wrenched out of the wall, trailing wires. She jumps back up onto the bed and swings the lamp with all her might, slamming the base against the ceiling.

There's a tremendous crack, and plaster dust rains down from a narrow dent. Elise hears a gasp.

'I see you, fucker!' she screeches, swinging the lamp again to smash another moon-shaped hole in the ceiling.

Something moves in the darkness above. Shifting fabric, maybe part of a jacket. Elise lunges, but it slithers out of reach before she can grab it.

Footsteps are clomping up the stairs. Elise ignores them. She's done getting rescued. She's done feeling helpless. *She's* going to be the one to catch this killer.

If she was right about the jacket, the intruder's face should be right about . . . *there*. She hurls the lamp again, bashing a third hole. Through the gap she sees not a face, but a tattered sneaker.

She jumps up to catch it, but the foot disappears, and she ends up gripping the lip of the broken plaster. It comes loose in her hand as the intruder thumps away, hopping from one beam to another, maybe planning to escape through the tarpaulin-covered hole in the roof. Elise looks around frantically for a way to slow them down.

Then the intruder takes a misstep, landing on the plaster rather than a beam. A leg erupts from the ceiling in a shower of dust. Elise hears a squeal of frustration or pain. She jumps off the bed and grabs the leg with both hands, like Tarzan swinging on a vine. The plaster collapses, and suddenly Elise is falling. She lands on her back on the floor, and the intruder crashes down on top of her, swearing and grunting, black clothes turned grey by all the powder.

The intruder rolls off and swings a fist at Elise's head. Coughing, she twists away and the blow glances off. She drives her knee into the intruder's crotch, crushing something soft and fleshy. Her attacker yells in pain, and Elise realises that he's not Madden.

She goes to block the window, but the intruder runs for the door instead. He wrenches it open and comes face to face with Whitmey.

Before Whitmey can make sense of the scene—a stranger in front of him, Elise behind, holes in the ceiling and plaster dust everywhere—the intruder shoves him backwards. Whitmey flails, and as Elise tackles the intruder from behind, all three of them tumble off the landing and down the stairs. Elise covers her head with her arms as she thuds against the steps, the walls, and other people's elbows and kneecaps.

As they reach the ground floor and roll to a stop, she whips a hand out and grips the intruder's wrist before he can go anywhere. Whitmey groans underneath them both. Kiara is already standing over them—she grabs the intruder, too.

Elise grins up at her. 'Cracked the case,' she tries to say, but what comes out is an explosion of dusty coughing.

As Kiara drags the intruder to his feet, Elise realises he's just a boy, no more than fifteen.

'Let me guess,' Kiara says. 'Seb Basking.'

Kiara

'I didn't kill anybody, okay?' Seb snarls.

Rick Basking's son is thin, with bulging eyes and pointed ears like an elf. Under the dust, all sorts of stains mark his clothes: sauce, grease, spray paint, maybe mud. He looks like an abstract painting.

Kiara wishes she'd paid more attention when Rohan said the real estate agent's son was a vandal and a troublemaker. She'd dismissed it as unrelated. A basic mistake—in a town as small as Warrigal, everything is related.

She conducts the interview on the porch, recording it on her phone. The others are inside. The kid won't open up in front of a woman who just pushed him down the stairs, or a big, burly cop like Whitmey.

Elise was reluctant to leave her alone with Seb; she thought he was too dangerous. But Kiara has met plenty of killers, and this skinny, shivering wreck isn't one. No way did he break Dominic's skull with a bottle or slash up the other victim. Seb doesn't even look strong enough to lift the axe that Oscar was supposedly attacked with.

She's happy to let Seb *think* he's a suspect, though. 'I'm guessing we'll find your prints all over this house,' she says.

'I come here sometimes. Whenever Dad's being an arsehole. That's not a crime.'

'Actually, it is,' Kiara says. 'Just because your dad has

keys to these places doesn't mean he owns them. It definitely doesn't mean *you* own them.'

Seb scratches at a mole on his right cheek but uses his left hand to do it. *Left-handed.*

'Trespassing,' Kiara says. 'Vandalism. Stealing rings of keys, and food—'

Something clicks in her brain: *stealing rings.* Her missing opal ring is small but valuable. Elise's bank statement suggested she's being blackmailed and is running out of cash. Yesterday Elise hesitated when Kiara asked if she'd seen the ring. Could Elise have *stolen* it?

The thought is so shocking that she almost forgets about Seb, who's still making excuses. 'I have to eat,' he's saying. 'That's not a crime.'

Anger surges into Kiara's chest. 'Is that your catch-phrase? Don't worry—plenty of food at Riverina.' There's no prison for teenagers in Warrigal; she means the Riverina Youth Justice Centre in Wagga.

Seb scoffs. 'You won't send me there.'

'That's correct,' Kiara says. 'The magistrate will do it.'

The boy looks unmoved.

Kiara swallows her rage and tries to get back onto her script. 'Well, today's your lucky day. You were here last weekend, right?'

'No,' Seb says.

'You sure about that? If you were here, that would make you an important witness in a homicide investigation. And if you tell me what you saw, maybe I'll let you off with a warning.'

'I wasn't here, so I didn't see anything.'

She stares him down, but he just glares back.

Finally he says, 'You're not allowed to talk to me without a parent present.'

'Is that really how you want to play this?'

His nostril curls. 'I'm not *playing* anything.'

Kiara stands up. 'Your funeral, kid. Let's call your dad.'

Elise

Elise watches from inside the house as Kiara locks Seb in the back of her car, his right wrist cuffed to the handle above the window. Elise doesn't feel sorry for him, exactly. Who knows how long he'd been watching them through that hole in the ceiling, or listening from inside the hollow walls? But it's hard to watch him squirm, a prisoner in that enclosed space, without thinking of her own ordeal.

No way out. No air. Can't breathe.

'So, he did it, right?' she says, when Kiara comes back into the house. 'He was the stranger in the raincoat.'

Kiara goes to take off her police cap, then seems to realise she's not wearing it. Elise knows the gesture well. 'No. Just a bystander.'

'Bystander?' Elise tries not to let the fury into her voice. 'He was watching me from the fucking roof cavity.'

'He was,' Kiara agrees. 'But he didn't kill anyone. No apparent motive, and I don't think he's strong enough to have dealt the killing blow to Dom or swung that axe at Oscar.'

'He was strong enough to ride a bike up the mountain.'

'Electric bike. And he has a difficult family situation,' Kiara says.

Elise's eyes narrow. She's heard that before, from people who have no clue how difficult a family situation can get.

'His mum recently died of cancer, and his dad isn't coping

well,' Kiara continues. 'So he runs away a lot, squatting in the houses his dad manages, or sometimes camps nearby. His dad doesn't call the cops because he doesn't want his kid tangled up in the youth justice system.'

Elise has experience with that, too: parents covering for their children, who then grow up and do irreparable harm. 'So what, he gets to keep terrorising the town until someone presses charges? Shit, I'll do it. That kid should be in jail forever.'

'He's not the killer, Elise. He's a kid who's lost his mum.'

'But he was here last weekend, right? He must have seen or heard something we can use.'

'He says he wasn't here,' Kiara says.

'What about the camp site your suspects saw?'

'He's lying, obviously. But there's nothing I can do for now—he's sticking to his story.'

'Why?'

Kiara shrugs. 'Hates the police, hates women, hates the world. Basking will be here in an hour to pick him up—maybe he can convince Seb to tell us the truth.'

'Like he convinced him to stop breaking into houses?'

Kiara rubs her temples. 'I can't do this right now, okay?'

'Do what?' Elise asks. They're just talking.

'I can't fight with you about this.'

'Are we fighting?'

Kiara sighs. 'No. I don't know.'

Elise flinches. Here it is again. Kiara pretends to want Elise's help, to enjoy her company, but actually, Elise is just one more thing to be managed.

Kiara forces a smile. 'You want a cup of tea?'

'Sure.'

She waits for Kiara to go away and boil the kettle. Then she walks out the front door and marches across the gravel towards the car where the boy is being held captive.

As Elise wrenches open the door, Seb hides the fear behind some teen bravado. 'Hey, bitch,' he says.

She gets in beside him. He shrinks back, as though she might hit him. She'd like to. But instead, she takes a breath. 'You know, I lost my mum a while ago,' she says.

Seb glares at her.

'It was rough,' Elise adds. 'It still is. Every day I reach for my phone to ask her for help, or to vent about something or other, and then I remember she won't answer. The funny thing is, I didn't call her much when she was alive. I didn't realise how much I needed her until she was gone.'

Seb grunts. 'You're saying "time heals all wounds" or some bullshit like that?'

'Listen to me. It doesn't get better, ever. I will never stop needing my mum, even though she'll never be there for me again. If you're waiting to wake up one day and realise you're over it, then you'll be waiting until the day you die. Which might not be too far off, the way you're going. You look like the sort of kid who's headed for alcohol and probably drugs. Then suicide, or a fatal head-on collision, or maybe stabbed to death in prison.'

Seb looks appalled. Apparently no one else talks to him like this. 'Get fucked, lady,' he says.

'*You* get fucked.' Elise leans in so close their noses almost touch. 'You know what I did when my mum died? I didn't start breaking into houses, or spray-painting dicks on fences, or perving on strangers. I went to her funeral, I cried a shitload, and then I went back to work. I'm a paramedic, by the way. I might be the one who pulls your body out of that car wreck when you're twenty-one.' She jabs a finger at Seb's thin chest. '*Everyone has lost someone.* You, me, that cop you were just talking to, all your teachers, whichever poor sucker has to scrub your graffiti off the walls—everyone. But the rest of us aren't using it as an excuse to be a ratbag. We're just doing our jobs. You ever think about your dad? How hard it must have been to lose his wife and then, on top of that, have his son transform into a total dipshit?'

The door opens behind her. Kiara grabs Elise's arm and yanks her out of the car.

'Elise!' Kiara's voice is low and cold. 'What the hell are you doing?'

'Grief counselling,' Elise says.

'Get back inside.' Elise has never heard Kiara sound so angry.

'Why did you even bring me here?' Elise demands. 'If you won't let me—'

'Get—back—inside.'

'Fine.' Elise trudges away towards the house.

Then she hears Seb say, 'I didn't kill that guy, all right?'

She turns back. She can tell from Kiara's expression that she heard it too: *that guy*. Not *those guys*.

Not *anybody*.

Seb witnessed one of the deaths. Just one.

'Okay,' Kiara says, 'who did?'

LAST SATURDAY

Seb

Seb crouched on the bough of the gum tree, four metres above the ground.

This was one of the most useful trees around. Strong branches, close together. Easy to climb, no nests or beehives. During the day Seb could see through the windows into the living room and all three bedrooms. But now it was night, and the curtains were drawn. He could only see the back deck in the moonlight.

He was frustrated. He'd gotten up before dawn on Friday and skipped school so he could spend the morning riding his e-bike along the highway. He'd chipped the motor to override the speed limiter and packed a spare battery in case the primary went dry halfway up the mountain. This time he hadn't needed to take any tiles off the roof to break in— he'd stolen his father's key. The two-storey, three-bedroom mansion was way out in the bush, away from Dad, his teachers, everyone. Seb had expected a weekend in paradise.

But soon after arriving, a car had rumbled up the driveway. Seb had grabbed some food from the fridge and stuffed it into his pack, then opened the ventilation grille in the east bedroom and squeezed through the hole in time to avoid being spotted. He'd hid inside the wall for hours, legs cramping, before there was a noisy argument on the deck about a hot tub. Seb had used the distraction to push open the grille, crawl out of the hole and slip out the front door. It had slammed behind him, but no one had come out to investigate.

He'd optimistically hoped the holiday-makers would only stay for one night, leaving him with the rest of the weekend to hang around, a prince in his own private castle. He came back on Saturday evening to find the lights out, even though it was still early. He'd thought he was in luck, until he'd heard moans from inside. Just now there had been a thunk, followed by a brief scream.

Seb had two options. He could spend another night shivering in his stolen tent, which he'd pitched on a previous visit, in case of this exact scenario. Or he could pedal through the dark for six hours to the townhouse where his furious father would be waiting.

Seb and his father were trapped in a feedback loop. When Dad found out Seb had been skipping school, he'd started driving him to Warrigal High and frog-marching him through the front door each morning. With no freedom during the day, Seb had taken to sneaking out at night with a spray can. So Dad had started dead-locking the doors. That made Seb feel even more trapped, so he started climbing out the window. Dad installed bars. And so on.

He didn't know how long he could last like this. It had felt romantic and adventurous during the summer, stealing food from open-air markets and lying on soft grass under the stars. Now he was cold, and tired, and hungry. But so what? Maybe it didn't matter if he starved or froze to death. He remembered Mum shrinking away to nothing in that chemo chair, wearing a bandanna that made her look like a pirate. Smiling at him with her creepy, eyebrowless face. Seb didn't want to end up like that. The sooner he was gone, the sooner everyone could stop giving him those sad looks.

Visiting his mother in hospital had been hard, so he'd avoided it whenever possible. Now he knew *not* having visited her was even harder. He tried not to think about it, to live with no regrets. But there wasn't much to distract him out here.

A scraping sound startled him.

He peered at the deck. One of the men staggered out through the sliding door that led to the east downstairs bedroom. One of his hands kept reaching out to the side, like he was steadying himself on invisible furniture.

Seb glared at the guy, hating him and everything he stood for. People said teenagers were irresponsible, but look at this grown man, so drunk he could barely stand, grinning after a night of crazy sex. Seb wasn't an idiot: he knew what the groans and grunts he'd overheard meant.

Then again, the guy was fully dressed, in a suit and tie. And there was something weird about his hair—way longer on one side than the other.

The guy reached the hot tub and slowly, determinedly clambered into it. He didn't even take off his clothes. He had to be very, very drunk.

Apparently not drunk enough, though. The half-submerged man picked up a champagne flute resting on the side of the tub. He peered into it, like it was a crystal ball. Then he looked around for a bottle to fill it with. A puzzled frown crossed his face.

As the guy turned, the dark mass on the side of his head glinted in the moonlight. It wasn't hair. It was blood.

A chill crept down Seb's spine. The guy felt around for a bottle, patting the sides of the tub. His hand roamed back and forth, slower and slower. Eventually he stopped moving.

After what felt like a long time, Seb slowly lowered himself down to the next branch, then the next. His shoulders burned. The guy didn't react, staring at Seb without seeming to see him.

Soon Seb's nerve broke. He jumped, fell the last metre and a half, and hit the ground with a splash of dead leaves. Then he just ran, hurtling down the trail until he reached the safety of his tent. He crawled inside and lay there, breathing heavily. No sounds pursued him. Did that mean the guy had been unconscious, from alcohol or a head injury, or both?

Seb told himself it wasn't his problem. *Fuck that guy. Fuck everybody.*

He lay down on his mat, cocooned himself in his sleeping bag and closed his eyes. But sleep wouldn't come.

LAST SUNDAY

Clementine

Clementine watched the handcuffs jingle to the floor. The handcuffs from Cole's bag. Her husband's bag. Why had the handcuffs been in her husband's bag?

Felicity raised an eyebrow. 'Are you an undercover cop?' she asked Cole. She didn't look perturbed, because it hadn't been her, bound to that bed, a hand over her mouth, too afraid to make a sound.

Clementine had believed the man was Dom. He always took things too far, and Felicity had warned—promised, even—that he was aggressive. So, he must have put the cuffs in Cole's bag. But why? And *when?* He was dead straight afterwards.

Oscar glanced at the cuffs only briefly. 'Cole, you kinky bastard.' He was searching the next bag for batteries.

No, Clementine thought. She turned to her husband.

He didn't meet her gaze—he was looking nervously at Isla.

He thinks it was her, Clementine realised. *He thinks she's the one he chained up. Choked.*

Cole finally glanced at Clementine. She saw the moment he realised what he'd done, his mouth falling open, his cheeks going red.

'Clementine?' he said stupidly.

She turned and fled.

'Wait!' he cried from behind her, but she was already running through the hall.

She'd never run from her husband before. She'd always run *to* him—whenever a shoot went to another model, whenever a photographer turned out to be a creep, whenever yet another pregnancy test was negative. She hadn't realised how fast he was. She could hear his shoes slapping the tiles behind her, and she found herself sobbing with fear.

'Wait!' he shouted again.

She ran up the stairs two at a time, but Cole could manage three, his thumping footsteps gaining on her. She made it into the bedroom, slammed the door behind her and locked it. The handle wiggled. She pressed her palms against the wood, in case the lock failed.

'Clementine,' her husband said, 'let me explain.'

'Go away.' It came out as a whisper, so she tried again. 'Go away!'

'I didn't know it was you.' His voice was muffled by the door.

A bubble of hysterical laughter came up Clementine's throat. 'Oh, okay! That's fine, then.'

'If I'd known, I never would have—'

'No, I get it! You thought you were raping Isla. Completely understandable.'

'I didn't *rape* anybody!' She could hear the horror in his voice.

'You never asked for consent.'

'We all consented before—'

'I agreed to have sex. I didn't agree to be cuffed to the bed and fucking *strangled.*'

'I thought you enjoyed it!' Cole sounded honestly perplexed.

'I was just lying there! Is that what you think enjoyment looks like?'

Clementine had heard of fight or flight, but last night she seemed to have found a third option: freeze. As soon as she'd realised a big, strong, potentially dangerous man had total power over her, her body locked up and her brain shut down. She just lay there while he took what he wanted.

If she had screamed, she would have screamed for Cole.

'But this was what you wanted,' he was saying now.

She clenched her fists. 'Don't you dare blame this on me!'

He ignored her. 'You'd dropped hints that you were keen to try something a bit rougher than—'

'Are you honestly pretending this was for my benefit? You *just said* you didn't know it was me!'

'That's the point!' He sounded frustrated. 'I love you! I never wanted to hurt you!'

'But you wanted to hurt *someone*, right? That's been your secret fantasy all along. And you never trusted me enough to admit it.'

'Can you blame me, given how you're acting right now?'

'This isn't my fault!' Clementine snarled.

Cole rattled the door again. 'Will you just let me in?'

'And that's not the worst part. You brought the handcuffs.'

'Heaps of couples experiment with—'

'And you clearly didn't intend to use them on me.' Her heart was in her throat. 'Meaning you knew the partner swapping was going to happen before we even left Warrigal. *Right?*'

Cole stayed silent behind the door.

'But you weren't the one who suggested it,' she continued. 'Felicity said it was Dom's idea, meaning that the two of you discussed it.'

'I never discussed it with Dom,' Cole insisted.

'What about the ten thousand dollars?'

Silence. He knew exactly what she was talking about.

'I thought you'd given yourself a bonus, because the gym was so profitable. But you've been acting like the business is struggling, always fiddling with your little spreadsheets and your stupid app. And Felicity knew we've been trying for a baby, which means Dom told her, which means you told Dom. The money was from him, wasn't it?'

'I wanted to tell *you*—'

'You fucking *sold* me!' Clementine screamed. 'You offered him the chance to fuck your wife, without a condom—'

'I said that to *you*—'

'So you could keep the gym afloat and try out all your sick, twisted fantasies on some other woman.'

'It wasn't like that.' He sounded like he was crying.

'What was it like, then? *Explain*.'

'The money was a gift, to help cover the next round of treatments. I never discussed the sex with Dom.'

'Bullshit.'

'I swear. It was Oscar who—'

'Oscar was in on it, too?' Clementine was aghast. 'So all three of you got together and decided to pass me around, like . . . like . . .'

'Please just let me in.'

'Go to hell.'

She tried to drag the lacquered chest of drawers over to block the door, but it was too heavy. She used the bedside table instead, and dumped a heavy suitcase on top of it. Then she ran into the ensuite, slammed the door, sat on the lid of the toilet and cried.

Cole

Cole sat on the landing with his back to the outside of the bedroom door, tears streaming down his cheeks. Part of him had always known it would be like this—that a monster was caged inside him, and that Clementine must never, ever find out. He had sensed that if he let it loose, it would smash through the foundations of his whole world and leave it to crumble.

But he'd told himself it would just be one night. He wouldn't even get too wild—no flogging, no biting, no electro play. Clementine wouldn't know it had happened, and Isla wouldn't know it had been him. Those dark desires would be out of his system, and he'd be able to focus all his energies on being a good husband and, soon, a good father. This could even help them conceive. Once the fantasy was over, he could enjoy regular sex again, which might make him more fertile.

He'd been a fucking fool.

He tried the door again. Still locked. He could maybe break it down, but that would terrify Clementine even more. He banged the back of his skull against the door, *thump, thump, thump*, as though he could give the monster a concussion.

A flame of anger grew in his chest. This was all Oscar's fault.

Last week, Oscar had turned up at the gym unexpectedly. Cole had hoped he was there for a membership. Oscar didn't seem to be the type, but many of Cole's customers were like that: they signed up because they wanted to get fit but then didn't want to do any actual exercise, apparently thinking the membership alone would get the job done.

Oscar had glanced around at the empty gym, then asked Cole a bizarre question: 'Have you heard of the Monty Hall problem?'

'The what?'

'It goes like this. You're on a game show, and there are three doors. One has a million dollars behind it, but you don't know which one. You pick door number two, but the host opens door number three instead, showing you there's no money there. Then he asks if you want to stick with door number two, or switch to door number one. What would you do?'

Money was so tight right now that even a hypothetical cash prize left Cole salivating. 'If the guy's trying to convince me to switch,' he said, 'I guess I'd stick with door number two.'

'No—you're supposed to switch,' Oscar said. 'That way you have a two-in-three chance of winning.'

'Isn't it fifty-fifty?'

'No, it's two in three. Scientists proved it.'

'That doesn't sound right.'

'Look, it doesn't matter. That's not what I'm here to talk to you about.'

'Thank God,' Cole said, with a nervous laugh.

But as Oscar laid out the plans for the following weekend, putting forward his proposal, Cole's relief vanished.

'I don't understand,' he said.

Oscar kept his voice low. 'Felicity and Dom are already on board. I think Isla will go for it. I just need you to talk to Clementine.'

'You want to . . .' Cole wondered if this was the point at which he was supposed to punch Oscar in the face. That would be the honourable thing to do. 'You want to have sex with my wife?'

'No,' Oscar said. 'But you want to have sex with mine.'

Now Cole definitely wanted to punch him: not because it wasn't true, but because he wished it wasn't. He'd thought about Isla a lot over the past year. He loved Clementine deeply, but the more difficult things became—with the failing business, the fertility treatments, the empty nursery—the more he fantasised about a completely different life. A parallel universe, where he and Isla had got together in high school and he'd ended up somewhere other than here.

'And here's the thing,' Oscar said. 'I reckon she's keen on you, too.'

Cole found himself looking around, as though this might be a prank. Someone could be recording him for social media. 'I would never cheat on Clementine,' he said, trying out the words, feeling them in his mouth and throat.

Oscar ignored this. 'Look. I'm not interested in your wife. I want Felicity.'

'You do?' Cole was startled by how bluntly Oscar admitted this.

'More than anything,' he said, in a way that sounded either romantic or crazy. As he explained more details of the plan—the house with the three bedrooms, the lights going out, the women each choosing a room—Cole felt like he, too, might be going crazy.

'Felicity will tell me in advance which room she's going to pick,' Oscar said. 'I want you to steer clear of that room so I can have it. That gives you a two-in-three chance of sleeping with Isla.'

To Cole, the maths still didn't sound right. But before he could say so, a customer walked in.

'Just consider it,' Oscar said, and vanished like a wraith.

That night, Cole couldn't sleep. Oscar's proposal was unthinkable, but here Cole was, thinking about it. Maybe Clementine would enjoy this? Cole had noticed how she always chose the seat opposite Dom's, and listened so closely when he talked, even though he had such a big voice that you couldn't help but hear. Cole hadn't worried about it, knowing she would never cheat. But if he gave her permission . . .

A horribly tempting thought entered his mind: *if Dom slept with my wife, would I still feel like I owed him?*

There was something else, too. Cole's own dark desire, like a tumour deep within his heart. Things he longed to try, but not on his delicate wife.

Isla was kind of wild. She'd let Dom film her that one time, hadn't she?

Cole was too cowardly to try to talk Clementine into the partner swapping, as Oscar had requested. But after a few nights, he'd sent Oscar a message: *two in three aren't good enough odds.*

Oscar's reply was immediate. *Hang on.*

Five minutes later there was another message. *Sorted. Felicity will make sure Isla picks the right room.*

Just like that, it was too late to back out. He felt like he'd already been unfaithful, even though the event hadn't happened yet.

The next day Cole put on a hat and sunglasses and went to a sex shop, where he bought the handcuffs. He lingered a while, looking at the gags, plugs and needles, but told himself: *no.*

In that bedroom on Saturday night, he listened to the way the woman breathed when he touched her. He concentrated on the feel of her silky skin, and the underwear that was nothing like anything Clementine owned. He believed she was Isla, so he put her on a leash and let himself off it.

Now he was alone outside a closed bedroom door. He could faintly hear his wife crying. If only he'd told her what he wanted to try. Now she'd found out the wrong way, and there was no going back.

'Fucking Oscar,' Cole muttered. He wanted to kill the bastard.

Oscar

Oscar was in the downstairs bathroom, thinking.

He wasn't hiding, exactly. But he'd needed somewhere private to process what he'd learned. If someone came in, he planned to tell them he was checking if he'd left a shirt in the washing machine. He'd opened the lid of the machine to make the ruse more plausible.

Not that anyone was looking for him. In the living room Felicity and Isla were arguing about the car key, and Clementine and Cole were yelling upstairs. It sounded like they'd ended up in the same bedroom during the partner swap. Oscar didn't know why that was such a problem— they'd obviously slept together before or, if not, that explained why they couldn't conceive. He could tell them that, and charge a fertility consultant's fee.

Oscar's problem was this: he had thought Clementine was in bed with *him*. And if not, who had that woman been?

Not his wife, that was for sure. Isla's touch was always cold. She fucked like a starfish—

He terminated that thought. Backspaced it. That was the *old* Oscar. The new, post-near-death-experience Oscar would never disrespect his wife like that, not even in his head.

But there was no denying that the woman Oscar met in that bedroom had been wild and eager, her nails raking his back, her teeth on his ear. It could only have been Felicity—and that changed everything.

After truth or dare, he'd been on his way back from the bathroom while the others packed the dishwasher. Felicity had squeezed past him in the hall and unexpectedly leaned close, her hand on his waist, her lips almost against his ear. 'See you in my room,' she whispered, and pointed to the door, making sure he knew which one she meant. Then she flashed a smile that made his loins throb, before she disappeared into the bathroom. Everything seemed to be going according to plan.

But that night, he couldn't get the right bedroom. Dom pushed past him, taking it first. He'd seen which room Oscar wanted and taken it *because Oscar wanted it*. Dom's cruelty was endless. Even in death, Oscar hated him.

Devastated, Oscar had walked into the other downstairs bedroom and found a woman he thought was Clementine, but he now knew was Felicity.

She had picked his bedroom rather than her own—and lied about it later. That meant she'd told him where to go not because she wanted him, but because she *didn't*. She had made love to him so eagerly because she thought he was someone else. This explained the bizarre end to the encounter: he'd brought her nearly to her climax, or thought he had, but then she suddenly recoiled, scrambled off the bed and ran out the door. Felicity must have realised who he was.

The thought would have broken Oscar's heart, if he'd still been fixated on her. Now he barely registered the insult—he had bigger problems. If he'd been with Felicity, and Clementine had been with Cole, that meant Dom had been with Isla.

Right before he was found with his skull smashed in.

Oscar knew Isla and Dom had dated in high school, and it had ended badly. Isla never wanted to discuss it, and Oscar hadn't pushed for details. He only knew whenever Dom was around, Isla seemed stiff, angry. But could she be a murderer?

No. Isla's innocent, he told himself. *I just have to prove it.*

He slipped out of the laundry, into the hall. The argument upstairs was still raging, Cole shouting at a closed door, Clementine's voice muffled behind it. 'The money was a gift, to help cover the next round of treatments,' Cole was yelling. *What money?* Oscar wondered. But the talking from the living room had stopped.

He eased around the corner as silently as a ghost. No sign of Isla or Felicity—they had to be on the deck. The row of bags was by the wall, unguarded. He'd searched Isla's bag before, but he'd only been looking for batteries. He'd ignored everything else, and perhaps missed a clue. With a last glance at the door to the deck, he unzipped the bag and rummaged around inside. It was hard for him to see what he was doing, this close to sunset—but he didn't dare switch on more lights.

Tops, pants, socks. A useless phone charger. A sheet of paper with details about the house, along with check-in and check-out dates—Isla never travelled without a printed itinerary. In a side pocket, Oscar found an envelope with Isla's name on it. It was open.

He hesitated. Even after everything that had happened, he didn't think of himself as a guy who would read his wife's mail. But what if the contents could confirm Isla's innocence?

Something else was tucked into the same compartment of Isla's bag. When Oscar saw it, his blood ran cold. He forgot all about the letter, stuffing it into his pocket as he pulled the damp, balled-up fabric out of the compartment. When he unfolded it, he found himself staring into the eyeholes of a grey ski mask.

NOW

Elise

Elise stands in the entranceway, watching through the window as the mud-spattered LandCruiser grumbles up the hill. It parks behind Kiara's car, and Rick Basking gets out. There are deep, exhausted wrinkles around his mouth, and he has the pallor that Elise associates with long shifts at the hospital. Maybe being a parent is a bit like being a nurse.

Seb kicks the dirt sulkily as Basking approaches. The boy avoids his father's gaze but still looks ready for a fight, fists bunched in his pockets.

Kiara has been waiting in front of the house. She steps into Basking's path and raises her hands in a calming gesture. She says something—Elise can't make out the words, just the tone: gentle but serious, statements rather than questions. Basking dodges around her and storms towards his son.

Seb opens his mouth, yelling some excuse or insult; teeth bared, nostrils flared.

Kiara grabs at Basking's arm, and misses. Basking closes the distance. Seb wrenches his fists out of his pockets and pulls one back to throw a punch.

His father reaches him first and wraps him in a fierce hug.

Seb's fist hovers in the air, his face buried in his dad's shoulder. Soon his arm falls, landing awkwardly around Basking's neck. His spine contorts with what might be a sob. The rest of his body goes slack, too. It looks as though

Basking is the only thing holding the boy up, but he also seems to be leaning on Seb, like they're two halves of a bridge, each able to stand only if they meet in the middle. Elise can't see Seb's face, but she can see Basking's, the tears streaming down his cheeks.

She wonders what it's like to have a father who loves you despite your mistakes. She wonders what it's like to lose the woman you love, yet still see her every day in your child's face.

A minute later, Kiara comes in.

'We need to know where he was at 10 p.m. on Sunday,' Elise says. 'When the second victim died.'

'Pack your things,' Kiara says. 'We're leaving.'

Elise frowns. 'Why?'

'Because this place is bringing out the worst in you.'

Elise recoils, stung. 'What exactly do you mean by that?'

'What do you mean, what do I mean?! You interfered with a witness. You—'

'I got him to talk!'

'Nothing he said will hold up in court. It wasn't recorded. You're not police. And what did we learn?' Kiara's voice is ice-cold. 'Dominic Pritchard survived a couple of extra minutes after he got hit with the bottle—that's all. Unless the kid is lying, in which case we learned nothing. After that stunt, there's no way his dad will give me the chance to interview him properly.'

Elise flounders. 'Dominic was attacked in the bedroom, not on the deck. That's worth knowing.'

'Just go pack.'

'How am I supposed to help you if—?'

'I never needed your help!' Kiara growls. 'I brought you up here to keep you safe from whatever mess you've gotten yourself into this time.'

This time. Elise is speechless. She doesn't know which implication infuriates her the most: that she can't handle her own problems, or that she's to blame for her own abduction last year.

For a moment, the only sound is the whirring extractor fan in the kitchen.

'Fine,' Elise says. 'I'll pack.'

She walks away, eyes burning. In their bedroom, she stuffs her clothes into the suitcase. She goes into the bathroom and grabs her toothbrush, razor and moisturiser, then chucks them in the case and slams the lid. She leaves Kiara's outfits and toiletries where they are. Kiara can pack her own shit.

The words echo around her head: *whatever mess you've gotten yourself into this time*. What else did Elise expect? She's not a cop. She's just a plus-one. How could she have deluded herself into thinking she was useful?

She drags her suitcase towards the door. As she glances around for anything she might have forgotten, she notices the stack of documents Kiara left on the bedside table. Atop the pile is a copy of a letter, paperclipped to a photo of the envelope, along with a note from Jennings confirming that the fingerprints on the corners are a mixture of Oscar's and Isla's. No mention of prints on the letter itself.

Elise has read it several times. But something has finally clicked.

Dear Isla,

I'm leaving—don't pretend to be surprised. I'll be seeking full custody of Noah. Please don't fight me for him. You know full well that any magistrate would side with me if they found out the truth.

—Oscar

Kiara and her colleagues haven't worked out what truth he was referring to. A drug addiction? Abuse of the child? The letter seems to give Isla a motive to kill Oscar. But it was Dom, not Oscar, who got clobbered with a champagne bottle on that first night. No one can make sense of it.

Before Elise heard Seb's story, she hadn't realised how chaotic that evening must have been: the darkness, the unfamiliar house, the moans and thumps from three bedrooms. Dom had opened a door, stumbled across the deck and climbed into the hot tub without anyone noticing. What else might have happened in the confusion?

Was it possible that Isla swung the bottle at Dom, thinking he was her husband?

LAST SUNDAY

Oscar

The ski mask fell from Oscar's hands, landing back in Isla's bag. He could see the reflective goggles in there too, and the black raincoat. He steadied himself against the wall, feeling like he might throw up.

Perhaps Isla had seen one of the flirty texts he'd sent Felicity. When they proposed the partner swap, her anger must have boiled over. She'd swung the wine bottle in a fit of fury—only to discover that she'd killed Dom instead of him. Today on the trail, she'd fallen behind deliberately so she could retrieve the axe.

Oscar's instincts screamed at him to run out the front door and flee down the hill—never mind the rain, or the dark, just get as far away from this house as possible. But if Isla had found the messages, she might come after Felicity next.

Oscar had never loved Felicity, not really. He barely knew her. The obsession had been a mirage, cast by his struggles with fatherhood. The events of this weekend had made him long for his normal life, and his interest in Felicity had evaporated. It was also clear that she'd only ever pretended to like him. But he couldn't just leave her to die—

'What are you doing?'

He whirled around. Isla stood right behind him, as still as a statue. Her big, dark eyes bored into his. She was holding a wine bottle.

Act normal, he thought. 'Nothing.'

She glanced at the bag next to his feet. 'Nothing,' she repeated.

'I didn't find anything.' Cold sweat pooled in his armpits. 'No batteries, I mean. Or keys. We're stuck here.'

Raising the bottle, she asked, 'Drink?'

He forced a smile. 'No. Thanks.'

'Okay.' She lowered the bottle but didn't put it down. 'I don't like you being out here by yourself.'

'I don't like it, either.' Oscar didn't dare ask where Felicity was.

Isla cocked her head. 'Are you feeling okay?'

'Yep. I'm great.'

This was such an obvious lie that she laughed, a tinkling sound he'd hardly heard since Noah was born.

Noah. Oscar missed his son so much. He swore that if he made it out of this alive, he would be the most attentive, loving father on earth.

'What are you thinking about?' Isla asked him.

His hesitation made the truth sound like a lie. 'Noah.'

'I miss him, too.' She wrapped her arms around Oscar. He let her do it, not wanting her to realise what he knew. One of her hands crawled down his back; the other was still holding the bottle. He felt like a little male spider, about to be devoured by the big female.

'Felicity has first watch,' she said. 'She's outside. You're second, right?'

He nodded.

'Come to bed, then,' Isla said. 'Get some rest.' She released him and sashayed away. As she passed the kitchen bench, she put the wine bottle down—like she was promising not to hurt him, if he did what she said.

Oscar looked around. Felicity would be circling the house, keeping an eye on the bush, not knowing that the danger was inside. He could go out there, but what if Isla caught up to him before he found her?

Act normal, he thought again. He took a deep, shaky breath, and followed his wife.

Oscar and Isla showered together before bed. They'd often done this when they first moved into the same apartment, their bodies close under the lukewarm, sputtering spray. But after the baby was born, someone had always needed to look after him. They had started taking turns showering, and even when Noah grew older, there had been no more shared bathing.

The downstairs bathroom had two shower heads, so there was no need to get too close to each other. And yet Isla—cautiously, shyly—joined Oscar under his flow. 'We shouldn't waste the hot water,' she said. 'Don't know how long it will last.'

His heart hammered. 'Right.' *Act normal.*

'I have to tell you something.' She raised her elbows and massaged some foam into her hair. He often saw her naked, but it felt like a long time since he'd really looked. The length of her neck as she lifted her face to the spray, the smoothness of her shoulders, the curve of her hip. The crescent moon shadows under each breast, the triangle of fuzz between her legs.

His own body, which had let him down the last time they'd tried to make love, was more than ready. The thought of having a second child had crippled him, but the knowledge that his wife was a killer didn't seem to pose a problem.

'Okay,' he said.

'It was me.' She held his gaze. 'In the bedroom, with Dom.'

'I know.' Oscar was too frightened to come up with a convincing lie.

Her eyes widened. 'You *know*?'

'I was with Felicity, and Cole was with Clementine, so . . .'

She nodded slowly. 'Right. Process of elimination.'

He swallowed. 'What happened?'

'I told myself if I ended up with Dom, I'd walk out as soon

279

as he was naked. Leave him hanging. I wanted to teach him a lesson—that he couldn't just take whatever he wanted, whenever he wanted it. But when he touched me, I was sure he was Cole. He was so . . .' She looked down at her naked feet. 'Well, I let myself get carried away.'

Oscar's chest felt tight. What was she saying?

'Then I felt some hair,' she continued. 'On his nipples. And you know how Cole's always been weirdly hairless?'

Oscar laughed nervously. 'Yeah.'

'It's strange, right?' She giggled. 'Do you think he waxes, or what?'

'Dunno. We don't talk about that stuff.'

'I don't want you to wax, for the record,' Isla said, touching his chest. 'I like you as you are.'

He said nothing, blinking water out of his eyes like a newborn.

'So, when I realised I was with Dom, I . . .' Her smile faded. 'I freaked out. I just hated him so much.'

'Why?' Oscar asked.

Then she told him about the video. How, when she was seventeen, she'd let Dom record her. How he'd promised never to tell anybody, but how the video had nevertheless spread through the school, then the internet.

These days, revenge porn was a known issue. She would have told a teacher, or the police, and he would have faced consequences. But back then, she'd been embarrassed, and had tried to stop anyone from finding out about his crime. Her friends acted like it was her fault, that she should have known better than to let him film the act, and eventually she'd started to agree with them. Dom grew up and became a big success, while Isla was too ashamed even to try.

There were tears in her eyes. 'I should have told you years ago.'

'I understand,' Oscar said, and he did. This explained almost everything. Why Isla went quiet whenever the others talked about their high school years. Why she tried so hard to avoid being photographed. Why she covered her body so carefully in public. Why she always looked at Dom like he was a live snake in the corner.

But why had she attacked Oscar on the trail? Had she found the messages, or was something else going on?

'This afternoon, in the bush . . .' he began, but couldn't find the rest of the question.

'I'm sorry,' Isla said, and she looked like she meant it. 'You must have been so scared.'

The image flashed through his mind. The axe, slashing through the air towards his face.

'Can I make it up to you?' She pressed her body against his. He was afraid she would feel his racing heart.

'You don't have to do that,' he said.

She squirted some soap onto her palm and reached down, smiling as she found him, a gentle squeeze. 'Let me anyway,' she breathed, and pressed her lips to his.

Oscar froze for a split second, then melted into the kiss. He closed his eyes and explored her with his hands, letting them creep down her spine towards her buttocks.

She's going to kill you, he thought. *Push you over. Say you slipped on the soapy floor.* But he didn't stop, probing her lips with his tongue, pressing his chest to hers. Some ancient piece of genetic code had taken over, telling him that danger mattered less than love.

Isla

Isla lay in bed with her hand resting on Oscar's naked sternum, one leg draped across his thighs, like she was claiming him. She kept her eyes closed, pretending to sleep. She suspected he was doing the same thing. He hadn't moved in a long time, but his breaths weren't deep or slow enough. She knew his rhythms.

When he agreed so readily to the partner swap, she had been furious. Her once-devoted husband had tried to trade her away, even after she stuck by him through his years of gloomy bitterness. But now she felt an eerie calm. Dom's death hadn't been part of the plan, but after the shock wore off, the rage had started to trickle away, too. She closed her eyes, searching for it, and found nothing. Perhaps it had always been Dom she was angry with, not her husband.

Her desire for Cole had dissipated as well. It wasn't just seeing the handcuffs spill out of his bag, though she had found that off-putting. It was the way he'd turned bright red and stammered, giving Isla a glimpse of how he would someday look and sound as an old man. Her crush on him had instantly become a fond memory rather than a painful regret. And then, once she'd dismissed Cole, she'd realised that Oscar wasn't so unattractive after all. At worst he was a droopy houseplant who would become beautiful again with a sprinkle of water. The weight of his body next to her was a comfort.

But was it too late to salvage things, after everything she'd done?

She hugged him closer. She wished she could stop time, and live in this moment forever.

'I love you, Oscar,' she breathed in his ear.

He didn't react. Maybe he really was asleep.

The long day was catching up to her, the sound of the rain making her drowsy. She yawned, her mind starting to wander, her thoughts becoming ethereal, dreams filtering through the cracks. Her limbs grew heavy. When she was balanced on the edge of sleep, about to tip over, Oscar moved.

Isla was immediately alert, but didn't open her eyes. She kept her arms and legs slack as he slowly manoeuvred himself out from under them, then climbed out of bed. Where was he going? The toilet, perhaps? No—she could hear the rattling of his belt, the rustling of his coat. He was getting dressed. Was it time for his shift on watch already?

Isla remained still as Oscar slipped out the door and closed it behind him. Then she looked at the clock, glowing red on the bedside table. It was only 9.44 p.m. Where was he going?

She lay there, thinking. Then she rolled out of bed and started pulling her own clothes on.

Oscar

Oscar had never been so confused. In the past few hours he'd felt scared, betrayed, horny, then scared again, a winding road of emotions that left him nauseated.

He still loved his wife. Insane, but true. Once they got home, he'd find a good lawyer who would get her off for Dom's murder, arguing that the recording had triggered mental impairment, or something. Oscar wouldn't tell the police about the attack on the trail, and none of the others could prove it had happened.

But he couldn't protect her if she hurt anyone else. And if Isla had found the deleted texts, Felicity might be in danger.

She was supposed to be outside, on watch, but on his way to the front door he spotted her in the kitchen, leaning on the bench in the shadows, both palms flat against the granite, head down.

The deafening rain dashed against the roof, an endless stream of white noise. The thunder rolled louder. The epicentre of the storm hadn't yet passed over.

'Hey,' he whispered.

Felicity's head snapped up. Her bleary eyes focused on his. 'What do *you* want?'

'We have to leave.'

'We can't,' Felicity sounded drunk but was probably just exhausted. 'No car key, remember?'

'Isla killed Dom.' Oscar's voice cracked. It hadn't felt real until he heard himself say it. 'She tried to kill me, too. We have to warn the others.'

Felicity's mouth fell open. 'You think *Isla* killed Dom?'

'I know she did. She told me.'

'She *what*?'

'I don't know why she attacked me. Maybe she knows about . . .' Oscar indicated to himself and her. The gesture was supposed to cover everything: the kiss at the party, the calls and texts she hadn't returned, then her abrupt suggestion of a partner swap, which she'd even more abruptly abandoned.

Felicity just stared.

'She's acting like she's forgiven me.' Oscar thought of how loving Isla had been in the shower. 'But I don't know what she'll do to you. Come on.'

He grabbed Felicity's hand.

She shook him off. 'I'm not going anywhere with you.'

He clenched his teeth. 'Keep your voice down.'

Ignoring this, Felicity said, 'I had a good life. I had a job, a car, a house, a rich husband who loved me. I made one mistake—'

Oscar flinched, and she seemed to notice.

Her lip curled. 'You were a *mistake*,' she continued, putting pressure on the bruise. 'Why couldn't you just let me go?'

'I'm trying to save you.' He reached for her hand again.

Felicity pulled it away. 'Stop touching me!'

Over the crackling rain, he heard a faint scuffle. He sensed someone standing in the hall behind him. Watching. The hairs on the back of his neck bristled.

She's here, he thought.

Clementine

A scream pierced the air, and Clementine jerked awake. The back of her skull thumped against something made of wood. A slow ache spread across her spine, and she realised she'd fallen asleep seated, leaning against the bedside table to stop Cole from forcing the door open. Now it was dark and cold. The rain roared like static on an old TV, turned way up.

She got to her feet, trembling. What was happening?

Another shriek from downstairs: 'Help! Somebody!'

Clementine hesitated a second longer, then dragged the bedside table aside and opened the bedroom door.

She bit back a shriek. Her husband's silhouette filled the doorway, exactly where he'd been when she slammed the door hours earlier, as if she'd turned him to stone.

'What's going on?' she heard herself say.

'Don't know.' If he was frightened, he didn't show it. He tromped down the stairs.

Baffled and frightened, Clementine followed. The screams got louder as they descended, as though they were making their way towards hell.

They reached the hall. At the other end, there was a vivid red smear on the tiles, leading away around the corner towards the kitchen.

'Oh God,' Clementine whispered.

Cole just kept walking.

When they emerged from the corridor, they saw where the trail led. Oscar was sprawled next to the oven in a lake of vivid red. Felicity was kneeling over him, still shrieking, both hands clamped around his neck. At first it looked like she was strangling him, but then Clementine saw more blood oozing between her fingers. Someone had slit Oscar's throat, and she was trying to hold the flesh together.

'Felicity,' Cole said.

Her gaze snapped up, her eyes filled with tears. 'Help him!' she cried. 'Please!'

Oscar was clearly beyond help. He had turned white, his eyes staring blankly at the ceiling. Another one of their friends, gone forever.

Minutes earlier, Clementine had never wanted to see Cole again. Now she found herself clinging to him, as though he might be swept away.

'What happened?' she asked.

'He wanted to save me, but I . . .' Retching sobs stole the rest of Felicity's sentence.

Cole crouched beside her. 'Felicity. Listen. Do you know who did this?'

'He told me to run . . . but when I looked back, Oscar was . . . he was . . .'

Clementine looked around the room and spotted an empty slot in the knife block. A trail of bloody smudges that might have been footprints led from the pool around Oscar to the back deck. The door was open, a smear of crimson on the handle. The wind howled outside.

The deck had direct access to Isla's bedroom.

'Isla!' Clementine shouted. She sprinted out the door.

The deck was deserted. Clouds had swallowed the moon, so nothing was visible beyond the safety rail. Clementine could have been on a ship, sailing across a black sea.

She pounded on the sliding door. 'Isla!'

No answer.

She wrenched the door sideways and entered the darkness

of the bedroom. She fumbled around until she found a light switch and flicked it.

The room was empty. She checked in the closet, and under the bed. No sign of Isla—but there were smudges of blood on the floor. The killer had been through here, *after* slitting Oscar's throat.

What would the killer need from Isla's room?

Clementine's head spun. *No*, she thought. *It's not possible.*

Isla had hated Dom since he leaked the video. She had seemed cold to Oscar all weekend, and had disappeared right before the masked maniac attacked him with the axe.

But she was Clementine's best friend. She couldn't be the killer. Could she?

Clementine locked the sliding door and hurried back through the hall to the kitchen. 'Isla's gone,' she heard herself say.

Cole appeared to realise what this meant. 'I'll check the front door.'

'Don't go out there!' Clementine called, but he was already out of sight around the corner.

Clementine crouched next to Felicity, trying not to look at Oscar. The blood was everywhere. The coppery smell made Clementine want to vomit.

'Was it Isla?' she asked. She couldn't believe it.

'What?' Felicity sounded like she was in shock. She wiped her nose, leaving behind a moustache of blood.

'No one's out there,' Cole said from behind her, and Clementine stiffened. She hadn't heard him come back in. 'I've locked the front door.'

'She has a key,' Clementine reminded him. In her head, she was screaming, *We're so fucked.*

'Okay,' Cole said. 'We barricade ourselves upstairs. At dawn, we head down the hill—with protection, this time.' He took three more knives from the block. He handed one to Felicity, who looked dumbly at it. He held out another for Clementine: a paring knife, small but sharp.

She accepted it, feeling sick. She couldn't picture herself wielding the blade as a weapon. She'd never so much as slapped someone.

It's just a deterrent, she told herself. *Like a nuclear warhead.*

Oscar's grey eyes were focused on the ceiling, his mouth open like he was trying to warn her about something. Clementine forced herself to touch his face. It was cold, slack. He was gone.

'Come on.' Cole led them into the hallway.

When they were halfway along, thunder boomed, and the lights all went out.

'Shit,' he muttered. Clementine heard him clicking a switch uselessly.

'The storm must have knocked down a power line,' she said.

'Or Isla found the fuse box,' Cole said. He still didn't sound scared. He took Clementine's hand, and led her up the stairs. She couldn't shake off the mental image of herself in prison garb, climbing towards the gallows. Two people were dead. Her husband was a sadist. Her best friend was a killer. Everything was wrong.

When she reached the landing at the top of the stairs, she looked back. Felicity was gone.

'Felicity?' Clementine whispered, after a few seconds.

The echoes of her voice died away. No response. Her skin crawled.

'Come on, Clem,' Cole said.

'Something's happened.'

A lock clicked, and the front door groaned open.

Clementine's breath caught in her throat. *Isla's back*, she thought. 'Felicity! Hurry!' she hissed.

'Get in.' Cole pulled her into the bedroom, then slammed the door.

'We can't just leave her!' Clementine insisted.

'I'm not dying for her,' Cole replied. 'And neither are you.'

Clementine's heart thudded against her ribs as she

watched him drag the lacquered chest of drawers into place, barricading the door again. He made it look easy.

For hours he had begged her to let him into this room. Now he was in.

Clementine's knuckles were white around the handle of the paring knife. She listened, but downstairs was silent. The house sounded empty. Had the front door been Isla entering, or Felicity leaving? But Felicity wouldn't go outside, where the killer was.

Unless she knew the killer was *in*side. Unless she'd realised it wasn't Isla who cut Oscar's throat.

He told me to run, she'd said. Had she been talking about Oscar, or the killer?

Clementine's gaze fell to her husband's hands. For the first time she noticed the blood on them. 'How did that happen?' she heard herself ask.

Cole looked down. 'Must be from the handle of the back door. I locked it.'

'Oh.' Clementine hadn't seen him do that. She remembered what he'd asked Felicity—not *Who did this?* but *Do you know who did this?*

She backed slowly away, hoping Cole wouldn't notice.

He did. 'What's wrong?'

'You owed Dom money,' she said.

'Is now really the time to discuss that?'

'Did you think killing him would clear the debt?'

'The money was a gift,' Cole said calmly. 'I don't understand what you're saying.'

Clementine could tell he understood perfectly. 'What did you have against Oscar?'

'Nothing,' Cole said. He still hadn't put down the knife.

'Other than your crush on his wife.'

Cole's voice was soothing. 'I didn't have a—'

'But that wasn't the main reason, was it? You just needed me to open this door. You thought a scream from downstairs would—'

'It wasn't me.' Cole advanced on her. He still *looked* like her husband, but there was a monster underneath.

'Stay back!' Clementine shrieked, brandishing the paring knife.

He stopped. 'It wasn't me,' he repeated, like a robot.

Clementine hadn't stared so intently into her husband's eyes since they made their vows. She wanted so badly to believe him.

The knife quivered in her grip.

NOW

Kiara

Elise seems to be staging a small rebellion. Kiara can hear her clattering around the kitchen, chopping and grating, apparently making dinner. Even though it's only five o'clock, and they're supposed to be leaving.

Not that Kiara is ready. She's in the bedroom, staring at the clothes Elise has left out. The avocado scarf, the walking clothes—things Kiara brought in the hope that this might be a relaxing, romantic weekend. They're right next to the stack of crime scene photos and witness statements. What was she thinking, coming here?

She sits on the edge of the bed and sinks into the memory foam. She knows what she was thinking: that she could get Elise away from whoever was making those phone calls. Protect her. Relax her. Remind her that they can face any challenge, as long as they're honest with each other.

Instead of saving their relationship, this trip seems to have doomed it. But if Elise really did steal Kiara's mother's ring and sell it to pay off a blackmailer, then the relationship isn't worth saving. Kiara wonders if that counts as a silver lining.

Things could be worse. She remembers finding the Kellys in the upstairs bedroom, Clementine holding Cole at knifepoint.

The cordless handset rings—a burbling sound she associates with old people. Kiara finds it on the bedside table and recognises the number on the screen.

She answers. 'Hi, Sarge.'

'Kiara. Got an update for you.'

Rohan's voice is comforting. Being alone doesn't usually bother her—she can sit in a police car on the side of the highway for hours without a problem. But when she's with Elise, and Elise is angry, the isolation hurts. Nothing is so lonely as a relationship that isn't working.

'I'm on holiday,' Kiara says.

'Yeah, I told my wife about that. Turns out I was wrong— she thought a minibreak at the murder house was a terrible idea. Shows what I know about women.' He laughs.

Kiara sits on the bed next to the mountain of clothes. 'You called to tell me that? Because you're a little late.'

'No. I called to tell you Cole Kelly is missing.'

Kiara stiffens. '*What?*'

'After you found the kid, Cole's lawyer argued he should be granted bail, since there are now four other suspects for the murders.'

Kiara squeezes her eyes shut. 'Seb Basking isn't a suspect.'

'The magistrate disagreed.'

'What about the rape?'

'We haven't charged him. There's no prospect of a conviction without the victim's cooperation, which we don't appear to have. Clementine has amended her statement.'

'God damn it!' Kiara can't believe this. 'Why?'

'She wouldn't say. You know how it is.'

Victims are often reluctant to pursue charges in sexual assault cases, but Clementine seemed so determined. What changed?

'I gave Cole the usual spiel about not leaving town,' Rohan continues. 'But I had a hunch he wasn't listening. Sure enough, I just went to his house, and there's no one home.'

'Could he have gone after Clementine?'

'She's still in hospital. I've posted a constable outside her room at the hospital, but Cole hasn't turned up.'

'You checked the gym?'

'Yep. No one there.'

Kiara's fingers twitch, like she's typing. They don't have enough evidence to prove that Cole is the killer, and he knows it. So why would he run?

Maybe because there's something they haven't found yet. Something he thinks he can dispose of.

'Get a trace on his phone,' she says.

'Already did, but there's nothing from any of the towers. It must be switched off.'

A chill grows in Kiara's chest and spreads all the way to her toes. 'Or,' she says, 'it's in an area with no reception.'

Elise

The chopping board clatters onto the kitchen bench. Elise lines up two carrots and dices them as loudly as she can. They're bendy, and the zucchini is soft. When Constable Vickers was told to bring food, maybe she raided her own fridge and selected the things she was on the verge of binning.

Elise has no appetite. The smell of death still lingers in the house. But she's not going to give Kiara another excuse to complain. If they're hungry on the drive home, it's not going to be Elise's fault. She's perfectly capable of roasting vegetables. She can do all sorts of things by herself.

Kiara is in the bedroom, thumping and rustling, packing all the things Elise refused to pack for her. She scrapes the carrot slices onto a tray lined with baking paper, then gets to work on grating the zucchini.

When did things go wrong? Elise can't pin it down to one moment. A week ago she was sure she wanted to be with Kiara forever. An hour spent without her was an hour wasted. Bad shifts were made bearable by the thought that she could tell Kiara about them on the weekend. But now it feels like nothing she does is good enough. Kiara thinks she's irrational, emotional, unreliable.

They love each other. So why does it feel like she's walking upwards on an escalator that's going the other way?

Elise dumps some wedges of red onion on the tray and

splashes too much canola oil over them. She works the pepper grinder as though wringing a chicken's neck. *Is it too much to ask*, she wonders, *to be given the benefit of the doubt?* When she says or does something that can be interpreted a number of ways, couldn't Kiara choose the one that *doesn't* piss her off?

The kettle boils, and she pours the water into a saucepan. Then she realises she hasn't preheated the oven.

That's the worst part of all of this: Kiara is right. Elise *is* unreliable. She says things without thinking. She ruins the mood with dark comments. She can't even cook a basic dinner without screwing up.

Blinking back angry tears, she twists the temperature knob. A light clicks on inside the oven, but something blocks most of it out—a dark cloud on the inside of the glass.

Frowning, Elise pulls the door open.

A ghastly smell erupts from the oven and hundreds of flies boil out. A few are sucked up into the extractor fan, while others bounce off her skin and crawl through her hair, up her sleeves, down her collar, into her nose. She screams, and the flies fill her mouth, buzzing like live wires against her tongue.

She staggers backwards, flailing and choking, as Isla Madden's body rolls out of the oven and tumbles to the floor.

TWO HOURS EARLIER

Felicity

It's a two-bedroom, one-bathroom place with shuttered windows, peeling paint and a lawn overrun with weeds. The rest of the cul-de-sac isn't much better, sad little townhouses phalanxed up against one another under mossy rooftops. Felicity has been here a few times, since Cole is her husband's best friend—*was* his best friend—but she never realised how lonely the dwelling looked until now.

No one answered when she rang the doorbell, pounded on the door, rapped against the windows. Now she's parked at the end of the cul-de-sac, shivering. She hasn't turned on the heater, because the inside of the Tesla smells like Dom's cologne, and she doesn't want to displace the scent. If she closes her eyes, it feels like he's sitting beside her.

'God, I miss you,' she whispers.

Her husband says nothing, because he's not there. How is she supposed to go on without him?

An engine rumbles. Felicity opens her eyes in time to see a Ford Mondeo enter the cul-de-sac and park in the driveway. Cole is in the driver's seat. Someone must have loaned him the car while the police are examining the Tarago. Lucky Cole, having such generous friends. *He's a parasite*, Felicity thinks. *He takes a car here, ten thousand dollars there. He even tried to borrow Oscar's wife.*

She squeezes the steering wheel so tightly it creaks.

Journalists have camped outside the police station, and she's been following their feeds. She couldn't believe it when she saw the post: *30-year-old man released on bail.*

She already told the detective Cole was the killer. Surely Clementine said the same thing. Why did the cops let him go? Even if they can't prove the murders, he should be facing an assault charge. Felicity still doesn't know what went wrong on the night of the partner swap, but she overheard the argument upstairs last Sunday: she knows what Cole did to his wife. A chilling thought strikes her: if they'd all picked different bedrooms, it could have been Felicity getting chained up and strangled.

Then again, if they'd chosen differently, Dom might still be alive. Felicity would endure anything for that.

Cole gets out of the car, dressed in trackpants, running shoes and a polyester jumper. Fiddling with his keys, he strolls towards the house like a man without a care in the world.

If the police won't do their jobs, Felicity will do it for them.

She gets out of the Tesla and slams the door.

Cole hears the sound and turns, leaving his keys in the lock. His face is handsome and gentle as ever, but it doesn't fool Felicity anymore. She knows about his violent streak.

Dom would beg her to walk away, but he's gone. He won't talk her down ever again.

'Felicity.' There's no feeling in Cole's tone. A blank void behind his eyes.

Felicity's heart is racing, but she keeps her voice even. 'We need to talk.'

Cole nods slowly. He unlocks the front door and steps aside.

Felicity hesitates, her resolve waning.

Cole smiles. 'After you,' he says.

NOW

Kiara

Kiara storms into the police station and slams her fist into the forensic examiner's jaw.

Jennings flies sideways off his chair, tea arcing from the mug in his hand. He makes a startled grunt as he hits the carpet, bewildered and red-cheeked. His clip-on tie pops off.

'You dickhead!' Kiara roars.

She didn't intend to hit him. Wasn't expecting him to be here on a Sunday evening. She planned to file an official complaint against him with Rohan. But she got more and more worked up on the long drive back to Warrigal, the ammonia stench of maggots still in her nostrils, Elise sobbing in the passenger seat. So, when Kiara saw Jennings' smug, stupid face, sitting at someone else's desk, she lost it.

'How dare you!' he blusters. He tries to pick himself up off the floor, but Kiara kicks him in the side, so hard her toes hurt. Hopefully his ribs hurt more.

'You didn't check the oven!' she bellows. 'There another body! You left it for my *girlfriend* to find, you incompetent—' she kicks him again '—stuck up—' and again '—piece-of-shit, boozy fuckwit!'

Isla Madden has been dead this whole time. That changes everything. If Jennings had done his job properly, the magistrate might not have let Cole out on bail, and Elise wouldn't be in bed, sweaty and trembling like she has the

307

flu. Kiara isn't sure of the worst thing that could happen on a romantic weekend getaway, but finding a rotting corpse in the oven must be in the top five.

Kiara can hear Rohan running towards her. She ignores him, gripping Jennings' collar and hauling him into a sitting position. Their faces almost touch—she can see the cracked veins in his nose and smell the wine on his breath. 'Get out of my town,' she growls. 'Or I swear to God I'll—'

Rohan grabs her shoulder and yanks her so she falls on her arse. 'Detective!' he snaps.

The word pours water on her fury. 'Sarge,' she says, breathing hard.

'Go home.' He points to the door, like she might not know which way home is. 'Cool off. Understood?'

She bites her lip. 'Sarge,' she says again, then storms out.

The cold doesn't cool her off. The goosebumps under her leather jacket are just one more thing to make her mad. She wishes the weather could somehow be Jennings' fault, too.

She walks around to the side of the building and leans against the brick wall in the dark. She hasn't smoked since she was a teenager, but has the craving now. If she saw a butt on the footpath, she'd pick it up and try to light it.

She's furious with Jennings, but she's also angry with herself. She knew Elise was unstable and took her to a recently cleared crime scene anyway, with one key witness still missing. Kiara didn't think to check the oven, even though she'd noticed the smell. Now the case is unsolved—perhaps unsolvable, without Isla's testimony—and Elise is even more of a wreck. It's all Kiara's fault.

She blinks away tears and takes deep breaths. Holds her hands a fraction of a centimetre apart, feeling the energy between them—a calming technique Rohan taught her years ago, which sounded like hippie bullshit at the time. It seems like hippie bullshit now, too. She drops her hands to her sides, as miserable as before.

Jennings will tell the deputy commissioner. That will be

strike three. Kiara's first case as a detective will be her last.

She wishes she could tell Dad about this. He'd understand. He might even see the funny side.

She trudges back to her car on heavy legs and sore toes. Slams the door. Sits in the driver's seat for a while, her thoughts chasing each other around in circles. Then she starts the engine and heads home.

As she cruises past Kingo's, she sees that it's buzzing, by Warrigal standards. The windows have steamed up, blurring the lights inside: the media, maybe, drinking while they wait for an update. When they hear that a third corpse has been found, Kiara will need gumboots just to wade through their drool.

She drives over the spot where she and Elise found Anton Rabbek a month ago. No reporters came to town for him. A hit-and-run is less newsworthy than sexual misadventure, even though the victim is no less dead.

She passes Barton Street, where Dom and Felicity lived. The big townhouses are dark and silent, the trees smothering the streetlights. Kiara is almost home when she suddenly does a U-turn. She tells herself it's not because she isn't ready to face Elise: she wants to find out why Clementine changed her statement.

The hushed voices of nurses echo through the corridors. The lights in the ward have been dimmed. The whole place smells like Elise's uniform.

Clementine is at the window, her hands on her belly, staring out over the town like a ghost in an attic. The thin gown draped around her adds to the illusion. She's been here for a week. She has no physical injuries apart from minor bruising to her wrists and throat, but the psychological trauma must be significant.

She sees Kiara's reflection in the glass, and turns around. 'Visiting hours are over.'

Kiara says, 'How are you holding up?'

Clementine turns back to the window without speaking.

'We found Isla Madden,' Kiara says, watching her carefully.

'Oh.'

'She's dead.'

Clementine's shoulders stiffen. 'How?'

'She seems to have been stabbed.' Kiara is trying to guess if Clementine already knew this, but the back of her head is impossible to read.

There's a long silence, then Clementine says, 'We always assumed we'd die at the same time. Even when we were little kids. Our parents thought it was morbid, but it wasn't—I just couldn't imagine life without her. Literally couldn't picture it. So it seemed like my heart would stop when hers did.' She hugs herself. 'But here I am.'

'I'm sorry,' Kiara says, wishing she'd had a childhood friendship that felt like that.

'Yeah. Me too.'

The lights of the town wink out one by one as people go to bed.

'In a letter to Isla,' Kiara says, 'Oscar threatened to leave her and take their son.'

'What?'

'Did she mention the letter to you?'

'No. And that doesn't make sense.' Clementine's brow crinkles. 'Oscar didn't even seem to like Noah.'

'He said he knew something about Isla. Something that would make a magistrate side with him. Do you have any idea what that might be?'

Clementine considers this. 'You know about the video? With Dom?'

'What video?'

Clementine explains. Apparently Dominic filmed a sexual encounter with Isla when they were both in high school. The video somehow got out, ruining Isla's reputation.

Privately, Kiara calls bullshit on the word 'somehow'. Dominic would have shared the video himself. She's seen it a million times. This gives Isla a motive to kill Dom, but it wouldn't factor into a magistrate's decision over custody. If only there had been details in the letter. It was so vague, as if . . .

Kiara's breath catches in her throat. *As if Oscar didn't write it.*

'Did your husband know that Oscar didn't have a good relationship with his son?' she asks.

'I'm not sure. Why?'

If Cole was planning to kill Oscar, he could have faked the letter to shift suspicion onto Isla. But then why would he murder Isla afterwards?

'I thought you already caught the killer.' Clementine tilts her head towards the screen hanging from the ceiling in the corner of the room. 'I saw it on TV.'

Jurors aren't allowed to watch the news. Kiara wishes the same rule could be enforced on witnesses and victims, who often rewrite their memories to fit the narrative they're offered.

'We found a teenage boy,' Kiara says. 'He's a person of interest. But my lead suspect is your husband.'

'Cole didn't kill anyone.'

'That's not what you said the last time we spoke.'

'I already told you I didn't witness either of the murders. I *thought* the killer *might* have been my husband. I changed my mind.'

'What about the rape?'

'There was no rape.' Clementine won't meet her gaze. 'I consented.'

'Consent can be withdrawn at any time,' Kiara says. 'The second he put those cuffs on you—'

'I didn't withdraw it.'

Kiara can feel a headache building. Her job would be so easy if people just told the truth, in detail, immediately and resolutely. Instead, witness statements are like sand dunes, easily reshaped by a changing wind, or washed away at high tide.

She's so tired. Police work is never easy, but there are usually breaks. Twelve to sixteen hours of decompression in between shifts. She's been on this case around the clock for days, and she's sick of it. Sick of the whole job. She's actually looking forward to getting fired tomorrow.

She persists: 'While the two of you were barricaded in the upstairs bedroom, did Cole threaten you?'

'No.'

'But he brought a knife upstairs. That suggests intent.'

'So did I.' Clementine's voice is flat. Some people perceive a lack of feeling as a sign of deception, but Kiara has learned to suspect the opposite. Emotions are finite—after extreme experiences, there's often nothing left.

'If you thought he was innocent, why were you pointing your knife at him when I arrived?'

'Like I said, I was confused.'

'He must have told you to put it down. What did he say?'

Clementine sighs. 'I don't remember. Ask him.'

'I would, but he's missing.'

She whirls around. 'What?'

'The magistrate approved his application for bail,' Kiara says. 'He took off straight after.'

'They let him out?' Clementine's voice verges on panic. 'He might come here!'

'That's exactly what he'd do,' Kiara agrees. 'If he was innocent, like you say. But we both know he isn't. I think he'll be headed for the Queensland border, or—'

Clementine is pale, shuddering, her hands shielding her abdomen. 'He'll come back if he finds out.'

'Finds *what* out?' Kiara's jaw hurts. 'If you're so scared of him, why won't you help us prosecute him?'

Clementine is starting to cry. 'I don't know what to do.'

'Just tell the truth! Why do you think Cole is coming for you?'

'Not for *me*,' she sobs.

Her hands are still on her belly. It takes a second for Kiara to understand.

Shit, she thinks.

* * *

'What a mess,' Kiara says, as she enters the granny flat. 'Cole is missing. Clementine doesn't want him to be charged for assaulting her, because she's just discovered she's three weeks pregnant. They stopped the IVF treatments a couple of months ago, and he knocked her up the old-fashioned way. It's a fucking miracle. I can't tell if she thinks he's guilty of the murders or not, but either way, she doesn't want her baby's father to be in jail. Even though she's scared shitless, convinced he'll come back once he—'

Kiara rounds the corner into the bedroom and sees that Elise has a suitcase propped open on the bed. Guppy is prancing around her feet, yapping. At first Kiara thinks Elise is still unpacking from the trip; then she sees that clothes are going in, not out.

Her heart sinks. 'What are you doing?'

Elise folds a flannel shirt and puts it in her suitcase. 'Leaving.'

Kiara looks around. The house, usually filled with the comforting detritus Elise leaves behind, is immaculate. Panic starts to set in. Kiara deals with it the same way as always: straightening her spine, taking deep breaths, keeping her voice even. 'Going where?'

'That's private.' Elise slams the suitcase shut. When she tries to zip it up, the sleeve of a cardigan gets in the way.

Kiara reaches in to help.

Elise pulls the suitcase out of reach. 'Don't,' she says, sounding so sad that Kiara can hardly breathe.

'Hang on,' she says. 'You can't make a decision like this on the basis of one traumatic event.' She hates how dismissive she sounds. These days, smaller and smaller injuries are described as 'traumatic'. The word no longer seems adequate to cover the sight of Isla's rotting body, tumbling out of the oven.

'Our whole relationship exists on the basis of one traumatic event.' Elise has managed to close the suitcase. She lifts it like it weighs nothing. She's always been strong.

'I said I'm sorry.' Kiara bunches her fists in her pockets. 'I didn't know about the body. And I shouldn't have taken you to that house either way. It was a bad idea.'

Elise just looks at her. 'This isn't about that.'

'Then what is it about? Help me understand.'

'You don't trust me.'

'Because you won't tell me the truth!' Kiara snaps.

Elise opens her mouth, then closes it again. She looks stricken, as though she's the innocent party here—as though she hasn't lied to Kiara and stolen from her. Then Elise carries the suitcase towards the door, and Kiara immediately regrets the outburst.

She hurries after her. 'Don't go.'

Elise keeps walking.

'Please.' It's not a word Kiara uses often.

Elise looks back, one hand on the doorknob. Tears shine in her eyes. 'Come on, K,' she says. 'Don't pretend this is working for you, either.'

I can fix this, Kiara thinks. 'Let's not decide right now. I understand that you're upset, but—'

'It's all right.' Elise doesn't look angry anymore, just sad. She squeezes Kiara's arm. 'We tried, didn't we?'

Half the cops in town are divorced. They all say the job ruined their marriages. They came home each night upset by things their partners couldn't understand, or they didn't come home at all because they were working late, and eventually found they were living with strangers.

Kiara has tried so hard to prevent that. She took Elise with her, turning it into *their* job, not just Kiara's—and that only made things worse. Now here she is, watching the woman she loves leave. A headlight sweeps across the curtains, and Kiara realises a taxi is already here.

Elise takes the house key off her ring and places it on a side table, more neatly than she's ever done anything. She scoops up Guppy with one arm; he tries to lick the tears off her chin.

So this is how it ends, Kiara thinks. *Not because the sex has gotten stale. Not because of an infidelity. I lost her because I tried so hard to keep her—*

'Wait,' she says. Her head is spinning. There's one motive she never considered until now, and it's shining a light on everything from a different angle—changing the shape of some shadows, banishing others.

Elise turns in the doorway and forces a sad smile. 'I know what you're going to say.'

But she's wrong.

'Cole's not the killer,' Kiara says.

LAST SUNDAY

Isla

'She's acting like she's forgiven me. But I don't know what she'll do to you.'

Isla hovered in the hall, listening. Her eyes were wide. It was her husband's voice, but those weren't his words. Oscar would never betray her like this. Would he?

She had kept secrets from him, but hadn't imagined he was capable of keeping them from her. He never showed any indication that he was thinking something he wasn't saying. It didn't seem possible that Oscar had been living a double life—especially not now, after that moment in the shower when she'd finally told him about the video, and they'd made love for the first time in months.

But her husband had slipped out of bed and got dressed as though preparing to leave her here. Now it sounded like he'd just confessed to an affair with Felicity. What was going on?

Lightning flashed. Seconds later, thunder rumbled. The rain grew to a roar. It felt like the whole house might wash away, breaking apart as it tumbled down the mountain.

'Stop touching me!' Felicity was shouting.

Ever so slowly, Isla eased around the corner so she could peer into the kitchen. There was Oscar, talking to Felicity, head bowed. He reached for her arm, like he was trying to take her somewhere, but she shook him off. Isla couldn't see his face, but she could see Felicity's, twisted by cold fury.

Oscar stiffened, as though he could sense Isla watching. He started to turn around, but Felicity grabbed him by the front of his shirt.

'You ruined everything,' she snarled. With her other hand, she grabbed a knife from the block—

And slashed it across Oscar's neck.

Isla wanted to scream, but it felt like her own throat had been cut. The world went monochrome. Her ears rang. She watched the blood splash the kitchen cupboards as her husband, the father of her child, dissolved into a puddle on the floor. Felicity raised the knife above her head with both hands like a high priestess, ready to make a sacrifice.

Isla couldn't move. Her brain had jettisoned her body. A million years of evolution held her still so the predator wouldn't notice her.

It didn't work. Felicity, who had been about to stab Oscar, looked up. Her eyes lasered in on Isla, petrified in the entrance to the hall.

'Wait,' Felicity said.

The word was like a defibrillator. Energy surged through Isla's body and she turned to run, her feet squeaking on the tiles, her heart slamming her ribs, her nerves singing. She opened her mouth to scream for Cole and Clementine—

She heard a faint whistle behind her, something hurtling through the dark, and then felt a horrible tearing as a shaft of red steel erupted from her chest. Isla looked down at it in horror. She tried to grip the knife, but her arms wouldn't obey. The floor swung upwards to meet her, and she barely felt the impact. Thunder boomed again, and still she couldn't scream.

Footsteps padded across the tiles towards her. 'I told you,' Felicity said, sounding annoyed, 'to wait.'

Oscar

Oscar watched as Felicity dragged his wife's body into the kitchen by the ankles, leaving a lurid smear on the floor.

Don't hurt her, he tried to say, as though it wasn't too late. The sentence came out as a soft crackle through his ruined throat.

When Felicity hurled the knife, he'd thought it would miss. It didn't seem possible for a blade to fly that distance and do anything other than clatter to the floor. But Isla had been well and truly skewered, the handle dead centre in her back. Felicity must have been incredible in the circus.

He understood it all, now. She had told him which bedroom to pick because she planned to kill him in there, but she got Dom by mistake. She'd tried again with the axe. If only he'd let her succeed. Isla would have been safe.

Felicity rolled Isla onto her stomach and wrenched the knife from between her ribs. Oscar felt the pain as if the blade had been pulled from his own flesh. Not much blood came out—maybe her heart had already stopped.

But Isla couldn't die. She just couldn't. *What about Noah?* Oscar thought. *He needs his mum.*

Felicity rinsed the blade at the sink. When she turned back around she was unrecognisable, her mischievous eyes turned ruthless. This must be who she had always been underneath, but he'd never seen it.

And Isla, beautiful Isla, dying on the floor beside him. She had always been kind underneath. He'd been blind to that as well.

Isla's head rolled, and they locked eyes. She looked frightened.

It'll be okay, he wanted to say. But fluid had filled his lungs. Instead, he tried to take her hand. His arm weighed a tonne. Sweat prickled all over his body.

Isla's hand twitched. She was reaching for him, too. Neither of them had the strength to meet in the middle. A membrane of air separated their fingertips. Oscar saw a hopeless longing in her eyes. There had seemed to be so much time. But now he realised the gap between birth and death was narrow, and the space between marriage and death narrower still. They had been together for only a moment, and had wasted most of it.

At least they'd decided to love each other, in time to die side by side.

Night was falling. The world slowly spun. A terrible cold crawled towards Oscar. He didn't look at Felicity as she opened the huge oven door and started removing the racks inside. He didn't take his gaze off his wife. He couldn't go back in time and do things differently. But he could be with her, until the very end.

He tried to smile, but his lips were numb.

And then, there it was. Nothing changed in her expression, but he felt the moment she left, like a spark escaping from a bonfire, corkscrewing upwards to who knew where. Oscar sagged. She didn't need him anymore. His duty as her husband was done.

He watched Felicity push Isla into the oven. Then the darkness closed in, and he couldn't see anything anymore. He heard footsteps, a door sliding. Sometime later there was a scream. 'Help! Somebody!' Felicity sounded so real, so terrified, as if she'd flicked the switch from *robot* back to *human*.

But he heard something deeper, too: Isla's voice, whispering to him. He couldn't make out the words—she was too far away. But he could tell she wanted him to follow.

NOW

Kiara

'I remembered where we met before,' Kiara says.

Felicity smiles pleasantly. 'Oh?'

They're back in the interview room, with the peeling blue paint, the battered table and the camera. It's only 8 a.m. When Kiara asked her to come in for a follow-up interview, Felicity said she had plans for the rest of the day. Kiara assured her this wouldn't take long.

The deputy commissioner hasn't called to fire her. Maybe Jennings hasn't reported the assault yet. But Kiara is aware this may be her last interrogation as a detective.

She's going to make it count.

Outside the jewellery shop, Felicity looked like a zombie, shell-shocked after her husband's death. Now, even though it's early, she's wearing light foundation and her hair has been blow-dried. She's dressed casually in a T-shirt and jacket, but the clothes are new, the colours not yet faded, no scratches on the buttons, the stitching pristine. The crucifix around her neck has been polished.

Kiara gets the feeling Felicity has chosen the outfit carefully because she's nervous about this interview. She should be.

'You were a minor at the time,' Kiara says. 'That's why your name didn't show up when I searched the database. You called the police to say your boyfriend was threatening you with a sword. The emergency squad showed up, saw he was armed, and shot him before anyone could get his side of the story. Later they realised the sword was taped to his hands. There was a lot of meth in his system, though none of his friends or family said he had a drug habit. Except you, of course.'

'He hid it well. I'll always be grateful to the police for saving me.' Felicity squints. 'I don't recall you being there.'

'I was a junior constable. You probably met a lot of police that day.' Kiara opens her manila case folder and lays out her notes. 'Anyway, I know why you killed your husband.'

Felicity's eyes widen. 'I what?'

'It was because you loved him.'

She looks devastated, angry and confused all at once. 'Of course I loved him. But—'

'And you tried so hard to keep him that you lost him.'

Felicity stands up.

'I wouldn't leave yet,' Kiara says. 'Your lawyer will want to know what evidence I have as soon as possible.'

'I don't need a lawyer. I didn't do anything.'

The guilty summon lawyers faster than the innocent—Felicity probably knows that. She still thinks she can convince Kiara she didn't do it.

Kiara just looks at her. Eventually, Felicity sits back down.

'I have to say, I've seen plenty of people murdered over who they had sex with,' Kiara went on. 'This is the first time I've seen someone killed over a kiss. An overreaction, if you want my opinion.'

'I didn't kill anyone,' Felicity says. 'This is outrageous.'

'You made one stupid mistake: you kissed Oscar in your backyard, on the night of the party just after Dom bought the Tesla. I don't know why you did it, exactly. You've always been impulsive, haven't you? Easily bored. Prone to risk-seeking behaviours.'

'You don't know me,' Felicity snaps.

Kiara doesn't. But she knows people *like* her: dishonest, narcissistic, manipulative. She's put plenty of them in prison.

The signs aren't obvious, but they're consistent. Sometimes it feels like she's catching the same criminal over and over, wearing a different face each time.

Psychopaths typically have abnormal thought patterns and a hunger for attention. Kiara should have guessed the killer would turn out to be the stand-up comic.

'Oscar just wouldn't let it go, would he?' Kiara says. 'He followed you around like a puppy, wanting more. If he kept it up, you knew Dom would find out. So you came up with a plan. You were going to kill Oscar, and frame Isla.'

'What a load of crap.' Felicity's disbelief looks real, but Kiara isn't fooled.

'Rick Basking and Clementine Kelly both thought Oscar was delusional,' Kiara says. 'But he wasn't imagining it, was he? You'd been leading him on. A month ago, you started calling and texting him, though you both deleted the records. I assume you told Oscar to do that so Isla wouldn't find them, but actually it was us you were worried about. And rightly so—cybercrime has recovered some of the messages you erased.'

This is a bluff. Cybercrime only rescued two messages, and neither one was incriminating. But Felicity goes very still.

'To Dom, you suggested a weekend away,' Kiara continues. 'A chance to reconnect with his team-mates from high school. You told Oscar you intended to propose some partner swapping. You'd make it seem spontaneous, but you'd each lay some groundwork ahead of time with your partners and friends. On the night, you and Oscar could pick the same bedroom, and have a wild time together right under the noses of both your spouses. You told him it would be a thrill.

'Oscar thought you were desperate to have sex with him, but really you planned to bludgeon him to death as soon as he walked in the door of the bedroom. His wife would be the obvious suspect, but you thought you could make her the *only* suspect. You'd planted a letter about a divorce in her bag and somehow gotten her fingerprints on it. You threw in a ski mask for good measure—cops love finding ski masks in suspects' bags.'

Kiara keeps her voice calm, almost casual, like she can prove all of this. But thanks to Jennings' incompetence, any half-decent defence lawyer could get most of the forensic evidence ruled as inadmissible. This case cost Kiara the love of her life. And if she doesn't get a confession, it was all for nothing.

Felicity glares at her. 'This is offensive.'

Kiara leans forward. 'But Dom already knew about Oscar. He'd guessed the two of you had conspired to choose the same room. So when he saw Oscar try to get the west downstairs bedroom, Dom took it instead. Unfortunately, you didn't recognise him right away. You only hit him once before you realised—but it was enough.'

Under the fake disbelief, Kiara can see real pain. Felicity is haunted by her mistake. But Kiara doesn't care if killers feel guilty. She wants them out of circulation.

'You panicked,' she says. 'Not only had you killed the man you loved, you'd framed Isla for the *wrong crime*. Soon the body would be found, and everyone would reveal which bedroom they'd picked. You'd be exposed as the killer.

'But you're smart. In minutes, you had a new plan. You waited until you heard Isla leave the east downstairs bedroom and Oscar go into the shower. You covered Dom's head with his pillowcase to avoid leaving a trail of blood, then you dragged him into Isla's room and hid him under the bed, trying to confuse the situation so you wouldn't be the obvious suspect. Did you move the wine bottle upstairs then, or later? Probably later, right?'

She waits, but Felicity doesn't fall into such an obvious trap. After a moment, Kiara continues: 'You took the batteries out of the cordless phone and threw them into the bush, along with the key to the Tarago. But you'd made another mistake: *Dom wasn't dead*. Fatally wounded, certainly, but he regained consciousness. He would have been dizzy, nauseated and very confused. It's also common to feel cold after a severe head injury. And because you'd dragged him into Oscar and Isla's room, there was an exterior door leading to the back deck. So Dom sat up, walked out the door and climbed into the hot tub. *Then* he died. We thought he'd been attacked from behind by a right-handed killer while he was in the tub. But he was attacked from the front by a left-handed killer—you.

'After everyone else was out, you went back into the bedroom so you could supposedly *discover* Dom's body. But it was gone. You panicked again. You thought Dom had survived the attack and fled. I'm guessing you were pretty confused when you found him in the hot tub—until Clementine mentioned that people often wander around after a traumatic brain injury.'

'This is all bullshit,' Felicity says. 'Cole owed money to Dom. He thought killing him would clear the debt. How come you're not out there looking for Cole? You're wasting valuable time.'

Kiara won't be sidetracked. 'Your biggest problem was Oscar,' she goes on. 'If he told anyone the two of you had arranged to pick the same room, someone would work out what you'd done. That's why you got rid of the batteries and the key—so you could deal with him before anyone talked to the cops. When the others hiked down the mountain towards the road, you followed them with an axe, wearing the mask you'd intended to frame Isla with and the goggles Dom had packed for the hot tub. You attacked Oscar once he was alone, but he fought you off and escaped into the bush. You had to steal a bike from Seb's camp site and race up the driveway to make sure you got to the house before Cole and Clementine.

'That night, you volunteered to take first watch. You were waiting for everyone to fall asleep so you could murder Oscar in his bed—then he made it easy by coming out to the kitchen to talk to you. You slit his throat, but Isla saw you, and you had to kill her too. Now you were in real trouble. Isla was supposed to be a scapegoat for the police to focus on. But after all the effort you'd put into framing her, now she was dead and useless. You were running out of people to shift the blame onto. You'd killed five victims now—including your old boyfriend, the one with the sword.'

Kiara pauses, waiting for Felicity to correct her. If she says four, or three, or any number other than zero, that's an admission of guilt. Felicity has made that kind of error before. But she stays silent.

It was worth a shot, Kiara thinks.

'You couldn't let Cole and Clementine come downstairs and see you standing over both bodies,' she goes on. 'So you put Isla in the only available hiding place—the oven. Then you confused the scene a bit, walking to Isla's room and back, and screamed for help. You let the Kellys conclude that Isla had murdered Oscar, but you were careful not to say you'd actually seen her do it, because you were planning to tell the police it was Cole. So he and Clementine barricaded themselves upstairs, and you fled down the mountain.

'When you were in police custody, you told us the others were armed and dangerous. You were hoping we'd shoot first and ask questions later, just like we had with your old boyfriend. But this time I stopped them. You must have been devastated when Clementine and Cole survived.

'You nearly got away with it, though. That was quite a performance you put on during our first interview. You only screwed up once, and I didn't notice at the time.' Kiara gestures to the camera. 'But I watched the recording again. When I told you two people were dead, you said, *Two?* At the time, I thought that meant you didn't know about Oscar's death, but it's clear that you did, since you were standing over his body. You said *two*, because there should have been *three*.'

Felicity's brow furrows the tiniest amount.

'And no-one knew Isla was dead,' Kiara says, 'except her

killer.' She leans back in her chair, trying to look self-assured. 'Game. Set. Match.'

Please, please, please, she thinks.

'That's it?' Felicity says, surprised.

Kiara nods.

'That's all you've got?'

'It's enough,' Kiara says, but disappointment is already settling over her.

'That doesn't prove anything.' An amazed look creeps across Felicity's face. 'You have no evidence at all.'

Kiara persists. 'If you have another explanation for knowing about that third body—'

'I didn't.' Felicity sounds more confident now. 'I only said *two* because I wanted to check that I'd heard you correctly. That's it.'

'Bullshit.'

Their eyes meet. Felicity is lying, and Kiara knows it, and Felicity *knows* she knows it. But the forensic evidence is unclear, and there are other suspects with motives and without alibis. It can't be proven beyond reasonable doubt in a court of law that Felicity is guilty, so the Director of Public Prosecutions is unlikely to make the attempt. Felicity knows that, too.

Kiara has failed. The murders of Dominic Pritchard, Oscar Woodleigh and Isla Madden will all go unsolved.

Felicity stands up again. 'I'm very sorry to hear about Isla. Her family must be devastated. But dealing with my husband's death is a full-time job. If you have no more questions for me, I have to go learn what "probate" is. It sounds obscene—like a cross between "probe" and "prostate".'

'You're not going anywhere,' Kiara says. 'You're under arrest.'

A trace of a smile flickers over Felicity's face. 'No, I'm not. This is a voluntary interview. Everything you've said about what happened in that house is speculation.'

'That's true,' Kiara admits. She thumps the door, and Rohan enters. He stands in the corner, lanky arms folded.

'Well, then.' Felicity picks up her handbag from the back of her chair.

'I'm not arresting you for killing your husband,' Kiara says. 'I'm arresting you for killing your neighbour.'

Felicity's smile fades. 'My what?'

'It turns out you lived right next door to a hit-and-run victim: Anton Rabbek, born 3 February 1971, blood type A negative. He was killed not long before you booked in your husband's Jaguar to have a dented bonnet fixed. The bonnet was very clean, which was odd. I wondered, *Who washes their car right before they take it in for smash repairs?* But it hadn't been cleaned deeply enough—we managed to scrape some A negative blood from the cracks. We'll get a DNA match soon enough. I'm guessing Anton saw you and Oscar together, and you were concerned he'd tell your husband. Or maybe he mowed his lawn at 6 a.m., or maybe he had a dog that barked all night, or maybe you just killed him for fun—I don't really care. With the blood, we don't need a motive.' Kiara gets out her handcuffs. 'I can't get you for all five murders. But I can get you for one.'

Tendons bulge in Felicity's wrists and neck. Her lips pull back to expose her canines. Her hands uncurl, claws out.

But a split second later she looks calm again. Reasonable. Human. 'I want a lawyer.'

Kiara nods and closes her case folder. 'Good call.'

Five hours later, the preliminary paperwork is done. As Kiara walks through the car park, she finally feels like she can breathe. Another killer in custody, another victim avenged, the rest of the world a little bit safer. She puts her aviators on and tilts her head back so the afternoon sun can warm her face.

This is just the beginning. Kiara will have to brief the media. She has to collect victim impact statements from the families. Make sure her report is iron-clad, so some slick lawyer can't argue lack of due process. The trial could take months to complete, particularly if Felicity doesn't plead guilty, although Kiara is pretty sure she will: she's smart enough to know she'll lose in court.

The Tesla is here, in the car park. Kiara never saw it following her home from the real estate agency, so she can't prove it was Felicity who sabotaged her brakes. Maybe it was some other psycho. There's no shortage. But that's a problem for another day.

Kiara struts towards her own car—then hesitates. Turns around again. The Tesla looks like it's riding low at the back.

She doesn't have a warrant to search it. But she has a feeling, the kind of instinct she's learned to trust. She raps her knuckles on the boot.

For a second, nothing happens. Then there's a muffled moan from inside.

Even before Kiara breaks the lock and wrenches the lid upwards, she knows it will be Cole Kelly. When she sees him crammed into the boot, his head mummified in duct tape, she thinks, *Hey, I might get Felicity for those other murders after all.*

Epilogue

The funeral celebrant is a big woman with Harry Potter glasses who tells stories from the couple's lives in her rich, cheery voice. She does a decent job of acting like she knew both Isla and Oscar. Maybe she did. Small town.

Kiara doesn't have to be here. The killer has been caught—there's no need to study the congregation for signs of guilt. And she has plenty of other work to do, the herd of cold cases growing faster than she can thin it. But she's learned from those old, divorced, burned-out cops that this is important. If you stop going to the funerals, pretty soon you stop caring about the victims, and then you forget the whole reason you joined the force. She'll be at Dom's funeral tomorrow, and that of the next victim, and the next. She's just got word from Rohan that Jennings decided not to make the complaint, perhaps realising it would call attention to his incompetence. He's gone back to Newcastle. The deputy commissioner is pleased with her work. This wasn't her last case after all.

She stands near the back of St Barnabas' Church so no one has to go without a seat. It's cold outside, but the space is warm from all the hemmed-in mourners. Half the town has turned out. Oscar's sister came from Rotterdam, and his parents have driven from Maitland. Isla's mum and dad are here, looking frail. All the parents look like older versions of their children. It's strange to think that Oscar and Isla were just kids, once.

Isla's university friends, who scattered all over the country after graduation, have come. Kiara can tell who they are—their clothes and hairstyles make them seem worldly, or perhaps otherworldly. Many look shell-shocked; it's as though, faced with the dead, they're realising nothing they cared about last week actually mattered.

In the front row, Noah is sitting on the lap of Isla's brother. The boy looks at the twin coffins with the blank stare kids sometimes get around death. Kiara doesn't have much experience with children, but she knows it's important to keep them away from violence—not because they might get upset, but because they might not. They might decide it's normal, then build their worldview around that foundation. It's hard to know if Noah understands why his parents never came home from their holiday, but Kiara can tell his uncles love him. Hopefully that will be enough.

The only free seats are on either side of Clementine and Cole. It's like they're radioactive. Cole's head is still bandaged, his arm in a sling; apparently he broke it when he hit the ground after Felicity knocked him out with a garden mallet. His other hand is on Clementine's belly.

Kiara is surprised to see the Kellys sitting together. When Cole handcuffed and choked his wife, he scared the hell out of her, whether he realised it at the time or not. Clementine accused her husband of murder, and held him at knifepoint. How could any relationship come back from that?

Then again, they know one another better than they did two weeks ago. Perhaps there's more trust, not less. This whole experience may have taken their relationship to new heights—or new depths. Maybe that's what marriage means: having so much dirt on each other that you're inclined to forgive the unforgivable.

Felicity has remained silent since her arrest, which means the police don't know what she was planning to do with

337

Cole. But Kiara can guess, given what happened to the old boyfriend, and the neighbour, and the occupants of the two caskets. Felicity seems like the sort of person who finds the same solution to every problem. If Cole had disappeared forever, he probably would have been blamed for the murders at the house on the mountain.

The celebrant finishes her speech. Oscar's sister gets up. From behind the lectern, she speaks about her little brother with a sort of wonder. Some of her stories make people laugh, though Oscar's parents cry the whole way through. Everyone sounds likeable in their eulogy, even a man who was unfaithful to his wife.

She talks about how her brother called her out of the blue to talk about a beautiful girl he'd met at uni. As she describes the glow in his voice, and her own joy that he'd found someone he really clicked with, Kiara's nose stings, and her eyes are suddenly wet. There's somewhere else she needs to be.

By the time the pallbearers approach the coffins, Kiara has gone.

She meets Elise at the cafe next to the real estate agency: the cafe they first fought over, when Elise brandished the stained receipt. Elise is wearing a T-shirt and jeans with dirty knees. It doesn't look like she's brushed her hair or showered. She's beautiful, and Kiara's heart aches.

'Hang on a second,' Elise is saying. 'All six of them were in bed with their own partners?'

A man at a nearby table gives them an alarmed look.

'Dominic and Felicity never made it to the bed,' Kiara says. 'But yeah, Clementine was with Cole, and Oscar was with Isla. There was no partner swapping at all.'

'How could anyone have sex with their own spouse and not realise it?'

Kiara shrugs. 'Straight people suck. I think they'd all just . . . lost touch with each other.'

'It's ridiculous. If I was with you, I'd always know.' Elise hardly ever blushes, but now she seems very focused on the foam in her cappuccino.

Kiara smiles. 'Me too. I'd never mistake you for anyone else.'

Elise is silent for a long moment. Then she says, 'What will happen to Oscar and Isla's son?'

Kiara's smile fades. 'He's staying with his uncles. Apparently they've been trying to adopt for a long time. One of them said it was like an ironic curse—like he'd killed Oscar and Isla by wishing so badly for a child.'

'It's so sad.' Elise's voice cracks.

Reaching across the table, Kiara puts a hand over hers. 'Yeah, it is.'

A customer arrives, and the door bangs. Elise doesn't flinch at the sound, doesn't even turn to look. She's making progress. Kiara wishes she could be a part of it.

'I want you to know that I'm here for you,' she says.

Elise blinks. 'Here for me?'

'Even if you don't—' Kiara's throat closes up. 'Even if we're not together, I still care about you. Whoever's leaning on you, I can help.' She suppresses a sad little laugh. 'This time I promise my help will be helpful.'

Elise still looks confused. 'Leaning on me?'

'I know, all right?' Kiara says. 'I know someone is blackmailing you. I know they've been calling you from a private number, and that you were meeting them around here somewhere. I know you've been withdrawing cash. I know you took my jewellery to sell. But it's all okay. Whatever it is they have on you, I don't care. I'll still be on your side.'

Elise's eyebrows shoot up. 'You think I'm being blackmailed?'

'You're not?'

'About what, exactly?'

'Well, I don't know. I just said that.'

Elise giggles so much that a snort comes out. She covers her nose with her palm.

'What's so funny?' Kiara demands.

'It all makes sense now.' Elise takes a breath, getting a hold of herself. 'That's why you wanted to get me away from the town. It's why you've been so weird and possessive.'

'I wouldn't say I've been *weird*—'

'You've been very weird. And you're a terrible detective.'

'Hey!'

Elise reaches into her pocket. 'The person calling me was a jeweller. I took your lucky ring to get your finger size.'

Before Kiara can decode that, Elise produces a black velvet box. She holds it out. Kiara stares at it.

'I took this with me,' Elise says, 'on the weekend. But with the boy hiding in the roof, and Whitmey and Vickers hanging around, and the dead body in the oven . . . well, it never quite seemed like the right moment.'

Kiara is still staring. That can't be what she thinks it is.

As if reading her mind, Elise opens the box. A small cushion-cut diamond sparkles inside, set in a rose gold ring. 'I'd been putting it off. I wanted things to be a bit more stable first. *I* wanted to be more stable. Someone on Instagram said you have to be happy with yourself before you can be happy with someone else. But life is short. So I decided . . .'

Kiara is speechless. She thinks of all the clues she misinterpreted. Elise is right—she's a terrible detective.

Elise misreads her silence as reluctance. 'I know we're broken up now. But you deserve to know: you were it, for me. I never wanted anyone the way I wanted you.' She blinks a few times. 'I know I'm jumpy, angry, maybe too proud. But, maybe, if you felt like giving us another—'

Kiara throws herself across the table, knocking over a salt shaker, and kisses her.

'You're it for me, too,' she whispers.

The rest of the world disappears. Elise's nose is cold against Kiara's cheek, but her lips are soft and warm. Her fingernails trace up the back of Kiara's neck and weave themselves into her hair. Kiara puts one hand on Elise's chest, feeling the thumping of her heart. She barely notices the spilled coffee soaking into her other sleeve.

Elise still loves me, Kiara thinks. *She still loves me.*

She doesn't want to stop and soon realises she doesn't have to: they can pause this kiss from time to time, but they never have to end it.

She pulls back. 'You really want to get married, after what we've just seen? Lies, affairs, dead husbands?'

Elise smiles through the tears. 'There wouldn't be any husbands in our marriage.'

Kiara laughs, and kisses her again. 'In that case,' she whispers, without taking her lips off Elise's, 'the answer is yes.'

Acknowledgements

Every book is a group effort, but *The Wife Swap* would have been especially impossible without the following marvellous people.

Firstly, thanks to the wonderful team at Audible, particularly Radhiah Chowdhury and Karen Yates, for immediately seeing *The Wife Swap's* potential and expertly guiding the book towards it. Thanks also to the incredible cast of the audiobook. I wish I had your talents.

Thanks to all my partners in crime at Allen & Unwin, especially Genevieve Buzo, Shannon Edwards, Angela Handley, Isabelle O'Brien, Jennifer Thurgate and, as always, the devious Jane Palfreyman. Your dedication is incredible. Whether it's a whole new prologue or a missing slipper, there's no job too big or too small! Thanks to everyone at Embla Books, especially Melanie Hayes, James Macey, Helena Newton, Vishani Perera and Emma Wilson.

Thanks to all my loyal friends at Curtis Brown, especially Clare Forster, Talia Moodley and Benjamin Paz, for always backing me up on even the craziest ideas. It's such a privilege to be able to focus entirely on character and plot, knowing you have the business side well in hand.

Thanks to all my author friends, who make this job a little less lonely and a lot more fun. Extra special thanks to Sarah Bailey, Alan Baxter, Shelley Burr, Gabriel Bergmoser, Rae Cairns, Paul Cleave, Jessica Dettmann, Candice Fox, Sulari Gentill, John M. Green, Chris Hammer, Sam Hawke, Rebecca Heath, Rachael Johns, Jess Kitching, Veronica Lando, Ali Lowe, Dinuka McKenzie, Tara Moss, Michelle Prak, Hayley Scrivenor, Kate Solly, Benjamin Stevenson,

Fiona Taylor, Sarah Thornton, Karen Viggers and Greg Woodland.

Thanks to all the experts who read versions of the manuscript, including Elizabeth Cowell, Isobelle Evans, Shireen Faghani, Kate Goldsworthy, Katri Hilden, Juliette Major ('Another simile?! Stop it!'), Bill Massey, Detective Sergeant Emily McCallum, Minh Hiên, Jessica Perini and Damon Young. None of the characters are based on real people, and mistakes are my own.

I *would* apologise to all my friends in the stand-up comedy community, but I know you're not easily offended.

Thanks to my ever-supportive family, who are increasingly alarmed by my book titles but nevertheless keep encouraging me. You're all bad influences.

Biggest thanks of all to my wife, Venetia, who read this book one chapter at a time as I was writing it and whose enthusiasm was infectious. Her thoughts on costume design, set dressing and dialogue were invaluable. Thank you for telling me to write the book I wanted to write without worrying what anybody else might think. I love you so much.

About the Author

Jack Heath is the award-winning author of 40 novels for adults and children, published in ten languages. He wrote his first book in high school, and was published at 19. He worked in a fish and chip shop, a call centre, an electronics warehouse and finally a bookstore before quitting to write full-time in 2017. He lives on Ngunnawal/Ngambri land in Canberra, Australia, with his wife, their two children, several chickens, a few fish, and a possum named Oreo who lives in a birdhouse.

You can subscribe to his newsletter at jackheathwriter. com/news or follow @jackheathwriter on social media.

About Embla Books

Embla Books is a digital-first publisher of standout commercial adult fiction. Passionate about storytelling, the team at Embla publish books that will make you 'laugh, love, look over your shoulder and lose sleep'. Launched by Bonnier Books UK in 2021, the imprint is named after the first woman from the creation myth in Norse mythology, who was carved by the gods from a tree trunk found on the seashore – an image of the kind of creative work and crafting that writers do, and a symbol of how stories shape our lives.

Find out about some of our other books and stay in touch:

X, Facebook, Instagram: @emblabooks
Newsletter: https://bit.ly/emblanewsletter

Printed in Great Britain
by Amazon